MOON
BOUND

MOON BOUND

BY MOONLIGHT SERIES BOOK 2

CHELSEA BURTON DUNN

4 Horsemen
Publications, Inc.

4 Horsemen
Publications, Inc.

4 Horsemen Publications, Inc.
1497 Main St. Suite 169
Dunedin, FL 34698
4horsemenpublications.com
info@4horsemenpublications.com

Cover by S. Wilder
Typeset by Niki Tantillo
Edited by Sienna Skye

Library of Congress Control Number: 2022950249

Print ISBN: 978-1-64450-735-3
Hardcover ISBN: 978-1-64450-940-1
Audio ISBN: 978-1-64450-736-0
EBook ISBN: 978-1-64450-734-6

TABLE OF CONTENTS

 Moonbound

CHAPTER I

It was a rather cold March for being in Kansas City, but that didn't stop the individual outside the door of the locksmith shop from pounding on it relentlessly. Nor did the clearly labeled sign posted on the glass that read "Closed from 12 to 12:30 for Lunch." Vee glared out the glass door, lazily eating her sandwich, and sipping her can of off-brand soda. She certainly wasn't in the mood for this, even knowing the person on the other side of the door was easily a great deal stronger and faster than she would ever be. She kept her eyes firmly in front of her making it clear she was blatantly ignoring him, despite the monstrous noise of the fist threatening to break the glass door.

To further her irritation, her sandwich fell apart as she took a bite. This was the kind of sandwich catastrophe that couldn't be fixed, so you had to either

eat the individual ingredients separately or ditch the idea of eating it all together. She looked at her ruined sandwich with disdain instead of the real perpetrator of its demise. Lunch was officially ruined. With a more than frustrated sigh, she crumbled the paper it had been wrapped in and deposited it in the waste bin behind the counter. She knew she might as well see what the hell the man banging on the glass wanted, even if her thirty-minute lunch interval wasn't completely up. She walked slowly, leisurely to the door, taking her time as she pulled the keys from her jeans pocket and unlocked the deadbolt holding the door closed.

The tall, broad man yanked the door open as soon as the bolt cleared and stormed through forcing her to back up to make room for him. His large eyes, startlingly soft for such a burly looking man, burned with anger like an animal on the hunt.

"Could you not pause from your precious sandwich long enough to do that fifteen minutes ago?" he asked. His voice boomed and shook the glass of the door and windows nearly as much as his fist had. The normally smooth brown skin of his face was dotted with a bit of wiry stubble, but it didn't hide the white line that formed as he clenched his teeth from anger or the cold. She wasn't totally certain.

"Can you not read?" she asked defiantly, pointing to the sign without breaking eye contact with the fuming man. He sucked in a breath through his teeth, closing his eyes and trying to center himself. He could not lose his temper with her. Well... any more than he already had.

"Damnit, Vee! What the hell is wrong with you? I came here because I was told to."

"I can tell. When you come in just to chat, you usually don't attempt to break down my door. Why don't you go run back and tell Shane I'm not in any mood for whatever it is he sent you here for? I'm not here for you all to just harass at any given time, Tommy. I'm tired of this endless stream of drama you all keep bringing me into," she hissed, her eyes narrowed, and nostrils flared.

"That *we* keep bringing you into?" he practically growled at her, stepping closer so he towered over her. They were under the impression that she had gotten herself into this on her own. They made that quite clear with their increasing expectations. Helping someone in need wasn't an open invitation to invade her life on a regular basis.

"Get out of my shop," she said, her voice firm and stance unwavering. He was physically intimidating, but Vee learned a long time ago that even the most intimidating person was shocked when a small woman didn't cower at them, and that *they* would be the one to back down.

"I can't leave here. I'm following orders," Tommy said, a bit more calmly, obviously trying to be more rational despite the temper he had gathered from standing out in the bitter cold while she ate her lunch. Normally, Tommy was much more easy-going, but the bone-chilling winter air seemed to make him unreasonably grumpy.

"Call him then," she practically spit, turning on her heel to go back behind the counter. It was times like this that she wished they didn't have a friendship.

She hated yelling at him, but with this behavior, he deserved it. She didn't care how cold it was outside or how important Shane thought it was for Tommy to be there. She didn't appreciate him yelling and scolding her for not answering his demands.

He watched her for a moment as she turned off the message from the machine so calls could come back through. She then pulled out her tools for the lock she had been fixing before she stopped for lunch. She was completely ignoring his presence; he rolled his eyes and took out a rather small cell phone for such a large man, dialing the number to his boss.

"*What?*" snapped Shane's deep, graveled voice from the receiver. Vee held back the little jump she wanted to make at hearing his voice.

"She wants me to leave," Tommy said, his eyes shifting to look at her again. She was still pretending he wasn't there.

"*Well, that's not what I said for you to do. Did you explain why I sent you or did you barge in?*"

Tommy winced, watching the smug smirk spread on Vee's lips. Tommy's pause was enough to tell Shane everything he needed to know about how that interaction went.

"*Give her the phone,*" Shane growled as Tommy reluctantly handed the phone to Vee's small, outstretched hand.

"What, Shane?" she grumbled, wedging the ancient flip phone between her ear and shoulder as she continued with the lock.

"*I take it Tommy decided against using his words?*"

"What else do you expect?"

"I sent him to stay with you and give you the news."

"News?" she asked, raising a questioning eyebrow he couldn't see. He sighed on the other side of the phone, and she heard the sound of skin rubbing on skin. He was rubbing his forehead with frustration. It was a nervous habit of his.

"The Shawnee Leader is on his way for a meeting, and I haven't exactly been forthcoming about having you as an asset. I wanted you protected for the next few days until I'm sure we won't have any problems."

Vee rolled her eyes. The way he said asset, he might as well have said she was his property.

"I don't need protection. I'm sending Tommy back," she told him as she found the bent piece and unscrewed it carefully.

"You're not as strong as you think you are. You'll need Tommy if something goes wrong in the meeting," he said, his voice on edge with anger. She could imagine his eyes flashing from warm brown to gold as his voice dropped dangerously. She tried to resist the way the sound of his voice made her feel. She flicked a glance at Tommy to be sure her sudden rush of emotion wasn't detected and looked away when it was clear it hadn't been.

"I didn't sign a contract. I'm not your employee or anything else. Tommy goes back, and I don't hear from you unless you want a lock replaced or a safe installed. Got it?" Before he had time to answer, she snapped the phone shut and swiftly tossed it to the hulking man in her small shop. She had forgotten how satisfying it was to hang up on someone that way. Tommy caught it and looked surprised, which amused her, and stood

there for a long moment, simply trying to wrap his head around how that conversation had played out.

"What are you doing? Shoo," she said, waving her hands as if they would magically rid him from her sight.

"I can't believe you talked to him that way." His voice carried a tone as surprised as his expression, thick brows raised on his forehead and eyes wide.

"Well, I did. Now go," she said, pointing to the door and narrowing her eyes, daring him to protest. Any other day she would have been fine with him sitting in her shop and chatting with her but knowing he was on orders; she didn't want him within a hundred feet of it.

"Fine. Bye, Vee," he murmured, stuffing the phone in the pocket of his jacket and leaving the shop much more quietly than when he came. She didn't normally dismiss him like that when he came to visit, but usually he was only there to chat for a moment between assignments, not *guard* her.

Vee gave a sigh of relief as soon as he was out of sight. She made quick work of the lock, replacing the bent part, placing the newly fixed product in a box, and walking back to the inventory room to stash it on the shelf. As soon as it was in its designated home amongst her inventory, her distraction was gone, and in its stead her anger came back.

She couldn't believe the audacity of those men. Shane was often calling on her to have a look at the children of his people. His pack. It hadn't really bothered her until the requests became more like demands. Over the course of the past nine months, she found herself almost constantly in their presence, with barely an evening to herself. She would have been fine with rushing out to someone's car, who unfortunately locked the keys in the ignition at three in the morning, but that was her job. She could always ignore those calls or decline the job. *She* was the boss. But in Shane's world, he was the boss, and he had extended that to include her as someone he could order around as well apparently.

Well, she was finished with that.

After about fifteen minutes of rearranging her inventory, trying to calm and distract herself from her own irritation, the bell sounded, letting her know someone entered the shop.

"Be right there!" she yelled from the back room. Most people in the neighborhood knew her and wouldn't steal from her; she wasn't that concerned about leaving a customer up front for a minute or two. Most of the things out there were display, and her register never held much cash. If they were going to buy something she had to go in the back to retrieve it anyway.

She walked back out to the counter quickly to see to her new customer after dumping the contents in her arms onto a wheeled cart. The girl who had just entered her store was short, her hair curling around her head to fall barely below her chin as she stood just in the door, still in her school uniform. She smiled as soon as she saw Vee, her eyes dancing, and dashed to the counter. Lori was Tommy's younger sister and Vee's occasional employee.

"Why are you out of school? It's not even one," Vee asked, raising her eyebrow, but smiling at the teenager, nonetheless.

"Tommy got me out early. It was cold, and he didn't want me to wait in the car," she said, hopping up on the counter so she could sit. On weekends and sometimes after school Lori would come to help around the shop. It was especially helpful to have someone there if Vee had to do a house call. Not having to close the shop down completely meant more foot traffic.

"He's still not gone?" Vee asked, her irritation coming back full force.

"'An order's an order,'" she said, poorly mimicking her older brother's deep baritone. Vee laughed and shook her head as she walked to the windows, peering out to see him sitting. He sheepishly looked at her from his truck, just out of view from the counter.

"Fine… Why did he get you out of school?" Vee decided to ask. She succumbed to the fact that she wasn't going to get away from him easily.

"The Shawnee leader. All the kids are getting out of school for their protection detail before he arrives. I'm surprised Shane didn't send his son to you instead of Tommy. He's so overprotective of you," Lori said, grinning like the giddy schoolgirl that she was.

"Apparently all those men are. I don't think their wives would be too pleased to hear that." Vee, being the new and interesting thing to look at, seemed to draw the attention of all the men associated with Shane. Well… at least they were quite apt to want to protect her. She never got any specific feelings that they were unduly drawn to her, except maybe Shane, himself.

She didn't think she was that attractive; she was petite and rather plain-looking. Her pin-straight, dark brown hair was layered and fell just below her shoulders with bangs that framed her face. She kept the bangs, not so much for the style, but as a sort of mask. For some reason they made her feel like she stood out less. The only thing she thought she had going for her were her large emerald eyes that peered out behind the brown curtain of her hair.

"But Shane doesn't have a wife, Vee," Lori said, batting her eyelashes. "He can afford to crush on his best asset."

Vee merely shook her head, her eyes narrowing at the incredulous situation as she picked up her soda and took another sip. She was uncomfortable with attention. She was uncomfortable with the feelings she got from having *Shane's* attention, and she hated that she was dragged into all this nonsense with him. It did seem to be inevitable, though, given what she was... whatever that was.

She was not exactly the most normal person, however relative that term is. A normal human would not be able to do the things that she could, nor would a normal human know the things that she did. She could sense all the preternaturals. Depending on what they felt like she would know what type they were, from Fae to Vampire, she was able to tell. She could also feel the emotions of others, and with great concentration, occasionally manipulate them. She didn't know why she was this way or how it came to be that she inherited these abilities. From what little she remembered of her parents, she did not get it from them, and her sister had always been normal.

Lori and Tommy were both preternaturals. Lori was part of the reason she was involved with Shane and

his irritating politics and posturing in the first place. They were Werewolves. Vee was not any sort of shape-shifter, however. She didn't change into anything under the full moon or otherwise. She was always herself and was in no way related to the Westport Pack, other than her knowledge of the world they lived in. She had known of the pack for quite a while, having noticed various gatherings around the city and their frequent need for new locks. They, however, didn't seem to know anything was particularly different about her until an unfortunate incident.

Because of her unique ability, she managed to save Lori from shapeshifting on a busy street and savagely murdering the group of friends she was with while they had been wandering the Westport area one night as Vee was locking up her shop. After that, Shane's pack wouldn't leave Vee alone, and Lori was frequently "popping-in" her shop to spend time with her. Lori was grateful for what Vee had done for her; Vee could feel it every time she came. She didn't mind Lori, she even gave the girl a job, but if her parents and the pack had been more watchful of their children coming of age, especially their daughters, Vee would still be hiding from the preternatural world as she had been before Lori's change.

"So, what's the big deal with the Shawnee Leader coming?" Vee decided to ask after grabbing another soda for Lori.

"I'm not sure. All I heard was he's a Werewolf pack leader from the Kansas side. Sometimes the packs converge on matters or run together on the full moon. I haven't ever gone with them when there has been a gathering like that. I hear he's mean, and he's been demanding answers from Shane for a while," Lori said, before cracking the can open and taking a sip.

"Demanding answers about what?" Vee asked, brows furrowed in confusion.

"I'm assuming about you. Werewolf rumor mill has been going ever since... Downing," Lori said, hesitating to mention the Were that almost killed Vee last summer. Vee's face crumpled a little at his name involuntarily. He was dead. She knew that, but remembering what he did to her... what he could have done had Shane not...

She didn't want to think about it.

"What about the Sha? Is there any danger of bringing them into the picture?" Vee asked, trying to force the thoughts of Downing away from her mind but immediately cringing as she waited for the answer about the Sha. *They* were a living and dangerous potential threat.

The Sha were the leaders of all the Were-packs, they were a group of the oldest family of Weres, and they even oversaw the other Were-creatures. They weren't Werewolves, but true shapeshifters, who could change into any animal they chose. Their magic stemmed from something different from the Fae and the Witches, who could also shapeshift, but not quite in the same way. Most people believed they were the originators of the Were-trait. The only difference was that they could not make a human into one of them. A Sha could only be born, which was why there were few, despite their power. If they were brought into the picture, there would certainly be trouble.

She had narrowly avoided being brought before them when they came to the city to deal with Downing months ago. Vee supposed she had Shane to thank for that. He seemed to keep their inquiries about her at bay, at least for the time being, but the last thing she needed was yet another group of preternaturals nosing their way into her life.

"Probably not right now. The issue would have to go a very long way before anyone brought it to their attention," Lori said, shrugging and eyeing the empty store. "Why is it so dead in here today? Isn't Friday a day full of forgotten keys and broken locks?" Lori asked, causing Vee to laugh.

"That's usually Mondays. First day of the week people are in a rush. Saturdays bring out the drunks who forget things," Vee said with a smile, making Lori chuckle. Lori was usually in the store when it was busier.

Tommy decided to barge back in at that moment, letting the frigid air chill the two ladies at the counter.

"Jeez, Tommy! A little notice before you bring in the cold?" Lori said, wrapping her sweater around her a bit more. Her skirt was the only thing over her bare legs, and Vee could see the goosebumps rise from her skin.

"Sorry. I didn't want to waste the gas. Do you mind if I just sit in here? I can't leave or Shane's going to lose it," Tommy said, rubbing his hands together trying to bring warmth to his frozen digits. She scowled. Not that it was Tommy's fault, but she was certainly not pleased that these two were interrupting her day. It might not have been eventful, but she enjoyed the simplicity of her day-to-day life. It especially irked her when it was pack business that was doing the interrupting.

CHAPTER 2

Vee put Lori to work, having her clock in and update the inventory on the computer in the back while she grabbed another lock to repair. The rest of the afternoon wasn't terribly eventful. Tommy seemed to intimidate the few customers that came in to look around. Even though she had let him stay, he knew she wasn't happy about it and it continued to sour his mood. He wasn't very well versed in hiding his emotions from others, so his glowering look made the last customer, a little old lady, take two steps inside and then head right back out without a word.

She had a few calls, but nothing to put on the books, which was disappointing. At about 4:00 p.m., Vee looked at the clock and sighed before glaring at Tommy as he sat watching out the window.

"I might as well close up shop. I'm not going to get any customers with your intimidating mug loafing about my store," she said glumly, setting her beverage on the counter to shut everything down. Lori and Tommy chuckled from opposite ends of the shop.

"I don't think I'm nearly as intimidating as you are. I don't care how small you are, I bet you scare off more customers than I do," Tommy said through chuckles. She looked up and narrowed her eyes at him as she set the phone recording to her "Closed" message and pulled her rather thin winter coat and bag from under the counter to put them on. The coat had been one of her first purchases when she came back to Kansas City a little over ten years prior. Her layers of light jackets had not been enough when the bitter cold swept through the city that first winter back home. The decade hadn't been kind to it, and now it was quite tattered and barely kept her warm.

"Go to the car. I'm going to set the alarm, and then you can follow me to my apartment," she murmured, waiting as they shuffled back out into the cold and into Tommy's truck, which he started before the doors shut. With her one ungloved hand, she pushed in the code to turn on the alarm and waited for the first of the aggravating beeps before she hustled out herself.

As she was locking each of the deadbolts, she noted to herself how strange it would be for those siblings to see her little home. The only person outside of Durran, Vee's best friend, who had seen her apartment was Shane; however, he had not even been in the interior of her abode. Her door and, unfortunately, her pajamas were all that had been in view when he had come over to talk to her months ago. Even though she considered Tommy her friend, she wasn't in the habit of sharing her only place of real solitude. She turned and looked at the two of them, hands on the heat vents of Tommy's truck, grinning at her. She shook her head, going to her own decrepit car, a 1990 Chevy Lumina.

As the key went into the ignition, she said a silent prayer to the universe that it started, so she wouldn't have to ride in the tiny cab of the truck between those two. She sighed with relief when it managed to turn over. She pulled out onto Westport Road and waited at the horrifyingly long light on Main Street. She stared at the two empty store fronts that used to be comic bookstores, pondering their absence. She always thought it strange that there were barely any comic bookstores anywhere in the city, and yet for a time, there had been two on the same street. Now they were both gone, and the only stores of that nature could be found in suburbs.

Following Main for a few minutes, she finally got to Thirty-Fourth Street. She took a left, which luckily didn't leave Tommy behind for her to wait on. She usually took the back ways, to avoid left turns as much as possible, but she hadn't wanted to sit and tell them the directions to her home while standing in the freezing cold. Tommy had been there before, but that had been so long ago she doubted he remembered the way.

Her street came up quickly, and she parked easily enough in front of her building, watching as Tommy passed her by to find another open spot. She knew this was going to be a long night, if not a long few days, with two Werewolves keeping her company—against

her will and on orders from their pack leader—but there was really nothing she could do about it.

An order's an order.

Tommy and Lori made their way up to the apartment complex door, just as Vee was unlocking it. The hallway was cold, but as they made their way up to the third floor it got a little better. The Weres had warmer bodies than she did, so she knew the break from the biting wind was good enough to keep them from being chilled. She, however, shook a little as she pushed her way into her door, switching on lights and heading straight to the thermostat that sat on the wall beside her refrigerator. She tried to save any way she could, even if that meant her apartment was nearly as cold as the unheated hallway while she was gone for the day.

When she turned back around she noticed the two of them looking over her humble one-bedroom apartment. Their eyes weren't scrutinizing, just curious as they took in at all the various things she had about. She wasn't necessarily messy, just a little cluttered. Books sat in piles on the end tables by her two futons, DVD and Blu-ray cases were strewn on the floor at the base of her television, and her coffee mug from the morning still sat at the little ledge off her tiny kitchen. Other than that, and a neat stack of mail, it was clean.

The kitchen was separated from the rest of the space by a tiny wall with a window opening. As if the people who renovated the building had thought people would be entertained here. This small apartment was meant for one and so were the other apartments in this building. No entertaining happened in any apartment here. It was part of its appeal.

There wasn't much to the space. The walls were painted a grayed lavender and most of the floors were a bleached wood, with scattered bathroom rugs for comfort on her bare feet. She had a small card table with two chairs pushed in a corner and her futons and TV took up the rest of the space. Beyond that there was a small hallway that held three doors; a tiny linen closet, a bathroom, and her bedroom which was about half the size of the living space. She wasn't rich, she was a locksmith, and she was all by herself. She didn't need much space.

"Um… can I get you guys something to drink?" she asked nervously, fidgeting a little as she pulled off her coat and slung it on a chair.

"I'm good," Tommy said, looking at Lori who shook her head and smiled.

"'Kay. I'm going to do a few things. Watch TV or something," Vee said, turning to head down the tiny hall that led to her bedroom. She entered it, taking off her shoes and replacing them with her worn, black slippers. For a moment she just stood there, looking around and unsure of how she felt about the situation. She realized she had been holding her breath since they came in, and she let it out shakily.

She thought about calling Shane and giving him a piece of her mind, but that wouldn't change the scenario at all. It would only prove to irritate her more about him sticking his thumb in her business, as usual. He was heavy-handed and tended to overlook her independence. It was never malicious, and she knew that, but it was a boundary she had tried to set previously— that she wouldn't constantly have bodyguards. He had,

for a time, respected that boundary, but clearly, he had just decided that invisible line was worth crossing.

If this meeting with this other pack leader was so important, and so potentially dangerous, why didn't he just call her about it himself instead of sending Tommy in to do it for him? Their relationship was… odd, but she felt like he could have avoided a lot of her anger had he just been more forthcoming.

She took another deep breath, deciding she needed to push how frustrated she was with Shane from her mind. She padded back into the living area and looked over to see Tommy stretched out on one futon, while Lori was flipping channels cross-legged on the other. Vee smiled to herself for a moment. If anything, Werewolves knew how to make themselves comfortable in any situation.

"Chinese food sound okay?" she asked them, getting only approving sounds and feelings to match. It was a bit early to order dinner, but with how slow delivery was this time of year on a Friday it would be an acceptable time to eat when it arrived.

She went to the kitchen, pulling open a narrow drawer full of takeout menus. She never understood why apartments redid kitchens but left these absurdly narrow, useless drawers and cabinets in their wake. The only things she could fit in the cabinet below the drawer were thin bottles of liquor and baking sheets, the former she would be sure to get out later that evening after Lori either went home or passed out. She looked through the menus until she finally came across the one she wanted, closing the drawer with her hip and flopping on the futon next to Lori, since Tommy was taking up all of his.

"Alright, what do you want?" she asked, turning first to Lori, whom she knew would be easier to please.

"Large beef with broccoli and some crab rangoon, please?" she asked, smiling sweetly.

"And for your brother?" Vee asked, nodding her head toward the massive man who had taken over her usual spot. It had a better angle for the television, so of course he sat on that one.

"A large orange chicken and a large combination fried rice," he said, turning his head from the explicit reality television show long enough to answer and give Vee a wink, to which she rolled her eyes. Internally, she was happy he seemed to have gotten out of the funk he had been in at the shop. Perhaps since she had decided to calm down, he had relaxed back to himself.

She dug through her bag to find her phone, dialing the number and placing their order. As she listened to it ring, she smiled at the fact she was not ordering for herself for once, but it was tainted with the knowledge they were ordered to be there. She had chosen to be alone, but she couldn't fool herself that it made her happier to be around them. That had been a strange revelation recently, what with all the new people in her life. Her loneliness was a choice she had made, and not necessarily something that made her happy.

As she sat down, she watched the commercial that Tommy seemed so enthralled with and decided to ignore the idiocy. She turned to Lori who was feeling the exact same way.

"So, are you staying, or are you leaving me alone with your brother for the night?" Vee asked, suddenly feeling very uncomfortable with the idea of being alone in her tiny apartment with Tommy, however friendly they may be. She enjoyed his company on outings or in her shop. Alone in her apartment might be too awkward.

"Dad's hosting the other pack members, and Mom went to St. Louis to stay with her sister. Last year I would have gone with her, but I can't leave the territory since I'm a member of the pack," she said, her feeling of resentment wafting toward Vee. Thomas, Lori and Tommy's father, was Shane's second. He also lived right across the street from Shane, so it made sense the other pack leader was staying with him.

It was rather uncommon that a girl would be born a Were with one human parent, but it happened. It was much more common for males. Lori obviously had conflicting feelings on the matter. On one hand, Lori enjoyed being part of the pack, the comradery and inclusion that came along with that, as well as some of her new abilities, but on the other, the older she got, the further away she got from her mother. Cora, their mother, understood being different to an extent, but only from having Werewolves for a husband and son for the last twenty-six years. That was probably why Lori enjoyed spending time with Vee so much. Vee may not have been a Werewolf, but she certainly understood what it was to be different.

"You're stuck with us, Vee," Tommy said, gesturing to the duffle bag and stuffed backpack by the door that Vee hadn't noticed previously.

"Packed overnight bags and everything," Vee commented, her eyebrows nearly to her hairline. Having company for dinner felt good, but the bags sitting there with the implication they were sleeping in her apartment felt like she was having them move in, making her want a drink all that much more. Drinking obviously didn't help control her *gifts*, but sometimes it didn't matter. Her emotions seemed to be out of control enough already, since she was fluttering between enjoying that they were there and filling with anxiety over it.

"We're only here until Shane gives us the okay. Then we're out of your hair," Tommy said, obviously noticing her tensed state and increased heart rate.

"It's not your fault. I could kill Shane, though," she murmured as she watched Tommy toe his shoes off and attempt to set his feet on the coffee table. Her threatening glare had him thinking better of it.

"You're lucky Mom isn't here. She would rip you a new one for trying to put your feet on the furniture," Lori said with a satisfied smirk as he put his socked feet back on the floor.

"I live alone now, Lori. I can put my feet on whatever furniture I want," he grumbled, feeling embarrassed for having tried it at Vee's.

"It's not the gesture I care about, but you have nasty man feet, no offense," Vee said, making a mock disgusted face toward his grey socks, that she suspected used to be white.

"None taken."

Vee shook her head at the TV, it was still on the reality show, which in her opinion was nowhere near reality. Why people enjoyed these shows, she would never know. Lori toed the strap of her backpack, pulling it in front of her on the floor before she started unzipping it.

"Homework?" Vee asked, watching her unload book after monstrously huge book.

"Just a few Trig problems," Lori grumbled with distain. The thought of math had both Vee and Tommy cringing.

"Don't be asking for my help. I'm no good at that," Tommy said, eyeing the Trigonometry book like it would bite him.

They sat in comfortable silence for a while. Tommy flipping channels haphazardly, and Vee reading while Lori cursed under her breath about the problem she was working on.

Just then there was a buzz at the intercom by her door. She wandered to it and pressed the 'talk' button.

"Yes?"

"Delivery?"

"Be right down."

Grabbing her wallet, she rushed down the stairs and opened the front door. The deliveryman gladly took her money, handing her the food and rushing back to his car, shivering as he went.

The aroma of Chinese food engulfed her nostrils. After her disappointing lunch, she was starving. She rushed quickly back up to her apartment, slamming the door closed, into the kitchen to cut open the bags of food. There was no point in fighting with the plastic bags. The thin, clear plastic somehow made them impossible to open without cutting or tearing them anyway.

She opened each container, organizing the food according to who wanted what, before she wandered back in the living room to place them in front of her guests.

"Drinks now?"

"Soda," they said in unison, not looking away from the TV and homework.

She grabbed three sodas, tucking them under her arm before she grabbed her own plate and three sets of chopsticks. She sat beside Lori again, handing out beverages and utensils. Lori had put her books away and placed a movie in. It was a dry comedy that had Tommy scratching his head, while the girls thoroughly enjoyed themselves. Lori helped Vee clear the food once they were finished, Tommy having completely emptied his containers, while he chose the next movie. It was a gory action movie they all enjoyed; however, Lori and Vee secretly planned to make him watch another of their choosing once it was over.

Halfway through Tommy's choice Vee's phone rang causing her to jump up and rush to the counter where she'd left it. For some reason she picked it up without looking who it was, assuming it was someone who locked themselves out of their house or car.

"Hello?"

"Vee, how's your company?"

Shane.

Her happy mood brought on by enjoyable company faltered, although hearing his voice made her heart beat a little oddly for a moment.

"Fine, Shane. Why are you calling?" she asked, keeping her voice a little flat, to show her frustration.

"He arrived and is staying with Thomas. I haven't gotten a specific timeline on how long he's planning to stay."

"So, you don't know when I get my life back?" she snapped, letting the last word end with bite.

"I'm sorry," he offered softly, only making her scoff.

"Yeah, I'm sure," she said sarcastically, ending the call promptly.

She hadn't even turned around to go back to sit when Tommy's phone began ringing.

"Boss?" he answered.

"Give her the phone," came Shane's voice. A normal human wouldn't have been able to hear so clearly from that distance, but her ability to hear just as well as the Weres only made her fume, knowing she wasn't getting out of this conversation like she wanted to.

"What?" she very nearly barked as soon as a very skittish Tommy handed the phone to her. She smiled internally, knowing Tommy was usually much more dominant. Somehow she brought out the helpless pup in many of the Weres she knew.

"You need to calm down! I'm trying to protect you from exploitation!" Shane yelled, causing her to pull the phone away from her ear.

"Protecting me from exploitation? What do you think you've been doing?" she yelled equally as loudly.

"Damnit! If I hadn't taken you in someone else would have. Vampires or the Fae would have gotten to you, and you would be treated a lot less friendly than what you've gotten from us. Or you would be dead." She could hear the growl in his voice as he tried to hold back his anger.

"The Fae would have no use for me. If my smell is so special, like you seem to think, I assume the Vampires would have attacked me by now. We had a deal, Shane. I didn't agree to have you treat me like a prisoner and have guards sent to my house while some meeting was taking place."

"Our deal was situational. I never promised I would never protect you again," he grumbled, going silent for a moment as if in thought. *"Just accept it, and we'll talk when he leaves."* And with that, the conversation was clearly over as the line went dead.

Vee growled in frustration as she glared at the phone, wanting to punch a wall.

"I'm having a drink. Sorry Lori," she said, not waiting for a response as she threw open the tiny cabinet. She grabbed the bottles of tequila and rum, a glass, a shot glass, and stomped back over to the futon to mix a rum and coke and fill a shot of tequila.

She took the first shot and sip, only looking up at her guests as she poured the next shot. Tommy gave her a pained look coupled with feelings of anxious concern that she felt from him. She felt similar feelings coming from Lori, and it only proved to make her ashamed of the screaming fit she had with Shane.

"Sorry," she murmured.

"It's fine. Just..." Tommy started, trailing off uncomfortably.

"I don't follow orders. I never have. I'm not in a *pack*. I don't have a leader," she tried to explain. She was used to doing things *her* way. Being on her own gave her that privilege and Shane had walked into her life

and decided, in his very dominant Werewolf way, that things with her would be going *his* way.

"But he feels like you're a member, even if you aren't one of us. That's not usually how it happens. Period," Lori said quietly. "It's about as rare as you are."

Vee looked over at Lori, a bit shocked. She wasn't lying. There was no burn behind Vee's eyes that would normally accompany a lie, but she couldn't quite understand the words the girl had clearly said.

She was thought of as a member?

She had never been accepted in anything. Not for her personality and not for what she could do. Even her sister, who raised her from the time she was ten, never truly understood or accepted Vee's abilities.

"Victoria, nothing's wrong, stop acting like there is," *Eliza said as she nervously began cleaning the house after* *news that they would be evicted. Money was always tight.* *Her sister had only been eighteen when their parents died* *and gave up college and the life she had expected, to take* *care of her younger sister. It was that or foster care for sweet* *little Vee.*

"But ... you're sending me feelings. It makes me want *to throw up,"* *Vee whispered, tears pooling in her eyes. She* *didn't understand how she felt other people's emotions any* *more than the people she told. It only frightened or enraged* *them. Her sister's pain was her pain, and the lie her sister* *said—no matter how innocent it was—throbbed in her* *head like an angry burn.*

"I'm not sending you shit! Stop pretending, or everyone's *going to think you're a freak!"* *Eliza screamed, causing Vee* *to cringe at the anger and confusion, along with the worry.*

She shuffled back to her room, curling up on her bed, to try and rid the nagging feelings of not only her sister, but also every person in the apartments around them.

It wasn't until later that she realized she could distinguish people who weren't quite human. They hummed at her or stung her, or she felt nothing at all, depending on what they were. And knowing from an early age, not only from her sister, but everyone else she mentioned her abilities to, that she wouldn't be accepted; she isolated herself, concluding that solitude was the only way she would survive. She would never be accepted, and no one would ever believe or understand her. Yet Lori just told the truth as she admitted Vee was 'a member.' Her anger was still there, but her anxiety was heightened. She wasn't sure she wanted to be included.

After years of thinking she would never truly be part of a family, thinking she would always be alone, she was now pulled into this pack without even knowing it, and it scared her. She took another shot of tequila, chasing it with her rum and coke. and She screwed the lids back on the bottles.

"If it's unheard of, why am I a member?" she finally asked after a long and uneasy silence.

"You helped Lori, and you're alone," Tommy said quietly. That only proved to confuse her further.

"Alone? What does me being alone have to do with anything?"

Tommy and Lori shared looks and cleared their throats simultaneously. Normally Vee would have

found that funny, but in her current state she couldn't find humor in anything.

"Other preternaturals have groups, or they frequently see each other. You… you have no others like you. You are completely alone. You don't even know what you are," Tommy murmured.

"You've been helpful and seem to care about some of us, even if we piss you off," Lori said, glaring at her brother. "Shane wanted to help you. He wanted to take you in," Lori finished, reaching out her hand to take Vee's but pulling back when Vee's body went rigid.

It was pity. They pitied her.

Shane pitied her.

"Take me in…" Vee grumbled under her breath, hearing the same words Shane had just said over the phone a few minutes before echoed in Lori's words. "I don't need to be taken in."

She stood, pacing for a moment.

"Do I seem like I need to be taken in?" she asked, not looking at either of them as she got a rhythm going with her steps. There was no answer from either of them. "I can't believe the audacity of that man."

She knew Shane had feelings for her, lust if nothing else, and obviously she was useful to the pack. Hearing that he felt sorry for her, that he felt like he needed to protect her like she was incapable of taking care of herself because she was alone, that was just unacceptable.

After several uncomfortable minutes of silence while she walked in a tight square, she started feeling stupid for having her little tantrum in front of them. She wandered to the furthest wall and opened the mahogany trunk beside the television to take out blankets for each of them.

"I don't have any other pillows. Sorry," she said, as they each took a blanket, their emotions wavering between pity and discomfort.

That's how she made people feel. Uncomfortable.

This was why she needed to be alone.

"Goodnight," was all she said, before she went back through the narrow hallway to her bedroom.

She knew she wasn't going to sleep much. The emotions of others would rouse her or change her dreams. As she pulled off her jeans, replacing them with loose pajama pants, she felt the exhaustion of the emotional rollercoaster that had been the last half of her day. She fell back onto her bed, cocooning herself in her comforter, and tried to block out the nagging emotions and vibrating presence that was associated with the Werewolves in the other room.

She tried to focus on her breathing and the slightly calming effect of the vibrations, instead of the conflicting emotions and mumbled voices from the front room. Slowly and finally, leaving the day behind, she fell into a restless sleep.

CHAPTER 3

As soon as he heard the distinct sound of Tommy's phone snapping closed for the second time today, Shane wanted to hurt something... badly. He was already dealing with another pack leader in his territory, which was always a precarious situation. Dominance games and potential take overs were always something to consider when other Weres came into the picture.

He was just trying to keep Vee safe. Why did she have to make everything so difficult?

He understood their agreement. He would not be constantly guarding her. She needed her space. But now word of her abilities had been made known to other packs. This could be dire for her. So, yes, he did feel obligated to have someone watching over her, protecting her while the Shawnee Leader was in town. She had exposed herself to his pack to save Lori, and he would be forever indebted to her for it. Yet he ached to be there, guarding her instead of Tommy and Lori. He wanted to stay at her quaint apartment with the prospect of laughter and talking. He wanted a scenario that didn't involve one of them getting angry.

Vee.

He didn't know why he was so fascinated with her. Ever since he first found out about her and smelled her scent, he had been consumed by her. Months had passed since then. He had known her almost a year at this point, and everything about her was still just as interesting and compelling as it had been at the beginning. His pursuit of her abilities had not been for her services necessarily, but more for her company. He thought giving her those tasks would make her feel needed and wanted. He thought that she would feel like she was part of the pack. Apparently, he had been wrong.

Or he had gone about his requests in the wrong way.

Of course, he did.

Having her yell at him for trying to protect her made him want to hurt things, hurt people. His eyes flashed a violent gold; his wolf touching the surface. He needed to calm himself. It was perfectly reasonable she would be defensive. She had very clearly told him she needed space and time. She told him she didn't want him doing this very thing. She would have probably been more accepting of the protection, had he just communicated with her.

Logic apparently held no place in his mind when it came to Vee.

"Dad?" came Patrick, his son, from the other side of the office door.

"Come in," was all he said in response, his voice low and rough with anger as he looked down at the paperwork on his desk without seeing any of it. His mind was elsewhere. Patrick wandered through; his head bowed in respect. He looked a lot like his father but obviously younger, being that he was still a teenager. Weres didn't age much after they entered adulthood, so Shane looked like he was in his late twenties or early thirties when he was actually quite a bit older.

"Did you need something?"

"Thomas is on the phone."

Shane's eyes looked over his son. He could see the nervousness of Patrick's body language, which only made him more suspicious of the phone call. If the Shawnee Leader had something to say before the meeting this would be the optimum time to call.

"Thank you, Patrick," Shane murmured, turning to the phone on his desk and lifting it. "Shane," he murmured in greeting, trying not to break the handset as he held it.

"Leib knows her name, what she does, not necessarily her abilities, but..." said Thomas in his gruff voice, lower since he was trying to speak quietly so his house guests wouldn't hear.

"How?"

"He didn't say."

"That changes things," Shane murmured absently, pinching the bridge of his nose.

This was becoming more and more complicated as time went on. With another leader being this aware of Vee, the Sha would soon follow. He couldn't protect her from them. He couldn't disobey them. They may have had inklings about her from their last visit, but he was hoping there would be more time before Vee had to face them.

"Time tomorrow still remains the same."

"How will you keep her from this?" Thomas asked, his voice anxious. He cared for Vee as if she were family. After Vee saved Lori, he too felt he was indebted to her.

"I'll think of something, Thomas. Don't worry. For now, your children will keep her safe," Shane said gently into the phone before he hung up.

The morning sun woke Vee, burning her cheek as it poured through the window and roused her from the subconscious. She rolled over, looking at the clock which unfortunately read 1 p.m. instead of her normal 5 a.m. She didn't set her alarm.

"Shit!" she hissed, hopping out of bed and rushing from her room to the kitchen. She started brewing the coffee while she pulled her dark brown, knotted locks away from her face and grabbed her phone from the counter.

No missed calls. What a relief.

"Coffee?" came Tommy's garbled voice from the living room.

She nearly jumped out of her skin, completely forgetting she had two other beings in her apartment. She realized she had been ignoring their presence since she woke, or rather, she had grown so accustomed to their vibrations that she was effectively blocking them. The idea that she had been blocking them out made her smile briefly. It would come in handy if she gave thought to how she managed to do it. She supposed she hadn't spent enough time in the presence of Weres to let herself grow used to the way they felt in her head. However, she quickly pushed it away as Tommy wandered in.

"Did you make enough for me?" he asked, smiling sleepily as he stretched.

"Uh… yeah…" she stammered, going to the cabinet and pulling out another mug to hand to him, tapping her fingers on the counter impatiently as she waited for the coffee maker to finish its brew.

"Did you sleep all right?" she asked, realizing how uncomfortable he and his sister must have been on her futons without pillows. Those futon mattresses were old.

"It was better than the ground. We've had to do that a few times," he admitted, smiling a bit at her.

"Sorry about the sour goodnight. I was having a bad day."

"I noticed. Don't worry about it," he said, touching her shoulder and sending her comfort. It only made her feel guiltier. "Oh, and I have money for dinner last night. Never got to pay you back," he murmured fishing through his pockets and pulling out a crumpled wad of cash.

"That's way too much. Just give me twenty, and we'll call it even," she said, and handed the rest of the wad back to him.

The coffee finished, and she poured some in her mug, glancing at him to hold out his. A few years as a waitress had shown her a great deal when it came to pouring coffee to outstretched hands. She didn't spill a drop before she placed it gently back in the warmer and turned to add milk and sweetener.

"You want anything in yours, or do you like it black?" she asked, glancing at him and shaking a sweetener packet.

"Black," he said, nodding in thanks as he took a sip. They both heard Lori stirring from the living room.

"We didn't wake her, did we?" Vee started, a little worried, but Tommy shook his head.

"No. She's a heavy sleeper. If she's awake, it is her own doing," he said, smiling at her concern.

He noticed how much affection Vee seemed to have over his little sister. There was a sort of protectiveness about the little locksmith that he admired. If it hadn't been for her, his sister would not be as light and happy as she was. True, Lori had to deal with things most girls her age didn't, but she did most of it with a smile on her face. She wouldn't have if she had massacred her close-knit group of friends.

"Morning," Lori grumbled, staggering into the kitchen and rubbing the sleep from her eyes. Her curly hair was in a crazed disarray on top of her head.

"Morning," Vee said, as she leaned against the counter of her small kitchen.

"Coffee?" was all the groggy teen managed to say as her eyes scanned the cabinets, trying to decide which one to open first for a mug to hold the precious elixir.

"You're too young to be drinking coffee, Lori," Vee said, as she reopened the cabinet and fetched another mug.

"Old argument, Vee. I'm plenty old enough. Besides, late nights with the pack make for hard school days in the morning. I have to drink it, or I would fail all my classes."

Both Tommy and Vee chuckled at the statement as she fixed her cup adding only sweetener before sipping it with a smile on her face.

"So…" Tommy started a bit awkwardly. "What's the plan for today?" he asked, scratching his chest absentmindedly.

This all seemed perfectly normal and abnormal at the same time. She had been quite put out by the thought of them staying in her little home, but they seemed very at ease and relaxed. Their comfort here, in her space, made her feel much more resigned about it. Having people in her small home wasn't so bad. Having people in her life was, perhaps, not quite so daunting, if she could enjoy the pleasure of drinking coffee and conversation with these two. This pack was changing her very carefully crafted view of the world. It was a lot easier to be lonely if you convinced yourself you prefer it that way.

"Well, since I'm stuck with you two; I guess I won't go to the shop. No point with how late it already is, and Saturdays are usually house calls. I had no appointments," Vee said, shrugging and trying not to care too much about the missed work. The shop was at a brief lull after Valentine's Day, and the cold tail end of winter made for less people leaving their homes, so house calls had dwindled a bit as well.

"No calls from Shane?" Lori asked, looking back and forth between her brother and Vee.

"Not so far," Vee said, with a similar shake of the head from Tommy.

"When's the meeting?" she asked, this time directed at her brother.

"I think it's later this evening. If he's not gone after that, we'll know there's trouble," he muttered, glancing over at Vee, who was a bit dejected by the idea of possible issues.

There was silence for a moment that began to get awkward. She hadn't ever had people over while she followed through with her morning ritual. She wasn't sure what to do next or if she should even try. But the awkwardness was growing, and she felt she should leave the room in some way, especially with how claustrophobic the tiny kitchen had become. It was a kitchen meant for one, and there were three people standing in it, one being large, hulking Tommy.

"I think I'll take a shower," she finally said, squeezing past them, coffee in hand, and made her way to the bathroom. A very hot shower seemed to be in order. Maybe that would help her refocus.

As the hot water finally began to pour, after nearly fifteen minutes of running, steam filled the room. She set her mug down on the tiny bathroom sink and started to pull off her clothes, before luxuriously stepping into the spray of the showerhead, letting the water cover and consume her. It was a simple pleasure but a pleasure, nonetheless. She would have been more than happy to spend her days showering if she didn't have things that had to be accomplished.

She was just pouring shampoo into her hand when she heard a phone ringing. Whether it was Tommy's or

hers she wasn't sure, but he answered it, speaking in his low voice. She couldn't make out what was being said over the sound of the water. After straining to make out the unintelligible words, she decided to ignore it. There was no way she was ruining her blissful shower over a stupid phone call, most likely from a stubborn Werewolf who sought to 'take her in' as Lori pointed out the previous evening.

With the suds rinsed from her hair, she began washing her face and body, enjoying the feeling of the grime being washed away and the fresh smell of her soap replacing it. She knew various Others, like her friends in the other room, could tell people apart simply from their scent. She was curious what she smelled like to them, given that she seemed to recall Shane mentioning that her scent was a bit different from other humans.

Was scent affected by soaps and shampoos? Or did the individual outrank any other scent that might linger on them? And why was she suddenly so preoccupied by how she smelled to the people in the other room, or for that matter, how she smelled to Shane?

The thought of Shane lingered her mind. And his scent...

She began recalling the time months ago when they had kissed. His touch, hard and demanding, but exactly what she wanted. The feel of his skin on hers lit a fire within her she hadn't ever experienced before. She felt her heart start to beat rapidly in her chest. She shook her head, ridding herself of the thought of him as she rinsed the remainder of the soap away.

No.

She could not think about Shane that way. Only trouble would come from that.

Tommy was still on the phone, but now she heard the television was on. Lori had probably become bored with whatever the phone conversation was. Wrapping herself in a towel, she quickly dashed into her room before being spotted by the massive man in the next room. She dried herself, thinking about what she might wear for the day. Normally she wore jeans and a t-shirt that didn't really show the shape of her body, but today, she decided to grab a more fitted shirt to go with her jeans. There was no reason not to. She wouldn't be stocking inventory or hauling heavy safes. It wouldn't be a constant bother to pull it back down as she worked because she wasn't working.

Once she was finished dressing and her hair was brushed, she wandered back out to see Tommy and Lori, both on the couch. But while Lori was sipping a fresh cup of coffee and staring at the TV, Tommy was still murmuring into his cell phone. It had been at least thirty minutes; what could he possibly be talking about?

"I know... but she won't like it," Tommy said, his voice obviously trying to be quiet and discrete.

"Is she out yet?"

"Yes. And she's standing right here, looking at me," Tommy said, having turned around to see Vee glaring at him, hands on hips.

"Hand it to her," came Shane's voice. She took it, making a mental effort not to be so angry today, even if he was being overbearing.

"Yes, Shane?" she inquired, placing the phone to her ear.

"Got a call. There's no way to avoid it. You'll have to come to the meeting." He paused for a moment, hesitating. *"I have to claim you,"* Shane said, his tone very clipped and business-like.

"Claim me?" she asked, eyes narrowing at Tommy, who was trying his best not to be part of the conversation, but she could feel his discomfort.

"I will explain it to you when you get here. We have a while before it starts."

"What is this meeting going to entail?" She was now pacing the room, listening to the floor creak beneath her feet.

"We will discuss matters like smaller non-wolf packs in the area as well as territory lines and new members. The last meeting was when Lori was introduced as a member." It was like he was somehow trying to soften the meeting idea to her, as if she would feel better about going to this foreign and uncomfortable event, knowing Lori had once had to go through it. The difference was Vee was not one of them.

"When do you want us?"

There was silence on the other end for a moment.

"You aren't going to fight me?" Shane asked, his voice giving away his surprise.

"I can fight with you in person. It will be more interesting that way. Now, when?"

"As soon as possible," he muttered, still obviously shocked.

"Am I to dress a certain way or can I wear my jeans?"

"Just be comfortable."

CHAPTER 3

"Got it." And then she hung up on him. It was rather satisfying, given how mystified he seemed to be.

"Let me get a few things, and we can go?" Vee asked her visitors, who looked and felt just as shocked as Shane had seemed over the phone. Vee never did anything that wasn't her idea without a fight. She turned, going back to her room to fetch socks and put on some boots. She decided to put on an open jacket to cover some of her figure as to not spur on any unnecessary lust from the meeting full of Werewolves tonight. All Weres battled their instincts. The beast within them so much more prominent, making things like attraction ten-fold more than that of a human.

When she reemerged Tommy and Lori were packed, dressed, and the television was off. This was certainly not the way she wanted to begin her day, but she figured any day that had to do with other preternaturals would be an unpleasant one.

She pulled on her coat and grabbed her bag, slinging it over her shoulder as she walked to the door. They followed suit, only stopping so she could lock her door before they headed out to their cars.

There was no need for her to ride with them. She had been to Shane's house on several occasions and headed there as soon as she pulled out of her cramped spot. It would take her about fifteen minutes to get there on a weekday, but it was Saturday. The roads were full of people who weren't working, so by the time she got on the other side of the creek it had been fifteen minutes. It would still take her another ten to get to his house, given how congested the streets were.

The large colonial house on Morningside Drive already had a huge number of cars parked both in the driveway and on the street. It was lucky the streets on that block were made to be much wider than normal, or people wouldn't have been able to drive down it. She parked a block away from his house, trudging up with her hands in her pockets, body quivering from the cold, onto his lawn. She didn't care if she wasn't supposed to walk on the grass; she was taking a short cut.

She rang the doorbell just as she heard Tommy's truck go down the street, parking in his dad's driveway. When the door opened, she felt like she had been hit over the head with a sledgehammer. The number of Werewolves in the house, the vibration she felt from their presence, made her want to lie down in the cold, browned grass and pray for it to stop. But she had to get this over with; she would grow accustomed to the feeling over time. The lanky boy who answered the door gave her a strange look, confused about her sudden discomfort.

Vee assumed the boy at the door was Jonathan Meyer, whom she had never met, but the similarity between him and John Meyer was uncanny. Vee had gone to see John about his youngest three-year-old son the month prior. He hadn't wanted Vee to come to his house, being far more skeptical about her sudden inclusion into the pack's affairs than most of the other Weres seemed to be, so she had met him here with Shane. John had been quite nervous as Vee looked over the younger boy that day, his eyes incredulous as he watched at her. She had told him that the tiny boy, like his older brother that stood before her now, would also be a Were.

"Vee," she said pointing to herself, making the boy nod and gesture for her to come inside.

"Shane is upstairs," he said, pointing to the stairs at the center of the entry where she stood.

She wandered up, her head slowly growing used to the constant vibrations with each passing moment. She had only been on the first floor of Shane's house. The stairs were carpeted with thick, mossy green fabric that looked far too expensive for her grubby shoes to be stepping on. For a moment she was worried that she might be smudging dirt from his yard on them, but she quickly decided she didn't care. Shane wanted to see her? He could deal with some stains for all her trouble.

The attitude she had been trying to keep down over the phone earlier was starting to rear its ugly head.

"Vee?" came his voice from a room to the right as she reached the top of the stairs.

"Yeah?" she said, not sure which door to go through to get to him. He opened the door to the furthest right, stepping out halfway. His shirt was unbuttoned, but the sleeves were rolled up, like he was dressed in what he wore from the night before. His dark hair was slightly disheveled, but it was enough to bring a certain amount of allure to him. His deep brown eyes took her appearance in.

She felt several emotions simultaneously. Some her own, others his, all confusing, especially accompanied by the sly smile that started in the corner of his mouth. She was still wearing her coat, so he was unable to see her more form fitting shirt, but it would be revealed

in time. She wasn't sure how she wanted him to react, now regretting her choice of attire for the day.

"Come in?" he offered, stepping aside so she could pass him. When she did, she looked at the surroundings. It was an office, reminiscent of older times, with deep earth tones and an ornately carved, dark, hardwood desk. He even had claw footed leather chairs flanking it. "Do you want to sit or...?"

"I'm kind of jumpy at the moment," she admitted, trying to settle herself with the torrent of emotions filling the massive house. The building seemed much smaller now that there were fifty people within it. The last few times she had been there the house only held Shane and a few other pack members, making the space within seem much more expansive, especially in comparison to her tiny apartment. Fifty-ish large Were bodies made any space seem small.

"Can I take your coat? It's gotten quite warm in here since the majority of the pack arrived."

She looked down at her coat, which she realized she was nervously clutching. She had to take it off; in comparison to the outside, it was a sauna in there. Slowly she peeled it off and placed it over her arm, instead of giving it to him. She could feel his slight desire at the hint of her more revealed figure. The jacket wasn't doing its job, but who was she to judge? She had just looked him over moments before and found herself getting lost in his chest every time it passed before her.

"So, what's with this meeting?" she asked, getting straight to business as he went to sit behind the desk.

"Shawnee Leader, Leib, has been hearing rumors about an unknown preternatural that has been helping our pack with various things," Shane said, looking up at her from his seat.

"So?"

"So? What do you mean?" he asked, a flash of irritation hitting her from him.

"What do they want with me? If they just want my help on occasion, like you, I would do it," she said, shrugging nonchalantly, only further angering him. This coming from the woman who was so enraged with him for sending people to protect her was now saying she would just go, drop everything, and help another pack?

"They'll want to take you. They'll want to claim you and use you. From what Thomas said, Leib seemed furious that I had kept something like this from him as though he is somehow entitled to know about *my* pack. I don't know what he would do to you, and I don't want to find out. You help us. You saved one of us. So, we will do the same for you," he said, having stood and moved around the desk to tower over her. He was looking down at her, holding her upper arms, and showing her just how much he meant his words. Empathy, protectiveness, slight pity, anxiety, anger, and affection all flooded her intensely when he touched her. Compared to her five foot four, he was a giant, and he was overwhelming.

"So, what then? *You're* going to claim me? You already feel like you've *taken* me in, don't you? So why not *use* me? You've practically done everything you say he's planning to do!" Her eyes burned with a rage that was kindled by his, eyes turning amber to match his

gold. His grip got tighter on her arms, and his nostrils flared.

"You are so stubborn it's unreasonable. I am claiming you so you can have somewhat of a normal life. Eventually you'll get yourself into danger, meddling with our or some other preternatural's business. You did it once; you'll do it again. If I claim you, you have allies. You can trust us. You can trust *me*, Vee," he said his voice softening a bit as he spoke. He was urging her to see reason, hoping she would feel his sincerity.

They stared at each other for a long while. She was tasting his emotions, feeling the truth in his words. He was being sincere. His emotions all culminating to show her he truly cared, and he was right. Nothing of what he said had been lies. Everything he told her about the Shawnee pack leader was true, and she had no way of protecting herself from an entire pack of Werewolves.

"How the hell does this work?" she asked, glumly, letting her eyes drop away from his intense stare. He slowly loosened his grip on her arms, letting his fingers run down the length of them, brushing her soft skin before he took a step away from her.

"There is a sort of ritual. It's only words, but it means I have claimed you. No other can touch you or cause harm to you without inciting penalty. That goes for the men of my pack as well," he said, causing her to cast him a wary glance.

"So, *you* claim me, and no man can, what? Touch me? I can't hug Tommy?" she asked.

"That is not what I mean by touch," he said, his expression very serious.

She began to laugh, outright cackle, at the very idea that not only was being intimate uncomfortable for her because of the emotions she could sense from any partner she had ever tried being with, but now she didn't even have the option.

"Well, that's just fantastic. Fine! Let's do it then! I wasn't going to be getting a boyfriend anytime soon!" she shrieked through her maniacal laughter. She really was going to be alone forever. Before, it had been of her own volition. Sad, but *her* choice.

Her reaction not only startled Shane but unnerved him as well. She was trapped by her own isolation, but he could tell she craved company. Someone truly closed off to the idea of others being in their life would never have risked what she did to save Lori or even entertained the idea of helping his pack as she had. Although they had discussed, after their kiss months ago, that they both weren't ready for anything more at the time, she didn't know the full extent of how Shane felt about her.

She would get a sense of his attraction to her, whether animalistic or otherwise. He never let anything beyond that go to her. After the last nine months of knowing her, he could not seem to let her be. He was always wishing for ways to bring her to him, to have her nearby. He craved any reason to see her. He desired her to the point it was painful, but he dampened that feeling for her benefit, not allowing her to feel the overwhelmingly strong connection that had grown from the day they met.

"It would only be for preternaturals. A claim for them to stay away, but you can continue with humans as much as you please. Of course, after tonight you will be public to the Others. All of the preternatural community will know you are not just a human," he said, warning her of the consequences.

She knew she was already in over her head and had been since the moment she learned that any of these things existed. It was only a matter of time before she was exposed to all of them. Why not now?

"I'll do it. You don't have to talk me into or out of it. Just lead the way to your kitchen, and I'll drink coffee until this ordeal is over. Then I'll go home and drink myself to sleep, okay?" she said, her voice thick with resentment and anger, while she could feel remorse flowing from him.

"I'm sorry."

"You're sorry my ass," she hissed, despite knowing his sincerity. She stomped toward the closed door to rip it open and head down the stairs.

"For god sakes, woman!" he growled, grabbing her by the wrist and pulling her back so they were chest to chest. "I'm trying to help you."

"It would have helped nine months ago to have left me the hell alone!"

"Well, we can't travel through time, can we?" he hissed, bending his neck lower so his forehead almost touched hers. "I've already apologized, and you've refused me. Since you're going through with the claim, I suppose you can go pout. Be angry at me for something I can't control. I'm only trying to make it better," he said, releasing her wrist and pulling away from her.

Without a second thought, she swiftly lifted her hand and slapped him hard across the face. For a moment there was a little red spot shaped like her hand, and it was silent and still. The whole house went quiet, waiting for Shane's reaction. He just looked at her, his eyes smoldering pools of golden lava, but strangely, she couldn't feel his emotion. She was instantly confused. She could plainly see a very intense emotion on his face, but she... she couldn't feel it. She almost stepped forward to touch him, hoping the touch would let her know what he was feeling but thought better of it.

If she had, she would have known the feeling he was blocking, withdrawing from, was the urge to pull her back to him and press his lips to her soft ones; to hold her and touch her and feel her. Not a handshake or an involuntary graze. No. He *wanted* her.

"Go get your coffee," he finally murmured, his voice so quiet and calm she was almost fearful of what his true feelings were. Did he want to hurt her now that she reacted that way? Should she try and apologize? The look in his eyes told her otherwise as she turned and went to the main floor, quietly passing other Werewolves, who only stared at her in awe as she made her way to the kitchen.

CHAPTER 4

She wandered through the large oak door that led to the kitchen and rolled her eyes like she did the first time she came to Shane's house. She hadn't seen the kitchen since the renovations were completed, having kept as close to the door as possible when here. The kitchen had been an unfortunate casualty of the rogue lone wolf, Downing, who had tried to kill her. The new kitchen held much of what she loved about the old houses in the neighborhood, but with a few more modern conveniences. Deep oak cabinetry topped with shining black marble covered the counters. A large industrial stainless-steel sink sat beside the high-tech coffeemaker and every other appliance in the place was shiny and new.

She poured herself a cup, rummaging through the cabinets for sugar, sweetener, even honey would have done the trick, but she came up with nothing. An arm reached out and pulled open a drawer, revealing an assortment of beverage sweetening items. She looked up at her helper, shaking her head as soon as she did. It was Patrick, Shane's son, who smiled a little at her. He was tall. He had filled out as if he were in his twenties, a new development in the past few months, and almost as handsome as his father, especially with that smirk slapped on his face.

"Thanks," she muttered, taking a sweetener packet and dumping it in her cup.

"No one gets to him like you do," he said, moving to lean against the counter as she opened the massive stainless-steel refrigerator, inspecting it for milk. Of course, Shane would have the fancy creamer that she didn't think was practical—a waste of money.

"As I recall, you've been quite a handful yourself," she said, pouring the expensive creamer into her coffee and taking the spoon Patrick handed her.

"But I'm his teenage son. I'm allowed to be trouble," he said, crossing his arms over his chest as she took her first sip of the coffee. It was so rich and creamy she wanted to curse the man upstairs for having money or hug him.

"I can be trouble to whomever I please," she muttered indignantly, eyeing the boy with suspicion. He was sweet but raging hormones coupled with the intense feelings of being a Were had given his father a lot more to worry about during these high school years. Car wrecks and fights were just the tip of the troublesome iceberg where Patrick was concerned, but

at that moment his face turned serious, arms dropping to his sides.

"Not after tonight, Vee," he whispered, looking at her with a mixture of pity and hope. He was trying to will her to understand the importance of this, and the weight in her chest only seemed to get heavier with the emotions she was feeling from him.

"Don't remind me," she muttered, glaring for a moment before she returned her stare toward the deep green walls of the kitchen.

Patrick, like Tommy and Lori, had always been nice to her, regardless of the fact she was not a Were. Several times she had allowed him to escape the wrath of his father by letting him work in her shop unpaid instead of whatever the pack punishment was going to be. She knew it must have been hard for a teenager to grow up as part of a pack, especially when normal human things were overridden for important pack matters, and your father happened to be the leader. He also lacked the balance that a mother would bring since his had been human and passed away at his birth.

Vee and Patrick talked for a little while, mostly about how school was going and if he wanted to work at the shop a little over spring break. Vee finally glanced at the clock on the wall oven and noticed it was only four in the afternoon. She was trapped there for another hour before the meeting, and she suddenly felt very uncomfortable about being there. It was always uncomfortable being in this house with its expensive furniture and professionally painted walls, but something about being the only person present within the confines of this house that was not a *real* member of the pack made it worse.

Tommy wandered in the kitchen with Lori hot on his heels.

"We were wondering where you were," Lori said, prancing over to Vee with cat-like grace.

"Found more coffee, huh?" Tommy asked as he opened the fridge in search of food. She hadn't fed the two of them before they rushed out the door. She silently admonished herself for being a bad host. There was nothing that could be done about it now, especially when all she wanted to do was hide in a closet until she was told to go home.

"If you mean the overpriced, absurdly decadent beverage I'm slurping? Then yes," she said, gaining a chuckle from the two younger Werewolves in the room.

"We heard the commotion earlier," Tommy commented, his eyes shifting her way briefly.

"Even over the block heads in the other rooms," Lori said, gesturing to the wall behind her where obnoxiously loud conversations between the males were taking place. "You okay?" she asked after she rolled her eyes at a sudden increase in volume.

"Fine, just angry. Your leader can be quite heavy-handed."

"He's being careful," Tommy murmured as he pulled out some roast in a plastic container from the refrigerator and began eating it with his hands.

Vee couldn't help the internal chuckle rising from her chest, knowing that, although his coffee was overly luxurious and his kitchen cost more than anything she had ever owned, he was at least sensible enough to

preserve leftovers. She guessed it was in a Werewolf's best interest to have their home heavily stocked with food. Werewolves ate a lot.

Just then she heard footsteps on the stairs, despite the loud conversations that had picked back up between the rest of the pack in the living and dining rooms.

"What the hell are you doing?" came Shane's rumbling voice from the entry. His anger washed over Vee like a tidal wave, and she nearly dropped her mug. "Did I say sit around like lazy idiots? Or did I *tell* you to get things ready?" he growled.

The house fell silent save for heartbeats and the now *very* intense vibrations from the Werewolves. As if he snapped his fingers, it sounded like a hundred soldiers got to their feet and started moving about the house. Moments later Shane pushed the kitchen door aside and let his glowering eyes fall on his three pack members that weren't doing something productive. One of whom was trying to put the roast back in the fridge without being noticed.

"Patrick, Tommy, go help the others. Lori, Markus just got here. He needs help with the groceries and making dinner. Will you assist?"

Lori nodded, going toward the back door where Markus was unloading his car as Patrick and Tommy quickly made themselves scarce. Once again, Vee was left alone with Shane. He lowered his eyes, moving around the counter island to her, but he did not speak. He merely opened the cabinet above her, grabbing a mug and moving to her other side to pour a cup of coffee. He didn't even add a sweetening agent or the fancy creamer he owned. He just sipped on his black coffee, leaning back against the counter of the island opposite her.

His shirt was still slightly unbuttoned, and she couldn't help but eye his toned chest. She imagined he was warm and soft to the touch, and she ached to push the rest of the fabric off his shoulders and examine his arms. She physically shook her head and closed her eyes. Again, she was thinking about him in a way that was far from useful. She was supposed to be mad at him, not ogling him.

"If you would like, you can use the computer or watch the television upstairs. No one will bother you up there," he said quietly. He smirked a bit when she shook her head and turned her focus away from him to pace the length of the kitchen. She did this partially to physically step away from him and partially to set her mind back on important matters, not how being near him made her feel.

"Shouldn't we go over this ritual before they get here? People do arrive early on occasion," she said, meeting his gaze and attempting to look intimidating. He sighed at her stubbornness. She was going to pretend to be angry, even if she couldn't stay that way. It was her way of taking some control over her situation. He understood it. It didn't mean he liked it.

"Fine. We should leave the kitchen before they come back inside and start cooking," he said, turning swiftly and heading toward the door. She pushed off the counter and followed him, passing through the dining room to the entry way and toward the stairs. She held back the chuckle that threatened at her

throat as she saw the men all quietly picking up trash, sweeping, and dusting.

She did notice the eyes on the two of them as they made their way upstairs once again. She couldn't help but feel a bit embarrassed, her anxiety picking up again realizing there really wasn't a safe place in this house where no one could hear. When they reached the second floor she was expecting to go back to his office, but instead he led her to the door immediately next to it.

He opened it, and they stepped inside. She stopped dead in her tracks as soon as she realized this was a bedroom. The room alone was the size of her apartment. The massive king-sized bed sat to the left of the room taking up a large portion of it, while matching deep cherry dressers sat across each other on the walls. There was a small table with a reading lamp next to a huge armchair and ottoman. Despite all that large furniture, there was still a huge swath of uncluttered space in between. Double doors opposite the bed were open, leading to a massive bathroom and walk-in closet.

"Could you close the door? You don't mind if I change while we talk?" he asked, not checking before he shed the shirt he was wearing on the floor and wandered into his closet to look through his selection.

She immediately ripped her eyes away from his defined back to close the door and turned back to see him laying one shirt on his bed before going to a dresser to retrieve socks. He noticed her expression then. She looked outwardly shocked and slightly uncomfortable, but the scent she was giving off told a different story. He smirked, watching her grip the coat over her arms for dear life, as if she were trying to keep herself from attacking him.

"So, the claim," he began as he sat on his bed, still shirtless, and leaned over to pull his socks on his feet. It was strange that that action could be seen as sexy, but for some reason Vee was having a hard time focusing. "I will formally state my claim on you, and you will accept it. Without your acceptance the claim will not be recognized. There's really not much more to it. The magic is in the words I say, and as long as you accept it, the claim is legitimate. A full mated bond can't be created without..." he trailed off, pausing to look up at her momentarily.

He wasn't sure how to tell her how a full mated bond worked. The magic of the claim begins it, but it's sealed after the pair ... well, mates. That normally didn't work unless both people were Weres, though. He wasn't certain about her magic, but the way he felt drawn to her was enough to make him believe they would be able to form a bond.

"After I claim you, you may have to answer questions Leib has about you," Shane continued, deciding to leave the bonding part out of it for now as he slipped on shoes she hadn't noticed were there. His last comment snapped her out of the haze she was in.

"What do you mean, questions?" she asked, her brows furrowing.

"He will want to know the extent of your abilities," Shane said seriously as he pulled his shirt over his shoulders but didn't button it as he walked closer to her.

Even Shane didn't know the extent of her abilities. He knew she was an empath, that she had better

senses than humans, and that she could tell the difference between preternaturals, even to the point that she
could tell which they were. He didn't know she could
occasionally influence an emotion or any of the other
things she had done on very rare occasions. She had
no control over some of them. They just... happened.
If Shane didn't know about it neither should anyone
else. He knew her well enough now that he could spot
her in a lie, and her heartbeat was probably ringing in
his ears as fast as a hummingbird's wings because of
her anxiety.

"What's wrong?" he asked, suddenly concerned
with her increased heart rate. He raised his hand to
touch her but let it fall away just as easily as if he
thought better of it.

She didn't know if she should tell him what else
she could do. The part of her that craved the safety
and security that she found in solitude hated all of this.
Years of carefully avoiding detection and here she was
less than a year from when she'd first revealed herself
to them. She was going to have to now share what
she could do with the Shawnee pack and therefore
the whole preternatural world. At that moment, she
wished she had never found out the reason others felt
different. She wished she hadn't left her sister's house
at fifteen. She wished she were as blissfully ignorant
as the humans that lived in the apartments around her.

"Vee?" Shane asked, worry flooding from
him into her.

"You want to know, Shane?" she asked, her voice
a little bitter. She closed her eyes and concentrated,
thinking of the calm serenity of a hot bath, a sunrise, a

baby napping, anything calm, anything different from the worry that was overwhelming both of them from Shane. Then she pushed it toward him, letting it cover him like a warm blanket. Instantly, she no longer felt his concern, She felt the effects of her ability. His hands fell from her arms, lax with the amount of calm he felt.

"You're... doing that?" he asked shakily, his voice as quiet as a whisper. She nodded her head, continuing to push it at him as she could feel the edges fighting with more deeply rooted concern and a bit of anger. "Stop..." he murmured, his voice soft as silk.

"No," she said, fighting back tears that wanted to fall from her jewel-colored eyes from the exertion of pushing and the fear that showing this ability caused.

"Stop," he said a bit more forcefully as the blanket of calm started to unravel at the edges. He was fighting it with more anger, and his voice was becoming harder as he began to regain some control. She shook her head, giving up, and letting the calm fall away, only to feel the full force of his anger and unease hit her.

She physically stepped back, dropping her mug and coat across the thick brown carpet. Quick as lightening he reached out and wrapped her in his arms before she could crumble to the floor. She was pressed to his chest and shaking.

"You cannot tell him that. Avoid telling anyone about that at any cost," Shane murmured into her hair, his anger subsiding. Only the anxiety and protectiveness remained.

"Won't he know I'm not being fully honest?" she asked, her voice muffled by his bare chest, lips moving over his skin.

Shane held back a shudder at the sensation and tried to stifle the arousal he felt by her inadvertent touch.

"Don't think about it, just—"

But just then a knock sounded at the door.

"Dad?" came Patrick's voice just before he opened the door to find Vee wrapped in his father's arms, and the room in the biggest state of disarray he had ever seen. Usually, his father's room was spick-and-span, save for the occasional piece of clothing. Never had he seen anything spilt on his father's carpet, let alone coffee.

"What is it, Patrick?" Shane asked, tightening his hold on Vee, so she could not pull away. She stifled the squeak of embarrassment that threatened to come out, her body going rigid under Patrick's gaze.

"I, uh..." Patrick cleared his throat, trying to remember why he came up there. "Leib and his men will be heading over shortly," he said after an uncomfortably long pause.

"So soon?" Shane asked, surprised as he released Vee but kept one arm around her waist.

"Like I said, people do arrive early," Vee murmured, pulling back into herself at the mild distance between them again. Shane glanced at her ruefully for that comment. She gave him a smirk, although it was tempered with embarrassment.

CHAPTER 5

Vee left her stained coat and broken mug where they were on the carpet of the main bedroom and followed the now fully clothed Shane down the stairs. He held her hand possessively. She assumed that claiming usually happened between couples, so this show of affection was to help solidify what Shane was trying to portray. She marveled at how natural it felt when their fingers had laced together at the top of the stairs, though. The skin contact gave her a full, uninterrupted stream of his emotions. Protectiveness, anxiety, comfort at her touch, and … that deep feeling again. She had felt it off and on in his presence and felt it grow over the months. She had felt it herself but usually tried to push it away before she thought about it too much. This time with their fingers locked together, it didn't waver from his end.

She didn't have time to think on it though. Just inside the door stood Thomas and three other men. One man was a step ahead of the others. He was tall and broad shouldered like most Werewolves, however his dark skin coupled with brilliant green eyes were undeniably beautiful, but also dangerous, like a viper. She felt wave after wave of suspicion coming off the man who was obviously Leib. His eyes met hers, and the way he looked at her made fear shoot through her like electricity. It doubled a bit with the hot feeling of lust that he radiated at merely the sight of her. She fought back the urge to curl her lip up with disgust.

"Leib. You're a little early. I don't think dinner is quite ready yet," Shane said, standing a few feet from the other pack leader once they reached the bottom of the stairs. They were sizing each other up; Vee could almost smell the testosterone in the air. Shane was a bit taller than Leib and his chest a bit broader. Based on the vibrations she was feeling, she could tell Shane was more powerful, which was odd. She hadn't noticed the difference between Weres as far as power went before. She wasn't sure if they were displaying this purposefully or if it became apparent when two dominant Weres were in the same vicinity.

"Well, perhaps we could get our business over with and enjoy our meal when it's ready," Leib said, his voice sounding like a growl that deceived the slight smirk on his lips.

Markus came around from the kitchen then. "Food will be ready shortly. I'll bring it out in a few minutes," he said to Shane, nodding his head respectfully at Leib.

"We can catch up a bit before getting into business," Shane said, trying to maintain a pleasant exterior.

Leib made a strange sound of approval, and they all moved over into the dining room. The table was large enough to seat twenty, which still wasn't enough for all the pack members to sit at together. It seemed almost too large for how few were going to be dining there on this particular occasion; Leib, his two men, Thomas, Margaret, Shane and Vee, with Markus and Tommy waiting in the kitchen on standby.

Vee was perplexed at how the other pack members, who had previously been filling the house, seemed to just disappear at Leib's arrival. She could feel them all, but it was like they had melted into the furniture. She had been under the impression the whole pack would be joining them, but she supposed if Leib didn't bring his whole pack the display of all the powerful beings under Shane's command would be more intimidating. She was realizing there were a lot of unspoken postering and power displays. Perhaps it was because in their wolf forms they could only communicate non-verbally.

They sat; Leib alternating between glowering at Shane and looking hungrily at Vee. She tried to avoid looking at him altogether.

"A lot has been happening here in your territory lately it seems," Leib started, folding his hands together in front of him on the table.

"Yes, we had a long stretch of peace. I suppose it's our turn for a little chaos," Shane said, squeezing Vee's hand under the table.

"What's a wolf pack without a little chaos?" Lieb grinned eerily. "I heard you had some extraordinary luck with your newest turned wolf. I didn't realize the circumstances when you introduced her last summer," Leib said, raising an eyebrow, his eyes switching over to settle on Vee's face.

"It was very fortunate," Shane said, trying to bring Leib's attention back to him, but his eyes were boring into Vee. It was as if he were trying to reach into her mind and take the answers he wanted. It was Vee's turn to squeeze Shane's hand. She was holding on for dear life. Everything about this exchange felt wrong.

"I didn't catch your name, Miss…?"

"This is Victoria Malone. And she's not what we're talking about right now," Shane said, making Leib's attention snap back to him.

Markus came through from the kitchen with Tommy in tow, carrying dishes of food. Vee could tell most of the food had come from one of the nearby Italian restaurants and been transferred to serving dishes. She smiled a little internally, distinctly hearing the words "groceries" and "make dinner" from Shane's mouth earlier. But she supposed this was better, seeing as how Leib came early. This would have been much more awkward had they been waiting on dinner to be fully prepared.

Vee's reluctance to let go of Shane's hand to eat was echoed by his own feelings, but they did, unlacing their fingers under the table and picking up their forks. There was silence for a few moments while everyone ate. Vee didn't have much of an appetite despite not having anything to eat yet that day. She picked at the food, but the others didn't seem to have the same issue, eating and helping themselves to more.

"Is this from that little place over here? In Brookside Plaza?" one of Leib's men asked, looking up at them from across the table, food still squirreled in his cheek. He seemed unaware of the shrewd look Leib shot him for speaking out of turn.

"Yes, one of our favorites," Thomas replied. Thomas was also giving off a protective feeling, sitting on the other side of Vee, flanking her as if he and Shane were shielding her. She suddenly felt bad for having been so childish about Shane sending Tommy and Lori to guard her. This man was not a pack leader like Shane. He was like the St. Louis leader, who was violent and domineering.

When she was a teenager, after she had run away to St. Louis, her friend Jack had told her and their other friends about that pack. He had escaped before he had been fully brought in as a member, and therefore was much harder for them to track down, even within the same city. From Jack's stories, that pack leader ran his pack like a mob boss going so far as to torture his own members to teach them a lesson.

She imagined Leib was like that. He clearly had a temper bubbling under the surface, just waiting for the opportunity to lash out. His sharp glances at the two men he had brought with him seemed to promise pain in their futures if they did anything out of turn.

"Have the issues with your pack died down? Last we talked your second was in police custody," Shane asked, beating Leib to the punch with the next topic of conversation once the eating slowed. Shane's words

had an additional edge to them. For a moment Vee didn't quite understand why, but then she realized how terrible a Werewolf in police custody would be. Not only for the Werewolf and the police but also the whole preternatural community. One Werewolf in jail or prison on a full moon and the secret was out.

"Charges have been dropped, but his little human girlfriend seems to be on the run from us," Leib said, again eyeing Vee.

"Oh. I didn't realize it involved a human partner. I didn't think most of your wolves went for humans," Shane said, his tone curious, but his feelings were not.

"Well, as you know, there aren't many of our kind to choose from," Leib snarled back, looking over at Margaret, who was trying her hardest to not show her deep hatred of this man. "You have more female Weres in your pack than any of the surrounding packs, Shane. You should share your women."

Vee felt his jealously but also a sick eagerness. Yes, there were more women in this pack than usual. Margaret was high ranking. Emily had been a lone wolf and decided to put down roots here. Frida was one of their best scouts, and of course, now they had Lori. Normal packs had one or none. Vee imagined it had to do with who Shane was and how he led them. Once you were in the Westport Pack you were safe. You were family.

"Should we move to the living room and discuss the more important matters?" Shane asked, choosing to disregard Leib's previous statement as his hand reached over under the table once again to hold Vee's.

They both immediately felt a little better with the renewed contact.

Leib nodded, and they all stood to make their way to the other side of the center hall. Shane and Vee sat on one taut leather couch, and Leib took the matching one opposite, his eyes moving to look at Vee once more. They were hungry, looking over her form in a way that reminded her of Downing. Like she was prey.

She watched as he deeply inhaled, catching her scent, and inspecting its flavor. She knew getting her scent was useless; she didn't smell like any preternatural.

"So, tell me, Shane. About this Victoria. You seem to be keeping her all to yourself," Leib said, glancing at their intertwined fingers, but not losing the arrogant smirk that had come across his face.

"She's a locksmith," Shane decided to say. Vee could feel him trying hard to remain composed. Just the way Leib was looking at her made him want to tear this man apart. His wolf was coming to the surface.

"And more than that, I hear. You've been hiding her away from us. Didn't want to share your new little pet?"

At the word "pet," Shane struggled to hold back a growl rising in his chest. He narrowed his eyes at the other pack leader, who was staring hungrily at what would soon be—at least in terms of preternaturals—his mate. It was at that moment that Vee felt the surge of magic in Shane. It was strangely reminiscent of when he was about to change, but his wolf was not fully in the forefront. She looked over at him, his lips parting in preparation to speak, and she could see the little smokey tendrils of magic starting to come from within him.

"I claim Victoria Malone as mine. My mate. All those who dare touch her shall pay penalty as dictated by me or the Sha. She is mine," Shane said, speaking the ritualistic words that would protect Vee from those who would hurt her. Vee watched as the magic swirled and encompassed both Shane and her as he spoke them. The feeling surrounding her was tingly and strange but not unpleasant. Leib turned his head to the nervous Vee and raised his eyebrows.

"And are you willing to accept Pack Leader, Shane Keenan's claim as your mate, Victoria?" Lieb asked her, watching her reaction to see if there was any uncertainty on her part. She could feel his anger just on the surface, having not been expecting to be blindsided by a claim; however, he was trying to remain calm, waiting for her response.

Vee looked down at her hands, one of which was still firmly clasped in Shane's, then back up at Shane's face. He wasn't looking at her. He was glaring at Leib, but she felt him. The words he said were powerful, meaningful, and he was giving them to her like he had when he cleaned her wound months ago. She was obviously unsure about this situation, but she knew Shane. Though he may have been irritating in certain circumstances and overly pushy, he wouldn't harm her. He had been doing everything he could to keep her safe. She trusted him.

"I accept his claim," she said with confidence, instantly feeling relief from Shane and fury from Leib. The magic that had surrounded Vee and Shane seemed to seep into their pores. Shane squeezed her hand again, taking his eyes off Leib to look at her face. There it was again—that deep feeling. His eyes echoed it.

"Fine," Leib growled, standing to pace the four-foot space in front of him. Most of his lust and hunger dissolved in him, fueling his anger and jealousy. "What is it that this *girl* can do?" he hissed, asking Shane not Vee. Vee fought back the irate comment that threatened to escape when he called her a girl with such a level of disgust. So, what if she was a girl?

"She is an Empath. She can feel emotions and she can also feel the difference between preternaturals. She was able to recognize that Lori was a Werewolf before she went through her first change with the moon," Shane explained, referencing back to Leib's earlier comment.

"The rumors were true, then. She knows what I feel right now?" Leib growled, walking over to their couch. He towered over her, waiting for an answer.

"You are angry, frustrated, envious—I assume of Shane's claim on me, and feel a bit ... aroused," Vee said, barely whispering the last bit as she attempted to control her face from showing her disgust. He snarled.

"And what else is it that she can do? How is she useful?" Leib now asked Shane.

"She saved four human girls from an attack that would have been accidental. We did not think Lori was going to have the trait. Victoria was useful," Shane said, his own anger starting to rise.

"So, her ability helped in that one instance?" Leib sneered. "Perhaps this was not worth a trip."

"Perhaps not. You have witnessed the claim and have found out what you desired. If you wish to stay

and insult my mate you may as well go," Shane said, standing to stare the weaker pack leader down. Shane's dominance was evident, and it crackled around the edges. It made Thomas and Margaret tense with predicted battle, standing as well in support of their leader.

"There are things you are not telling me, Keenan. But trust me; I'll know soon enough," Lieb said, casting one last look at Vee before he stomped out of the house, his men following behind.

The air stayed tense as they all listened to Leib's car drive off in the distance. Vee's heart was beating wildly in her chest. It was as if everyone in the house had been awaiting an attack. Once the threat was gone, they all sagged with relief. Shane sank back into the couch beside Vee, waving Thomas and Margaret away. He turned to her, eyes searching, trying to determine how she was feeling.

"Are you all right, Vee?" he asked, his voice soft and gentle. She turned her head to look at him, her face not giving away a single thing she felt. Inside she was screaming, confused, and yet relieved. Angry, yet scared. She wanted to yell at Shane because she knew she was stuck with this claim, but she wanted to kiss him for what he had done for her.

If she could not be touched neither could he. He sacrificed potential mates, claiming her to save her. Leib had been right. She wasn't that valuable, or at least that was what she thought. Helping Lori and going to see pack members' children to tell them if they were going to have the trait were the reasons they called her. They did just fine before her and they could again.

"Why did you just do that?" Vee asked, realizing now as she looked at him that it was more than just to protect her.

He reached over, brushing a lock of hair behind her ear and running his finger down her silky cheek. So far, he had tried to resist touching her this way, but he hadn't been able to catch himself.

"I—"

"The pack is going to eat now, Shane," Margaret said from the archway, interrupting him before he could say the words. In that moment, Margaret had been happy, relieved like the rest of the pack that had begun flooding back into the house. That changed; however, when she saw what she had interrupted, chagrin instantly taking over.

"Thank you, Margaret," Shane murmured, not turning to look at her as she immediately left them alone once again. "We can talk later," Shane said, smoothing his thumb over the top of her hand. She pulled her hand away, tearing her eyes from his and standing abruptly.

"I—I think I'll go home. This has been…" she stammered, looking around the room for an escape while she patted herself, checking for her bag. It was in that moment she realized all her things were still upstairs.

"You should wait until he's left the territory," he said quickly, standing as well.

"I can't *stay* here," she said, starting to feel anxious again and uncomfortable. Without Margaret's interruption, Vee wasn't certain what could have happened in that moment. Her heart was hammering against her ribs. Shane's touch on her cheek, the comfort and rightness

of their hands clasped together, was enough that she wasn't sure she would have been able to control herself had he simply leaned over and brushed a kiss to her lips.

"We can get what you need. You can go home as soon as we're sure he's gone," Shane said, trying to hide the rejection he felt. This further confused her. He wanted her to stay with him.

"Go be with your pack," she said, stepping back to put some distance between them. It had felt too good to be near him. She was struggling with conflicting feelings. Solitary was safe, but she couldn't really be alone anymore. "I think I'll go lie down for a bit. Where should I…"

"Just go to my room. I'll be up in a moment," Shane said, wandering away before she could tell him that was a bad idea. She was left standing alone in the living room. She wasn't sure if she wanted to return to that room to lie on his bed. It would only tempt the desires that she was already having difficulty pushing away.

Reluctantly, she sighed, heading back up. Perhaps if she fell asleep, he wouldn't tempt her. Perhaps if she managed to block out the violent buzzing that the multitude of Werewolves within the house were putting out, she would be able to fall asleep before he returned.

She went to his bed, shucking her shoes and climbing under the warm, down covers. Dreams and thoughts she tried so hard to evict from her mind resurfaced fiercely as she surrounded herself in Shane's scent. She tried to push the events of the past few days away, using the vibrations of the minds below to lull her. Exhaustion and the deep comfort that this bed provided seemed to allow her to drift off to sleep.

CHAPTER 6

When Vee first woke she didn't realize she was somewhere other than her bed, even given the fact that her bed was nowhere near as comfortable as the one she was sleeping in, and the cover that was wrapped around her body was far thicker than the one in her home. The sheets beneath her fingers were smooth and soft, not the pilled, threadbare sheets she was used to. She furrowed her brow, still not opening her eyes as she tried to figure out what else was wrapped around her.

She pushed her back against whatever it was, instantly realizing it was a body, warm muscle and bone, with arms wrapped around her torso. That's when she felt that familiar and comforting buzz of Shane. Her eyes snapped open, and she attempted to sit up. She was unsuccessful as his heavy arms pinned her to the

bed. Her heart began pounding instantly, adrenaline surging at the unexpectedness of this predicament.

"Shane?" she asked, her voice not trying to be quiet. In fact, she was starting to feel rather panicky now that she realized she was still in his room, in his bed. The sound still came out more meekly than she would have liked, but it was not a whisper, thankfully.

"Mm…" was all she got from him in return.

"Shane, wake up," she said, patting his arm at her waist. She managed to remove the mild panic from her voice that time, sounding much more forceful and like herself.

"What?" he grumbled sleepily, rolling onto his back and taking his arm with him.

She sat up as soon as she was free, moving as far from him as she could on the bed. He rubbed his eyes, blinking a few times before he looked at her. She was still in her clothes from the night before, her hair a bit frazzled as she stared at him with large emerald eyes like a scared puppy. She pulled some of the covers over her chest like she was exposed to him, as if she wasn't still fully dressed as she had been the evening before. He couldn't keep the amusement off his face as a wide grin spread across it, showing off his white teeth.

"Why are you in-in bed with me?" she asked quietly, noticing his bare chest as he pushed the covers down to scratch it. She took a moment to shift a bit, making sure her clothes were still firmly attached to her body as she left them when she fell asleep. They were.

"It's my bed," he responded, chuckling a bit as he put both hands behind his head and studied her.

"Why are you in it?" she asked, narrowing her eyes and clinching her fist in the comforter.

"A few pack members stayed the night. They took the other beds," he told her seriously. She knew he wasn't lying, but she could tell it wasn't the whole truth.

"Okay..." she grumbled, moving her eyes around the room as her mind raced.

She noticed his shirt laying lazily over the foot-board, and his shoes sat beside the bedroom door. It was awkward being in his room the night before. This was far more awkward.

"I think Markus and Emily have already started making breakfast," he commented, closing his eyes and sniffing the air. She could smell the coffee coming from below, but she wasn't going to let this go. They could have easily shared a bed without touching. It was big enough, but he was trying to change the subject.

"Why were you spooning me?" she decided to ask, ignoring the previous comment.

He sat up, maneuvering so he was sitting crisscross across from her. She glanced as the covers fell away from the lower half of him, letting out a small, but audible, sigh of relief when she saw he was wearing pants.

Shane gave a small smirk at her sigh, took a deep breath, and looked her square in the eyes.

"Why do you think, Vee?" His eyes started turning that brilliant gold as he looked at her, and once again she couldn't tell what he was feeling. Only when a Were was feeling a strong emotion would their eyes change so drastically, so she knew there was something boiling within him that he was blocking. She had never come across someone who actively tried to block their

feelings from her. Not that many knew what she could do, but it was still unsettling to see him clearly feeling something intensely and have nothing to go on but his words and his stony facial expression.

"How are you doing that?" she asked, her brows pulling together so much, the wrinkle in her forehead looked like an angry vein.

"What?"

"You're... blocking..."

She couldn't finish, all she knew was she needed to find out what he was feeling. Despite the awkwardness of waking with him wrapped around her, she had to touch him. She leaned forward, letting the covers fall from her as she reached out both hands, cupping them around his face. Instantly a flood of emotions assaulted her; possessiveness, lust, amusement and... She couldn't feel them all. He was feeling too many things at once. The power of them all hitting her so suddenly sent her off the bed and on the floor with a loud thump.

"Vee?" Shane said nervously, scrambling off the bed and onto the floor beside her. She had one arm covering her eyes, and the other gently reaching toward the top of her head. At least the floor was carpeted. "Vee? Are you alright?" he asked, his voice still tinged with worry as his hands hovered over her body, afraid to touch her.

"The next time you decide to block your emotions please don't let me touch you," she grumbled, moving her arm so she could rub her eyes. Shane let out a relieved, yet anxious chuckle, leaning back against the wall, but watching her with a wary gaze, nonetheless.

"That was… You just shot off the bed! I thought…"

"What? I was knocked unconscious? Dead?" she asked, opening her eyes just enough to catch a glimpse of his worried face. "I'm not that fragile."

"Fragile enough," he said, letting out a low rumble of laughter as she started to sit up. It was a little dizzying, but she managed with one hand cupped over the bump that was forming.

"I may not be a Werewolf, but I'm not glass."

Taking a breath through her nose, the smell of coffee and food assaulted Vee causing her stomach to lurch with hunger. The meager amount of dinner she had eaten the previous day was proving to not have been sufficient, and she was ready to remedy that by eating like a Werewolf.

"Coffee," she grumbled, rubbing her head and her stomach.

"Let's get you some," Shane suggested, amusement still lighting his eyes. He stood lithely with the slightest amount of effort despite his crouched position against the wall, walking in front of her and offering her a hand. She hesitated, making sure she could feel his amusement before she took it. Being thrown across the room was not on her list of things to repeat.

"Thanks," she said, releasing it quickly, as if continuing to touch him would scald her. She wandered over to the bedroom door.

She noticed when she got to the hall that the other doors were open as well, showing off several bedrooms with unmade beds and a TV room. The TV room had a huge, sectioned couch in black leather and an enormous flat screen television. She scoffed at the sight of

it. Shane's TV made hers look like the crippled elderly. Patrick was in, what she assumed, was his room, rummaging through the dresser that was against the wall surrounded by dirty clothes.

"Patrick, make sure you do your homework today. Just because next week is spring break doesn't mean you get to slack off," Shane called as they began descending the stairs.

"Planning on it," Patrick grumbled without looking up.

Vee smiled a little. It was such a normal, short conversation between a father and son. An outsider wouldn't have known with that short exchange that both of them were something other than human.

Vee managed to escape Shane's house by a reasonable hour that afternoon. She was back in her shop, despite it being a Sunday, trying to make up for the work she had missed. Even though she didn't get many customers in the shop on Saturdays, she knew it had been closed long enough to make a dent in her sales.

Shane grudgingly let her go, knowing Leib was out of the territory. When the rest of the pack had left his house she knew she needed to leave. One night in Shane's bed with him was one night too many. She may have fantasized about him, enjoyed his company, been claimed as his mate, but she had a hard time considering an actual relationship. She had spent the last ten years expecting to be alone forever, and it was hard to think of that changing.

He was as stubborn as she was and overbearing to say the least. She knew she felt his lust and desire before, but she had a hard time placing his true feelings. They had a connection, that she knew. A strange, immediate attraction the moment they met. An urging deep within her to know him and be near him had taken root within her. Despite those feelings not dissipating, only growing stronger after all these months, she questioned their viability.

She knew what true devotion felt like. When she would walk by an old couple, holding hands on the street, even if they didn't show any outward signs of romance, she could feel it within them. It was something about those moments that she wished there would be someone for her out there. Realistically she knew that wasn't the safe option. It was better for her to be alone.

Her head still hurt from hitting the floor that morning. A bump had formed that was tender to the touch, but she had had worse. What really bothered her was how the injury got there in the first place. Trying to feel his emotions while he was blocking her was obviously a dangerous pursuit. How was it that twice Shane had blocked his feelings? Once in his office and again today in his room. She couldn't tell by his reaction if it had been intentional or not, but it was still strange.

The bell on the door chimed, and Vee looked up to see Eliza, her older sister wandering in toting a small person with her. Mary, no longer the toddling baby she had been nine months ago but now a little girl. She was the spitting image of her mother, from the perfect complexion to the brown ringlet curls and the muddy brown of her eyes. The usual greeting Vee gave to customers died in her throat as she saw them. She had no idea how she was supposed to react to her sister.

The last time she had seen Eliza had been when Frank essentially threatened her life. Since then, she had diligently stayed away. Now, there Eliza was in Vee's shop.

"Eliza," Vee murmured with a nod, watching as her sister unwrapped the elaborate scarf from her neck.

"Victoria," Eliza sighed, walking forward to the counter. "You remember Mary?"

"I do. Hello sweetheart," Vee said, turning her gaze to the little girl, who had as much spunk as a frightened mouse. Her ringlets seemed to shiver with fear as she looked upon the unknown person. Vee truly regretted not being able to know Mary, who she had adored each time she had seen her. Of course, the little thing would be afraid of her. She was a stranger.

Vee looked back at her sister, giving her a quizzical eye as she inspected Eliza's emotions. She was uncertain and feeling a little guilty. That was not a good sign.

"Need a new lock? Maybe a safe?" Vee decided to ask. There were few other reasons why her sister would show up here, and though it was unlikely that she would buy something from her, she thought she might as well ask.

Eliza's eyes narrowed, and her lips pinched together in a thin line.

"No, Victoria. I came here to…" Eliza hesitated a moment, her eyes darting around uncomfortably. "To see how you were doing."

A little lie. It burned behind Vee's eyes worse than when she hit her head.

"I don't know why you bother lying to me," Vee said.

The mention of Vee's abilities made Eliza go rigid, and her eyes widened with fear. She had never liked to talk about it, preferring to ignore it.

"Frank found something," Eliza murmured, taking her hand out of Mary's and rummaging in her large tote-like leather purse. The way her hands shook made it a little less fluid when she took out the manila envelope and set it on the counter before Vee.

"What is this?" Vee asked, her eyes narrowing at the suspicious package.

"They're adoption papers. And a little more," Eliza said, attempting to put on a mask of smugness, when she was just feeling sincere sadness and guilt.

"Excuse me?" Vee said, eyes staring at the envelope before her as if it would jump out and bite her.

"He's been searching for quite a while. He wanted to make sure you had no claim to anything, being my sister. No reason to keep coming around and being part of our lives," Eliza told her, voice shaking.

"Is that what you want, Eliza?" Vee asked, her voice flat and emotionless as she turned her eyes up, looking at her sister's distraught face. Eliza lifted Mary into her arms, eyes welling with tears as she clutched the little one.

"We can't see each other again. I-I'm sorry," she said, protectively holding her baby. They looked at each other for a long moment. The understanding flowing between them. Eliza didn't want to push Vee away, but she had Mary to worry about. With Mary came Frank.

This was the life she had chosen when Vee left. "I'll leave you to it, then," Eliza finally murmured, breaking eye contact and turning, still clutching Mary as she stepped back out into the cold.

Vee sat there for a long time, staring at the thick envelope. She didn't know what she was feeling. Shock, perhaps?

The sky was darkening, and the street in front of her shop picked up traffic once again. She probably wasn't going to be getting customers in her shop for the rest of the night, but it seemed less lonesome to be in her shop than if she were to go home. She certainly didn't want to be alone with the *thing* her sister had left for her.

She reached her hand out to touch the foreign, offending object filled with papers that she didn't want to see. But even though it was just inches away, she couldn't bring herself to pick it up. She was afraid of very few things, but somehow this topped all of them. This had her shaking and unable to move.

There had been many times growing up when she thought she may have been adopted. Her sister had used that as a tool to tease her when they were children. And her parents and sister were not like her; no one had the abilities she did. They had all looked similar enough that she just chalked those thoughts up to paranoia. Vee's coloring was a little darker and her eyes the shocking emerald in comparison to her family's brown. She never wanted to question it, never wanted it to be true. Something about her long dead parents having not been her own hurt her.

The curiosity of who her real parents were burned in the back of her mind with increasing intensity as she stared at it. Were they like her? Would she finally get a chance to know what she was? She inched her hand forward across the glass countertop until her fingers brushed the envelope. With that small touch she had enough strength to pick the whole thing up.

The door opened with a ding, and she stared at the person standing just inside. She certainly looked strange, eyes wide, face having lost all its color, and one hand clutching the envelope with white knuckles.

CHAPTER 7

The person standing in the doorway had black hair that was cut short and splayed around her head in an appealingly messy manner. Her face ended with a pointed chin. She wore a dark coat covered in the rain that had started to pour outside, and she looked at Vee with her oddly reddish-brown eyes, confused.

"Are you alright?" Durran asked, moving toward the counter.

Her movements were slow and deliberate, with hands raised to show Vee she wasn't a threat. Vee wanted to laugh or say something witty to break the strange tension. She knew Durran wasn't a threat, but she couldn't get the words out. Holding the adoption papers that might tell her where she came from was terrifying, and the words got caught in her throat.

"Vee, what's wrong?" Durran's voice was like honey, raspy and low, but sweet enough to feel beautiful to the ears. She had the sort of voice that made everything she said feel important, but that was generally how Watchers got their way and avoided detection.

Her presence was without feeling. A void, instead of a vibration or buzz like humans and Weres, she didn't throb like the Fae, but she was still in her mind. Vee could feel her emotions however dulled they were. In that moment, Durran was cautious and worried. Vee sucked in a breath and found her voice.

"I-I'm okay," she whispered, sinking into the stool behind the counter and letting the envelope come to her chest.

"You don't seem okay," Durran commented, coming around the counter to stand over her. "What is this?" she asked, tapping the envelope with one finger and looking Vee in the eyes. She swallowed dryly, pulling it from her chest and sharing at it.

"Adoption papers."

"Ah." Vee looked up at her then, slight irritation covering her face with the simplicity of her acknowledgment, as if she had known. The idea was atrocious, so atrocious in fact, that she didn't want to even think it. Because if Durran had known, and kept that to herself... well, Vee would consider that a betrayal of trust, and she was already a little hesitant about how far she trusted Durran these days.

"What are you doing here, Durran?" she asked in a clipped tone.

"Checking on you. I heard you've been ousted," she said, humor evident in her voice, masking the true

emotions underneath. Durran was clearly grappling with anger and anxiety over the situation.

Vee very suddenly became angry. In the course of one night, the entire preternatural community knew who she was. Fantastic. She wanted to kill something, not that it would do her any good.

"Great," she grumbled, slamming the envelope back on the counter with an audible smack as she stood up.

"Quite a bit of trouble you've gotten yourself into."

"That *I* got myself into? Stupid Werewolves don't know when to leave someone alone! Now I'm stuck with them," she hissed, flashing an angry glare at Durran, who was still smiling despite Vee's hostility.

"Yes, I heard you agreed to the claim. I suppose that will keep you safe for the time being. Shane is powerful," Durran murmured, moving to lean against the counter beside her, a hint of jealously reaching Vee.

"I don't care how powerful he is. This weekend continues to get worse, and I have yet to see where or when my normal life comes back."

"It doesn't," Durran said seriously, her eyes flashing bright red for just a moment. "It hasn't been normal since you helped that girl."

"Beautiful," she groaned, covering her eyes with her hand.

"It's not so bad. Now I don't have to sneak away to see you. I can just say I'm going to see that unknown preternatural called Vee." She grinned, causing Vee to blush momentarily.

"Don't you have watching to do?" she asked, walking around the counter to her displays to inspect them. She needed to be busy, even if there was nothing to do.

"I'm doing what I need to be at the moment," Durran responded, not following, but watching her as she moved about the shop.

"Are you going to open this?" Durran finally asked after several minutes of silence, gesturing back toward the envelope.

"I don't know," Vee answered honestly. Her fear of the documents within that thin paper covering scared her more than the idea of the whole preternatural community knowing she existed.

"Can I?" Durran asked, reaching over to the counter, trying to snag it.

"No!" Vee hissed, stomping back over to the counter and ripping it away from her hands. "I… I don't know if I can handle it right now. Too much going on," she murmured, moving to stow it in her messenger bag.

"Do you realize it's seven? Have you eaten?"

She looked behind her at the clock on the wall. It was indeed seven. It was way past closing time on a normal day, and as her stomach now reminded, past food time.

"I'll take that noise as a no," Durran said, moving around the counter as Vee started turning things off and slipping on her thin coat to leave.

"I'll just go home and make something," she said as a goodbye. However, Durran wasn't leaving. She was standing in front of the door, waiting for her as if she didn't get the hint. Vee rolled her eyes, but set the alarm, rushing out the door that Durran was holding open for her before she turned back to lock everything up.

"I'll take you home."

"I can get home on my own," Vee admonished, rushing through the rain to her decrepit Lumina and getting in. She put the key in the ignition and turned, getting a few angry sounds from her engine before it sputtered and died. She leaned forward, pressing her head to the wheel and closing her eyes. If anything was going to make her life more miserable, it had to happen now. She didn't know if she could take anymore.

Durran knocked at the glass causing Vee to turn her head just enough against the wheel to see her smiling smugly from the other side.

"Fine," was all Vee said as she pulled her keys out and removed herself from the vehicle. The car would sit there until she could get it towed to a mechanic. She cringed, realizing then, it would be the long walk in the cold to work every morning and no trips out in the field. No car meant losing her biggest source of income.

They both walked up the street until they got to Durran's car, which happened to be a black 1990 Buick Century. Vee always liked the old Buicks, and she admired the comfort of the car as she slid into the passenger seat. 1990 had been a good year for this car. Chevy didn't seem to get that stroke of luck for the Lumina. Durran got in beside her and started it up with a roar.

"Now. What do you want to eat?" Durran asked, as she pulled out of the parking space and onto Westport Road.

"I'll eat at home," Vee said again, stubbornly.

"Fine," Durran snapped, losing the lightness in her voice, casting an awkward silence between them.

Durran had something for restaurants. Not only had they met in a restaurant, but she also often liked to pop in promptly at noon on Fridays when Vee would take her lunch break. She would force her to come out to eat; it was an odd little ritual that they had developed over the years. It had been strangely out of character that she hadn't come around the previous Friday but not unheard of. If Vee had been out at lunch with Durran, then she might have avoided the fight with Tommy.

Back when she had little social interaction other than customers, she welcomed Durran's interruptions, but this weekend had been a social sensory overload. She wanted to be alone. She had a lot to think about, mostly concerning Shane. Durran took the back roads to her house, the way Vee would have if she were driving. The streets they passed by were lit, and people were all settling in for the evening together. Durran pulled up in front of her apartment and turned off the car.

"Thanks," Vee said, unbuckling her seatbelt and reaching for the handle. Durran's hand shot out and grabbed her, causing her gaze to return to her eerily red-tinted eyes.

"This is not a good time to be alone and vulnerable," Durran whispered, suddenly far closer to her than she had thought they had been moments ago. Her face was drawn, brows slightly pinched, giving away the concern she felt that easily flowed to Vee.

"I've been alone for a long time," Vee said, her voice coming out more hushed than she thought it would with the sudden sense of intensity. There were too many dulled emotions flowing from the Watcher to

her. She couldn't get a good read of any of them other than deep worry.

"It's dangerous. They all know."

"They all know what?" she asked, her brows furrowing.

"I can't explain right now. You… you need to understand. The claim with Shane will only do so much. It only works on some preternaturals. Now that you're out, you're exposed. Some will want to see if you can do more than you say or show." Durran's words were coming out in a hoarse whisper. Vee had only seen a break in Durran's cool, calm exterior a few times in the past. It was a bit disconcerting.

"What do you mean?"

Durran was silent, looking her over for a moment. Her expression was pained, and her emotions were still muddled.

"I'll call Shane. You go inside," she murmured, before she released Vee's arm and moved away from her. Vee just sat there, staring at her, feeling confused. What was she talking about? Why would Shane's claim not be good enough to keep others away? It was irritating enough to have all these preternaturals give vague warnings. Could none of them just speak clearly and *tell* her what was ominous and threatening? What did she need protection from?

Durran had pulled out her cell phone and pressed it to her ear, ignoring Vee, indicating the conversation was over. Durran didn't particularly like the idea of calling Shane, but the Were had claimed Vee. He needed to take responsibility of that claim.

Vee took a deep breath and opened the car door, slamming it before she walked to the apartment building and disappeared behind the main entrance. Once in her home, she leaned against the wall, sighed, and closed her eyes. What happened to the solitary simplicity she had gotten used to? When she opened them again, she noticed the blankets Tommy and Lori had used only a few nights before. She didn't want to bother with picking them up. She just wanted to make a sandwich, watch some mind-numbing television, and crawl into bed.

But of course, that wasn't going to happen.

Her phone rang from the pocket of her coat just as she was taking it off. She pulled it out, glancing at the screen, even though she already knew who would be calling.

"Yes, Shane?"

"I'm coming over. Durran called me."

"Yeah, I assumed that would be happening," she growled, glaring at the door as if it were Durran.

"I'll be there in twenty minutes."

"I think I'll survive without you for twenty minutes. I've survived this long," she mumbled with indignation before she hung up the phone and continued with her coat removal.

Shane in bed this morning, Shane in her apartment this night. She was going to have a Shane overdose.

She moved to her kitchen, grabbing the ingredients for a fried egg sandwich and putting the bread in the toaster before switching on the television. The late-night drama was at least background noise to keep her

from overthinking as she waited for her food to cook and bodyguard to arrive.

She had just put the finishing touches on her sandwich as the buzzer sounded, letting her know someone was waiting for her. She rushed to it, pushing the intercom button.

"Yeah?"

"It's me," Shane said, sounding less than happy, probably because he was standing in the freezing rain. She thought about teasing him, pretending she didn't know it was him, but she decided against it, given the weather and his tone.

"Buzzing you in," she said before she hit the button to unlock the door. She waited patiently beside the door for him, listening to his heavy footsteps on the stairs until they stopped.

"I know you heard me, Vee," he said quietly from the other side of the door, causing her to chuckle as she flipped the deadbolt and opened it. He was drenched, and his expression hid nothing of the irritation he was feeling.

"Come on in," she said, turning around to head back to the kitchen.

CHAPTER 8

As she padded back through her apartment, she grabbed a soda and her sandwich before returning to the front room. Shane was removing his coat and shoes. She wasn't sure what he saw as he eyed the small space she called home. The subtle simplicity was not something he was used to, what with his massive house and his exquisite furniture. She had only ever let Durran in her apartment until recently. Durran had called it her fortress of solitude in the past, but now three additional people had seen her home.

She sat on one of the futons, directing her focus to the television instead of him. It was hard to do; however, given that his coat had soaked through, and his t-shirt was damp enough to show off the toned abdomen she had been crushed against just the night before. She did think briefly about how amusing it

was that he was wearing a t-shirt instead of his usual button down, coupled with a pair of jeans. She had never seen him in such casual attire.

The television show left much to be desired, but she wasn't sure she wanted to have a conversation with him yet. She felt the overwhelming tension threatening her. First, being claimed and outed and then her sister's bombshell. Claimed or not, they weren't in any sort of relationship other than friendship, and she wasn't sure she really wanted to discuss all her feelings with him.

She heard him move through the apartment to the kitchen, rummaging around for something. The thought of him going through her things was both curious and frustrating. She could have gotten him something if he asked, but he decided he was comfortable enough to do it himself. How could he feel comfortable like that in a place he had never been before? Instead of choosing to argue about it, she kept her body planted on the couch and her eyes glued to the show she wasn't paying attention to.

He reemerged from the kitchen and moved around the room, eyes glancing over her simple decor. It was much like he imagined over the past few months, only having seen a brief glimpse inside the one time. She didn't have much, mostly books and movies on shelves and some stacked on surfaces. The small card table just off the kitchen had her bag and stained coat strewn across it, with her mail stacked neatly in the middle.

Without a word, he sat on the futon several spaces away from her. She thought about mentioning that there was another futon, but she knew how much sass would be present in the comment. She really wanted to avoid a fight. She wasn't in the mood, and his presence there was enough to make her want to yell. It was unnecessary. There was no immediate threat to her safety.

The crack of a soda can being opened sounded through the apartment. She turned to see Shane lazily sitting back on the edge of the futon in his band t-shirt and worn jeans, sipping on the soda he had helped himself to. He turned his eyes to her and smiled from behind the beverage.

"You look startled," he commented.

"Do I?" she asked, turning her focus back to the uninteresting show.

"Apparently you don't like me casual?" he asked, gesturing to his attire.

"I don't dislike it. I just haven't seen it," she responded quietly, trying to keep her voice from being snippy. She regretted insinuating that she liked when he wore anything in particular, but she simply kept her mouth closed, avoiding confrontation of any kind. He didn't say anything else, but she could feel his amusement.

Her sandwich became too much after a bite into the second half. She stood to throw it away, but Shane grabbed her wrist to stop her.

"We should talk about... Well, we didn't really get an opportunity after last night," he said, the contact of his hand on her arm making Vee's heart pick up a little. His hands were rough, calloused, and strong. Somehow the feel of them on her skin when there were only the two of them in this small space was enough to make her breathing become uneven.

"I don't think I can handle that right now. I didn't even want to discuss anything with Durran. My intention was to be alone this evening," she told him, pulling her arm from him to break the contact. He narrowed his eyes for a moment. His emotions becoming a little jealous as soon as Durran's name was mentioned.

"Your Watcher is a little too overprotective of you for my liking," Shane said, his voice low and his eyes lightening slightly, a hint of the wolf underneath.

"She's not *my* Watcher, Shane. Just *a* Watcher who happens to be my friend," Vee said dismissively, rolling her eyes as she began walking over to the kitchen. She was trying to keep her calm despite the irritation and the utter absurdity that Shane being in her home was.

Was it irritation with him or her own stupid thoughts? It didn't matter.

She dumped the rest of the sandwich into the garbage under the sink and rinsed her plate.

Shane had followed her, leaning on one counter, but somehow blocking her exit at the same time. When she finished and set the plate in the sink she turned to him, giving him an irritated and questioning look. He clearly decided that wasn't the end of the conversation.

"You think she's not your Watcher?" Shane asked, crossing his arms and raising his eyebrow dubiously.

"I think I would know," she hissed, not being able to control the irritation in her tone anymore.

"If she wasn't your Watcher, she would have no interest in you. Watchers don't care for beings that aren't their own kind unless they are their ward, or they benefit their ward in some way."

"Maybe Lori is her ward, and she likes me because I helped her," Vee grumbled, however unlikely that was. She had known Durran years before she saved Lori from killing her friends. The reality of Shane's words were seeping in. Why hadn't she been more suspicious of her when she came to the restaurant every day all those years ago? Shane merely laughed at her attempted reasoning. It only proved to inflame her irritation to anger.

"What do you care, Shane? If she's my Watcher, why are you here instead of her?"

That silenced the laughter immediately and caused him to stand straight to his full and overwhelming height. She felt him, his possessiveness, his dominance, his anger, his lust. She felt it all, and yet, she stood her ground and stared him in the eyes, challenging him.

"You are my mate. If anyone has the right and responsibility to watch over you, to protect you, it is me," he said, his voice a growl, verging on inhuman. He had chosen the wrong words. Her anger flashed across her face, eyes immediately turning amber.

"I may belong to you in the eyes of the preternaturals, in the eyes of the Weres, but I certainly don't belong to any man, Shane. I don't follow orders. I don't need someone to be responsible for me. I don't need to be watched over. Get out," she said, her voice low and calm but deadly.

Shane's eyes burned golden, and his anger turned to fury. He walked forward, bending his neck to look down into her eyes.

"I'm not leaving," he said, his voice a low rumble that vibrated within her from the small distance

between them. He moved his hands up her arms and shoulders until they were on either side of her face. His touch gentle, despite the rough skin of his hands and his anger.

"Go," she said, her voice a little weaker with the contact. She hated he had this kind of power over her. She seemed to melt under his gaze, in his hands.

"No."

His hands pulled a little at her face, bringing their noses close enough to touch. She could feel his hot breath against her lips as his scent enveloped her. She fought the urge to go weak in the knees. She should have been denying him, pushing him away, instead she was breathing raggedly, awaiting his lips to touch hers.

He leaned in just a bit more to touch his lips to her soft ones. Just a gentle brush of his lips on hers. The feelings were overwhelming, intoxicating. *She* was overwhelming and intoxicating. What he had intended to be a soft kiss immediately turned fierce. It was as if that was all they needed for a dam to break between them. He felt Vee lose herself immediately at his touch, leaning forward into him, wanting, just as much as he did. It was just as powerful a kiss as it had been the first time their lips had touched. She made him feel like he had never truly known what love was before, now that he felt it for her. How could one woman make him want to beg and plead?

Vee reached up, running her fingers through his hair, pulling him closer. For all the words she said before, for all the times she told herself and everyone else she wanted to be alone, it was all washed away when she was with him. It was probably the reason she pushed him away so much. It scared her how strong her feelings were for him, how strong the emotions were that he was feeling for her.

She recalled, hazily in the back of her mind, that they were fully alone for the first time. No one to interrupt them. No one to stop them if this went too far. Part of her wanted to pull away, but that quickly dissolved when he lifted her to set her on the counter, bringing them level with each other, his hips resting between her legs. So many things were being said with this kiss. Their mouths molded together perfectly, hands clutching and caressing, searing heat in their wake. But as his fingers brushed the skin at the hem of her shirt, dancing there for a moment before he slipped them under to the skin of her back, his phone rang in his back pocket.

A low growl rumbled in his chest. The disruptive sound breaking the spell, making him pull himself away from her, ripping his back pocket to get his phone.

"What?" he growled, trying very hard not to break the fragile phone in his hand.

"Dad? Did I…"

"Just tell me what you called about," Shane said, trying to calm himself. Patrick didn't deserve to be snapped at. How could he have known? Shane closed his eyes for a moment, reaching up to rub his forehead, and moved out of the kitchen, leaving Vee sitting on her counter, shocked.

"Ethan called. He's coming home," Patrick murmured, from the other end of the phone.

"When?" Shane asked, his voice picking up energy, but not out of anger. He was excited and worried.

Vee knew Shane had another son. A much older son than Patrick, but she had never met him. Ethan's last visit was tumultuous, what with him being punished by the Sha for having mistakenly turned a serial killer into a Were.

"He was driving from St. Louis. Could be four hours, could be twenty minutes."

"Shit."

Vee was apparently more of an inconvenience than they liked to let on. She wasn't leaving her apartment to stay with Shane again. If he wanted to go home to greet Ethan, he would just have to do it without her.

"What are you going to do?" Patrick asked, his voice sounding a little nervous over the phone, but it was hard to tell what he was really feeling without being in the room with him.

"Call Tommy. Tell him I might need him. I'll let you know when I've figured it out," Shane said, turning to look at Vee who had exited the little kitchen and wandered toward the hallway.

"I'll let him know," was all Patrick said before Shane hung up.

"Go see your son," Vee said, not turning to look at him as she paused at the hall.

"You need to be protected, and we need to talk about this," he said gesturing between them.

"I don't think any immediate danger is coming. There haven't been any signs, and everyone in the complex is human, except for you," Vee commented, turning back to him.

"And you," he said, letting one side of his mouth go up in a cheeky smirk. She rolled her eyes, deciding to ignore his comment.

"Go home. See Ethan. Come back if you feel it's necessary." After she said it, she regretted it. She gave him an open invitation to come to her home whenever he wanted. This would not go over well later.

He was quiet for a moment, looking at her and probably weighing his options. He trusted her enough not to put herself in danger on purpose, and that was enough to have him go.

"Alright. But if you need anything. Call me. I'll be here."

"Deal," she replied, waiting in the hallway as he replaced his shoes, sopping coat, and went to the front door.

"I'll call you later, either way. Be safe," he murmured, looking at her for a long moment before he opened the door and left her apartment.

She couldn't help but sigh in relief as his footsteps hit the pavement outside, and his car started up moments later. It had been far too close in that little kitchen. She would have been putty in his hands if he had gone any further, and she still wasn't completely sure what her feelings were on the matter.

She steadied herself, walked to the door, and locked it before slumping back on the futon to finish watching whatever this dimwitted show was. But she couldn't focus on it. She touched her lips as she sat there, thinking back on the way it all felt. It wasn't just lust and possessiveness she felt from him. Even his wolf under the surface felt something more. She closed

her eyes, breath ragged again just at the thought. This was not just a simple crush or flirtation between them. It hadn't been, even months ago. There had always been a deeper connection there.

She shook her head, realizing she had sat there, lost in thoughts of Shane for quite some time. This was absurd. She got up, storming into her bedroom, angry with herself, and grabbed a pair of sweatpants from the floor. She hoped desperately that Shane would just stay home. She didn't want to fight with him, but everything was getting too strange. Over a few days she had way too many new things on her plate. This was the way things went for her. Long stretches of nothing at all, then days where it all piled on into one chaotic mess.

She flopped on her bed, mildly irritated at how uncomfortable it was in comparison to Shane's. She looked at her alarm clock, seeing it was bearing on 10 p.m. If she was going to wake up at her usual time tomorrow morning to open the shop, she would need to go to sleep. She rolled over, grabbing her phone from where it landed on her pillow and decided to text him. The last thing she needed was him waking her up with a phone call.

[Vee: I'm going to bed.]

[Shane: Avoiding the conversation, still?]

She rolled her eyes, imagining the smirk on his face.

[Vee: No, I just wake up early.]

She hoped it came off as indignant as she felt through the message. She imagined his eyes twinkling with amusement as he flashed a cheeky smile her way. She was swimming in dangerous waters, kissing him and thinking thoughts like this.

[Shane: Goodnight, Vee.]

She sighed, looking at that final message from him. She could have just left it at that, but she couldn't fight the flutter in her stomach as she reread the words.

[Vee: Goodnight.]

She laid back on her back, staring at the ceiling, knowing she wasn't going to fall asleep for a long while. She would be battling her mind and her heart before she would be able to find any sort of rest.

CHAPTER 9

Shane sat in the living room, rereading her text messages and trying hard not to continue being angry. The constant interruptions when he was with Vee were becoming quite the nuisance. And now, it seemed like he would never find that time to even have a conversation with her. They needed to discuss what their relationship was. He knew she didn't want her life to have to change, but she couldn't deny that she had feelings for him. He assumed part of her irrational hostility was because she was battling herself over the life she had made for herself and her actual desires.

Months ago, not long after they had met, Vee and Shane had discussed how neither of them were ready for any sort of relationship. He felt guilty for feeling so strongly about her so fast, especially when he had never felt that way for anyone before, even his late wife. As the months passed, he had realized his feelings were true, no longer denying that he and Vee were intrinsically connected. This wasn't something that was just going to go away.

Patrick came in the room, holding a glass of water, pulling Shane from his thoughts.

"I'm heading to bed," he told Shane.

"You're not going to wait up for Ethan?" Shane asked, a little surprised.

"From what he told me, well, you'll want to talk to him alone," Patrick said, his voice wavering a bit and skin tightening around his eyes, making his youthful face seem a bit more adult.

"What did he say?"

Patrick sighed, running his free hand through his hair, and looked at his father with anxious eyes.

"He's going to try to talk you into breaking the claim. He said a lot of harsh things about Vee," he told his dad, clearly unhappy about it. Shane wasn't surprised, but it didn't help his mood. Instead of being with her, protecting her, he was home, waiting for his son to come argue with him about his relationship with her.

"Great," Shane murmured, looking down at his hands as if they would hold the answers to all that ailed him. Unsurprisingly, they held no answers for him.

He felt slightly defeated, not wanting to argue about something he wasn't going to undo. The only reason he would ever break this claim would be if Vee wanted to. When the thought had come to him that placing a claim would protect her from Leib and any number of other preternaturals, it was like a piece of a puzzle was sliding perfectly into place. He wanted to claim her, and for her to claim him. He only wished he would have been able to do it prior, so it hadn't been about protection. He had hesitated too long, and now their relationship was forming a bit backward from how he had wanted it to go.

They heard Ethan's motorcycle coming through the neighborhood. Shane stood, looking at Patrick, who nodded as a goodnight, heading up the stairs to his room. The motorcycle engine shut off, and a few moments later Ethan came unceremoniously through the door, his duffle slung over his shoulder.

Shane went to him but was greeted with cold eyes.

"You went through with the claim, huh?" Ethan snarled, eyes flashing golden like his father's. Shane sighed.

"I did," he said very matter-of-factly, turning to head toward the kitchen. Ethan dropped his bag, slamming the door behind him before he followed.

"How could you do that? You haven't completed the bond yet have you? I can smell her all over you," he growled, watching Shane as he filled a glass with water and took a long sip.

"No. It's not completed. Just the claim."

"And it's going to stay that way, right? You don't actually plan on being stuck with that woman for the rest of her life?" His voice was laced with absolute disgust.

"What my plans are doesn't concern you," Shane said, trying to remain indifferent to Ethan's maliciousness.

"You're risking your pack! You're risking Patrick for this woman! The news about her has spread already.

Being associated with her is dangerous. Who knows what's going to come out of the woodwork!"

"Rumors were already spreading. I couldn't leave her unprotected," Shane said, his voice becoming sharper as his frustrations continued to increase.

"This is sick. Going after some weak preternatural. She's practically human. You already had a human wife. Wasn't that enough of a taste for you?" Ethan growled, nearly spitting as he brought up Patricia. Shane couldn't contain it anymore. His rage bubbled over the surface at the mention of his late wife.

"*Never* speak of her again! I don't want another bad word uttered from your mouth about Patricia. Do you know how much it hurts your brother when you speak about her that way? She's just as much a part of him as I am!" Shane yelled, slamming his fist on the countertop. It made a mournful sound, barely holding together with the force of his strength.

"It was a disgrace, and you know it. And here you are doing it again. At least we know your type. Human and weak."

Shane threw the glass across the room; it was all he could do to contain his violent impulse toward his older son. Ethan's eyebrows shot up in surprise, his body suddenly stilling with the explosion of glass and water. Shane was breathing raggedly through his nose, his eyes glowing with anger, a white line streaked across his cheek from his clenched jaw as he fought to calm himself.

Ethan had seen his dad angry, many times in fact, but he had never seen a reaction quite like this aimed toward him. They were both silent for a moment once the sound of the glass dissipated, and all they could hear was the subtle drip of water as it trickled onto the tile floor.

"You can insult me all you want, but leave Vee and Patricia out of this. Your hatred for humans as companions explains so much of your lonesome existence. Perhaps you are bitter because no woman, human or otherwise, wants to take you to their bed," Shane said more calmly now, but coldly.

"At least I'm not risking everything for someone who will die before me anyway," Ethan hissed back.

"She's not completely human, Ethan, we don't know how long she'll live," Shane said, a bit of his own fears creeping into his words. No, he didn't like the sinking feeling of outliving her, but he did have a small glimmer of hope, knowing that she at least was touched with preternatural in her. Maybe that would be enough to extend her life.

Ethan looked at his father quizzically. He had heard the rumors but didn't know what was true and what wasn't.

"So what rumors are true about her, then? How do you know she's not completely human?" he asked softly. Shane put his elbows on the counter, leaning against it and looking at his hands once again. All the rumors that had been floating around the community were true. That she was an empath. She knew how to tell the difference between preternaturals and humans. She saved Lori. She was targeted by Downing. None of those were the reasons Shane knew she was preternatural though.

"Because she's my True Mate," Shane whispered, closing his eyes. He had thought it a few times over these months, but now he knew it to be true. There was no way he could feel so drawn to her, to have his wolf and his human-self need to be with her so much, without it being true. Ethan's face crumbled into complete and utter confusion.

"That's not possible. She's not a Were," he said in disbelief.

"Maybe not, but it's true," Shane told him, looking up once again at his son, his expression that of unwavering certainty.

Vee had barely slept. Her dreams were filled with a mixture of fear and danger, Durran and Shane. She tossed and turned; each time she fell back to sleep, she was awoken again because of her dreams. Her mind had not slowed its racing, even as she went through with her routine, which was so wonderfully welcomed after the utterly bizarre weekend she had.

By the time she made it to lunch, she was emotionally exhausted. She had packed a sandwich in her bag, knowing she would have no way of going to grab anything quickly since her car was still dead on the side of the road when she had left the house in the morning. As she went to grab it, she was suddenly reminded of the other massive revelation of the weekend. Eliza's visit to the shop, and the envelope she would inevitably have to open.

But now wasn't the time.

She set the sandwich on the counter, averting her eyes from her bag, and cracked open her soda as she pulled out her phone to call her mechanic. She needed to get the Lumina towed before she got a ticket, or the city did it for her. One night sitting out on the street over the weekend was one thing. If it sat out there on a weekday, she would be paying a hefty fine for something that was barely worth repairing.

She got off the phone after making the arrangements for the tow and sighed as she looked up to see Durran darkening her doorway. She moved around the counter, sandwich in hand, and unlocked the door to let her in.

"What can I do for you today, Durran?" she asked, locking the door to keep back the bitter cold once Durran was inside.

"He left you last night. What good is he if he doesn't protect you?" Durran started, already in a foul mood.

"Yes, his son Ethan was coming. And guess what? Nothing happened once I was alone. How about that?" Vee said, a tight smile on her face before she took another bite of her sandwich.

"His priorities need to be on you right now. I don't care about his son," Durran grumbled, pacing around her showroom.

"Well, he does, and that's admirable of him. Obviously, you knew he left. Did you sit outside my apartment all night, then?" she asked, her voice accusatory. Durran stopped her pacing then and looked at Vee. Her emotions were all over the place, going from anger and jealousy to chagrin.

"Someone had to keep watch," she said by way of admission. Vee nodded, looking back down at her food. Vee let the truth of Shane's words the night before settle over her. Durran had basically just admitted to being Vee's Watcher. It had been a great source of topic in her dreams the night before. She had imagined fighting with Durran about not being honest, but perhaps a more subtle reminder of honesty and trust would do more than yelling.

"I'm still wondering when I'm supposed to get a say in any of this. I suppose I had the option to turn down this claim of Shane's, but I certainly never asked you to come watch my apartment."

In the past, Vee probably would have never spoken to her this way, but a line had been crossed and trust broken months ago. Vee still struggled to get past it. It didn't help the jealously and unfounded anger that Durran felt at nearly every mention of Shane. Vee still couldn't quite tell why those feelings were there. Was it that Vee had more people in her life now and wasn't at Durran's beck and call? Or was it something more?

Durran glanced at her briefly, guilt washing over her, but only momentarily, before her eyes shifted to Vee's open messenger bag. The envelope still sitting inside from the night before.

"You still haven't opened it yet?" Durran asked, making Vee turn to see where she was looking. Vee let her head droop a little sheepishly when she looked at the envelope.

"I just... it's all too much right now. I'm waiting until it levels out a little," she told her. It was mostly the truth. She just wasn't ready to admit the idea of looking

inside that unassuming package caused her complete and absolute fear. Did she want to know the truth?

"Aren't you curious?" Durran asked, her own intrigue piqued.

"I am, but..." Vee hesitated, looking at Durran with pleading eyes. She was silently begging her friend to drop this. She couldn't handle it right now.

Durran nodded, knowingly. This was part of the reason she hadn't sought out the information herself. It could overwhelm her, and send Vee into a mental spiral. Not something a Watcher wanted their ward to deal with, especially not right now with everything else going on.

"I'll leave you to it. It's nearly twelve-thirty," Durran said, unlocking the door and leaving Vee to her very disjointed and confused thoughts.

CHAPTER 10

Vee was finishing up closing, dreading her bitter cold walk home, when her phone rang. She had a mostly undisturbed day, Durran's visit notwithstanding, but of course Shane would call as she was finishing up for the night. Damn that man figuring out her routine so quickly into them knowing one another. She supposed the hours of her shop being posted on the window didn't lend much mystery about how she used her time.

"Yes, Shane?" she answered, wedging the phone between her ear and her shoulder as she started locking the inventory room.

"I'm on my way there," he said, his voice a little garbled over the Bluetooth connection in his car. He must have been driving on Ward Parkway, cell service was spotty on that road, at best.

"Why is that?" she asked. She didn't recall having told him about her car troubles the night before.

"Durran told me your car was dead last night when she called. I assume it hasn't been fixed yet?"

Damn Durran...

"I was just going to walk. It's really not too far," she said, beginning to slide her stained coat on. She really wished she had an acceptable spare, so she could stop wandering around looking like she didn't take care of herself. She would have to wait until next weekend when she did laundry to fix that.

"It is too far in this cold, and it's not safe right now," he argued, clearly increasing his speed to her location.

"Fine! Fine! I'll be waiting outside," she grumbled, hanging up the phone and going to set the alarm.

She had barely finished locking the door when Shane pulled up, clearly having raced the remainder of the way to her shop to avoid her trying to walk. She stepped into the car, the heat blasting away the freezing temperatures outside immediately. She hadn't ridden in his car before, but she wasn't surprised by how nice it was inside. Smooth leather and fancy, high-tech gadgets; it was clean and smelled like leather softener, cologne, and the unmistakable scent that was Shane. Very different from her car.

"I don't suppose you want to go to dinner?" he asked, as she buckled her seatbelt.

"I'm going to have to get the alternator replaced on the Lumina. Do you think I have money to go out to dinner?" she asked a bit snarkier than she had intended, but still giving him her most dubious face.

CHAPTER 10

"It could be a date," he said, making her eyebrows rise in surprise.

"A date?" she asked him, her expression unchanging though her heart pounded in her chest.

"That's what I said."

She glanced down at her clothes; stained coat, worn jeans, faded black t-shirt, and a frumpy over-sized sweater. She was pretty sure this sweater had a hole somewhere from where she snagged it on a key hook earlier that day.

"I don't think I'm really dressed for such an occasion," she said, semi surprising herself with the fact that her attire was the only thing that she really had reservations about going on a date with him. A restaurant was neutral territory, unlike most of their interactions, which happened at either her or Shane's house.

"I made sure to dress to match," he told her, making her look him over. He was, indeed, dressed casually again. His jeans were even worn on the knees, *actually* worn from years of use, not pre-worn for fashion purposes. How had they gone so many months without her seeing him this way, and now two days in a row?

"I..." she started, trying and failing to find another excuse not to. "I suppose," she muttered, as he started driving.

Shane knew better than to ask Vee where she wanted to go, she would only argue with him. He had already decided to take her to one of the more casual restaurants in Westport. Something close by that would allow her no time to change her mind as they drove. It was a Monday, so he hoped it wouldn't be busy and that they would have a little privacy.

They walked in, once he found somewhere to park. Vee had been surprised they found a spot so close to the restaurant. Usually they filled up quickly, but the nightlife didn't seem to be picking up. Perhaps it was because it was a Monday, or it was due to the cold. Either way, Vee appreciated that there weren't quite so many human minds for her to get accustomed to.

They easily got a table, a little in the back and decently far from any other diners. Vee sat down on one side of the booth, removing her bag and coat and putting them beside her. Shane did the same. The server came by with waters and the specials, and then left them to look over the menu.

Vee tried very diligently to focus on the menu instead of looking up at Shane, but she failed quite a few times. She wasn't completely comfortable with the fact that they were becoming … something. What that something was, she didn't know. She couldn't even deny her feelings for him when she was alone in her apartment anymore, let alone when he was sitting right across from her.

"It has been difficult finding time for us to talk," Shane said, eyes also cast on the menu and not at her.

"We could have talked last night, but…" she trailed off, thinking of what they had done instead, letting their emotions get the best of them. He glanced at her face then, seeing just the faintest blush rise to her cheeks as her heart picked up speed. A human wouldn't have been able to see the color touching her face, but he did. His hands longed to reach over and touch the skin there, to see if it was warmer with that rush of blood, but he forced himself to keep a firm grip on the menu instead.

"We do seem to get carried away," he said, smirking a little. Vee looked up just in time to see that smirk cross his lips.

"What exactly is it that *you* are wanting to discuss, Shane?" she said, setting the menu on the table and leaning forward, her face questioning.

"I thought we might like to figure out what exactly we are to one another. That may require a discussion."

She let that roll around in her mind a moment. Shane also set his menu down now, looking at her, watching her as her eyes danced, thoughts swirling behind there that he wasn't privy to.

"You first," she said abruptly, her eyes landing on his.

"First, what?" he asked, confused.

"You tell me what I am to you first," she said, placing her chin on her fist, waiting. She was admittedly being a little aggressive with her questioning, but she was putting up a defense. What if she didn't like what he had to say? What if it was only physical attraction he felt? Would that be enough for her? She would rather be disappointed first, than have spilled her feelings to him, only to have them not reciprocated.

The server came back right at that moment, breaking their eye contact.

"Did you two decide on what you would like to order?" he asked, pulling out a notepad from his apron. Vee realized she didn't even know what kind of food they served here, let alone what she wanted to eat. Her mind had been far elsewhere when she had been pretending to look at the menu. She pointed at Shane, making him go first as she skimmed the menu as quickly as she could.

"I'll have the meatloaf with a side of the mashed potatoes," Shane said, handing his menu over. Vee panicked now, deciding she would just eat whatever her eyes landed on next.

"I'll take the soup of the day," she finally said, not having any idea what the soup was at all, but to be honest, hot soup sounded fantastic on such a cold evening.

"Alright, I'll get those put in. Did either of you want anything to drink other than water?" he asked, and they both declined.

Once he was a distance away, Vee turned her attention back to Shane who was looking at her with an odd expression on his face. His emotions were dulled again, letting on that he was amused, but she could tell there was something more under the surface there. Blocking her again, though not completely this time.

"How do you keep doing that?" she asked, completely beside herself with frustration and curiosity over it.

"Blocking you?"

"Yes!" she said, exasperated, making him laugh.

"I'm not completely sure. I just know you can feel them, so sometimes I try to hold some things back," he told her with a shrug.

"Why?"

He took a deep breath then, propping his chin on his clasped hands, considering his words carefully as he looked into her eyes.

"I don't know if you're ready to feel everything I feel for you," he told her honestly. Vee didn't know what she thought his rationale was for blocking his feelings from her was, but that wasn't what she had been expecting.

"But you'll tell me, instead?" she asked, doubtful.

He studied her eyes for a moment, wishing he could feel *her* emotions. If he thought it wouldn't scare her away, he would just let her feel it. But they had been overwhelming for him, difficult to put to the back of his mind. It was strenuous to stay away from her, to give her the space that she needed for all these months. The last thing he wanted was for her to run away. She wasn't a woman he could crush to his side and force to be with him. Despite her calculated and routine life, he could see she needed her independence, her freedom.

Shane wanted Vee to choose him, to want to be with him. He wanted to go to sleep every night with her in his arms. In fact, the best night of sleep he had had since he met her was the night she was safely in his bed. It wasn't even the undeniable attraction; it was just the comfort of having her there. He had relaxed fully, knowing she was protected beside him, sleep taking him quicker than it had come in years. It was a strange sort of torture to smell her on his sheets the night before and not have her there.

No. These weren't things he could say to her. Not until he knew how she felt.

"I can tell you that this claim isn't something I take lightly. I will care for you in whatever way you'll let me," he said after several long minutes of silence while he considered what words would cause the least amount of damage to their budding relationship. Vee could tell he chose these words specifically. That they were true, but he wasn't telling her everything.

"Why won't you just tell me?" she asked, frustrated now. If she didn't already know her bodily reaction to touching him when he was blocking, she would have reached across the table and grabbed his hand. As it was, slamming her head into the back of the booth, while she still had a bump there from the last time she tried such a thing, was not the best idea.

"Will you tell me?" he asked, raising a skeptical eyebrow.

She sat back against the booth, glaring at him. How dare he turn this back to her? She chewed on the inside of her cheek for a moment, considering what to say. She wanted to be straight forward, but since he wasn't...

"I don't like change. I like my routine. My things. I like having my own time. I like making my own choices," she started. He sighed, closing his eyes, disappointment evident on his face. "But I like you," she continued, making his eyes snap back open to look at her. "And for some reason, even though you won't give me any sort of straight answers, I trust you."

Shane opened his mouth to say something, but their server came back then. Both Shane and Vee tried to smile as if they weren't having an extremely intense conversation. Vee could barely breathe as they were thanking him once the food was set down, her heart beating wildly. Had she really just told him she *liked* him? As if it was a simple crush? She looked down at her soup, instead of at Shane. She knew she was hungry, but it seemed affirmations of affections tended to override her need for food.

Shane sat there for a moment watching her face and listening to her heart. Just her heartbeat alone told him she wasn't telling him everything either. He picked up his fork and knife and began eating, prompting Vee to gather her spoon in her fingers. The silence stretched on for quite a few minutes as they ate. This felt almost as anxiety inducing as the dinner with Leib had been.

"What can I do?" Shane finally asked, not knowing how to form the question he wanted to but not wanting the silence between them anymore.

"What do you mean?" she asked, looking up from her bowl at his face once more.

"What is it that you need for me to do … to…" He still couldn't find the words he wanted to say. How could he simply ask her how to make her love him?

She didn't fully understand what he was asking, but she saw the struggle on his face. He was getting frustrated with himself. Had she made this powerful man trip over his words?

"Straight answers. You let me in. I'll let you in," she told him, pushing the half-eaten bowl of soup away from her so she could place her arms on the table. He set his utensils down on his plate, sitting back against the booth and looking into her eyes. They were both adults. Why were they playing this game?

"I—" he started but stopped when her eyes snapped away from him toward the front section of tables. Her heartbeat became rapid again, breathing uneven. He could smell her fear as she looked past his head and behind him.

He turned, following her gaze to see the couple who was standing at a booth only a few tables down from them.

"We need to leave. *I* need to leave," Vee said, scrambling to grab all her things from beside her in the booth before Shane could turn and ask her what was wrong.

"Take my keys and wait in the car," he said, not questioning her actions, at least not right now. They could talk about it later as long as she didn't try anything foolish, like walking home.

Vee snatched the keys from his outstretched hand and tried to quickly pass the couple by, but they had already noticed her.

"Ah, Victoria," Frank said, his tone smug as he stepped in front of her, blocking her way from the exit. "Did you like the little package I had Eliza give you?" he asked. Eliza had already slipped into the booth but was cowering in the corner of it. It looked as if she was trying to will herself to sink into the wall she had pinned herself against.

"I haven't looked at it yet. I've been busy," Vee told him, bringing her now amber eyes to meet his blackened ones, pupils dilated as if he were a predator watching his prey squirm. He didn't like her response, hoping whatever was held inside that envelope's contents was enough to crush her. A fact that made the idea of opening the envelope even more daunting to Vee.

Frank opened his mouth to say something, probably yell something at her, since his face was turning bright red. Rage was building within him but was stopped with his mouth hanging agape as he looked over Vee's head. She could feel the heat of Shane's body behind her, feel the power flowing from him. She was certain he was quite intimidating in the eyes of Frank. Shane was tall, well-muscled, and exuded raw dominant power.

"Vee, head to the car. I'll meet you out there in just a moment," Shane said, his voice low and threatening, though not directed toward her. Vee did not hesitate, giving one last look at Eliza and slipping past Frank to escape.

She gasped the moment the cold air hit her, taking just a moment to breathe it in and clear her mind a little, before she ran to Shane's car. Once in, she started it, finally wrapping her coat around her as she waited for Shane to emerge from the restaurant. She knew he was paying, but she wasn't sure what he was doing about Frank.

Shane really didn't have to *do* anything. He stood there for a moment after Vee had made her way past him and outside, glaring intensely down at the man. He seemed frozen in place, unable to take his eyes off Shane. The server came back through, slowing as he saw the two men standing in the aisle. Shane reached out his hand to the server, card already in hand, not breaking eye contact with Frank.

"Please run our bill for me. We need to leave," Shane said.

"Oh! Um ... of course."

Shane then turned away from Frank once the server had returned to their station to settle the bill and gathered his coat. He waited patiently, still glaring at Frank, despite not knowing the whole situation with these people and Vee, but knowing she was scared of that man was enough. He was human, so Shane didn't need to do more than be intimidating. The man reeked of fear with the small push of Shane's dominance. He was weak. A sad man that used manipulation to gain power, and power only to continue to manipulate.

"Who is he?" Frank hissed in Eliza's direction, unable to take his eyes off Shane. Eliza merely shook her head, whimpering quietly.

Shane held back the growl at the way the woman he was with cowered at not Shane's presence, but her husband's. Power should be used to protect, but this man was clearly using it in the worst way. He would need to find out exactly what this man had done to Vee. He could think of a multitude of ways he could break him, even some that did not involve his superior strength.

By the time he signed the slip, tipping well as usual, and walked back to his car, Vee was panicking in the passenger seat. He got in, and she audibly sighed with relief.

"Why did that take so long?" she asked, her eyes darting between him and the door to the restaurant.

"Just waiting to pay," he said honestly, pulling out of the parking spot.

"Did you say anything to him?"

"I don't even know who *he* is," Shane said, turning to look at her now that they were at a red light. Vee felt a twinge of guilt at that. She hadn't really told him about the situation with her sister. There were a lot of things Vee hadn't told him about yet.

"That was my sister, Eliza, and her husband Frank," she said while letting out a breath. Shane took that in for a moment. The fear he smelled from her the moment she saw him was shocking. Vee was not one to scare easily.

"Why does he scare you so much?" Shane asked, watching her fingers fiddle with her bag strap. Vee sighed, looking over at him, a sadness evident in her eyes.

"He's threatened me before. He doesn't want me as part of their lives, which means I cannot see Eliza. We didn't really see much of each other anyway, but last summer she asked me to change their locks…" Vee let out a shaky sigh. "That was some sort of breaking point for him. Seeing me in their home, I suppose," she told him, trying to steady the quiver in her voice.

Shane gripped the steering wheel. Preternatural threats he could handle. Humans, however, that took a more subtle approach.

"I wish I had known before," he growled, gunning it as the light turned green.

"You can't do anything about it, either way. I just need stay away," she said, attempting to make her voice more normal, feeling his anger coming through.

They lapsed into silence once again, Shane trying to calm himself and Vee simply not wanting to rile him any more than he already was. He pulled up to her apartment, shutting the engine off.

"As usual, we didn't get to finish our conversation," he said, looking over at her, his eyes back to normal. The short drive had given him enough time to reasonably calm down, since there was nothing he could do about the Frank situation. She smiled a little.

"Unfortunately, I think if I invited you up there we probably wouldn't finish it either," she said, raising her eyebrows a little, a bit shocked she let those words slip out. Shane laughed at that, a deep rumble of joy from his chest as he reached over to touch her cheek. She leaned into his hand a little, her eyes still focused on his.

"I really *should* come up there, Vee. Just to be safe," he said, trying to keep the thoughts of what happened in her kitchen from his mind. That wasn't protecting her, and he needed to talk to her before that went any further. He had to explain to her what might happen if they did let it go that far.

"As much as that sounds wonderful right now, I can't have you messing up my sleep. I get up very early, and I was fine last night, all by myself. I'll be fine tonight. Besides, isn't Ethan still in town?" she asked, pulling away from his touch. The loss of contact was almost painful. Her careful wall around her feelings for him was tumbling down rapidly.

Shane growled a little, at both the way she pulled from his hand and thinking that Ethan was any sort of good reason why they should spend the night apart, but he felt a little better knowing she had been okay the night before.

"Call me if you need me, please?" he asked, as she opened the car door.

"I won't need you, but on the off chance I do, I will call," she assured him, before closing the door and heading into the building.

CHAPTER 11

Vee woke to the angry sound of her phone ringing. She moved her eyes to look at the clock, seeing it was two in the morning. With a sigh she removed herself from the comfort of her bed and wandered to her phone, glancing at the unfamiliar number before answering.

"Hello?" she murmured sleepily into the phone. She hadn't been getting many middle-of-the-night-locksmith emergencies, and those were rather lucrative, so she had to rouse herself. There was no response, only ragged, uneven breathing on the other end. She furrowed her brow, her sleepy brain wasn't recognizing that this was slightly alarming, only registering the strangeness of it.

"Hello?" she asked again, rubbing her eyes and listening more intently to the noises in the background.

There was a low rumble—maybe a growl?—coming from wherever the person on the phone was and the breathing. "Who is this?" she demanded, even though her voice didn't have much force behind it, having just woken up.

The line went dead.

She pulled it from her ear and looked at it, confused and bit scared. Whatever that was, it didn't seem good. She thought to call the number back but decided against it. Perhaps it was a wrong number or a pocket dial. That breathing could have been someone sleeping, but why had it made the hairs on the back of her neck stand on end?

Her first instinct was to call Shane, but she knew how that was going to go. He would demand she come and stay with him, and she didn't want him to have any more fuel to keep her constantly guarded.

Then she thought about Durran. If she was her Watcher, shouldn't she have seen this? Shouldn't she know Vee felt threatened?

Her phone rang just the moment she thought that, and she looked at the caller ID, seeing it was Shane. She rolled her eyes.

"Hello?"

"Durran called. What happened?" he asked, his voice sounding a bit sleepy as well.

"Got a weird call, nothing to worry about," she lied, as she walked out to her living room to sit on a futon because she wasn't going back to sleep anytime soon.

"Nothing to worry about," he scoffed. She could practically see him rubbing a hole in his forehead. *"I'll send Patrick to get you."*

"No. Don't wake him up, and don't send anyone else to get me. I'm not leaving."

Hell would freeze over before she changed her life completely. Enough had happened in the past few days. She wasn't going to rush off to Shane's house every time she felt mildly threatened. If Shane thought she was going to move in with him now that they were ... whatever they were, he had another thing coming.

"You are obviously being targeted."

"And whose fault is that?" she hissed, responding to the irritation in his voice.

"Vee, just listen to me."

"I'll call Durran," she said, ignoring his previous comment as she ended the call and scrolled through her phone to find Durran's number.

She didn't have to wait for it to ring before Durran answered, her tone indifferent.

"Vee."

"Can you come here?" she asked immediately. There was a distinct pause on the phone.

"I don't approve of the fact your wolf let you call me. Why isn't he coming?"

"He wants me there. I don't want to leave," she told her, ignoring the way Durran had voiced her disapproval and referred to Shane as *her* wolf.

A sigh.

"This is his responsibility," Durran murmured, grumpily.

"And I don't care. You're my Watcher, aren't you?"

Durran said nothing, causing the silence between the two of them to become very uncomfortable.

"Fine. I'll just sit here alone then. I seemed to do just fine by myself before," she hissed, hanging up the phone and chucking it to the other futon. Any other calls that evening were going to be ignored.

Waking up at two in the morning was not enough sleep for her, but she could manage a workday on fumes. With her silver-plated switchblade on one side and her meat tenderizer on the other, she would be ready for anything that might jump at her. Or, at least as ready as she could be.

She flipped on the television to some mundane infomercial, practically playing it on mute so she could hear the sounds of the world around her apartment. A few cars driving around on the damp pavement, probably half-drunks on the side streets after leaving the bars. She heard Una's cat, Midi, jumping from the sofa to the floor below and pacing the apartment, like she was waiting to strike a foreign invader. Normal night sounds.

Other than that, little was happening according to her ears and what she was feeling from those sleeping around her. She watched the repeating infomercial and waited for something to happen, but as the sun started to make the sky pink with its morning arrival, nothing ever did.

She was now exhausted, slumped over with her weapons of choice still in her limp hands. The infomercial changed to the morning news, and she let the switchblade fall from her fingers long enough to rub her red, sleep deprived eyes and unmute the television.

"...*the person or persons were not caught, but the police are still gathering evidence. Mrs. Smith is still being held for observation at the closest hospital. If she stabilizes, she may be able to pull through. The other two people in the household, three-year-old Mary and forty-three-year-old Frank, were found in what appears to be a homicide…"*

Vee's tiredness vanished at the mention of the names. Mary? Frank? They had never specifically said 'Eliza,' but the horribly damaged front door, taped off by police, that they were now showing was… was definitely…

Vee scrambled to the other futon, grabbing her cell from the worn mattress cover and shakily scrolling through her phone until she reached Eliza's number. She still hadn't deleted it after Frank's threat. She never had the intention of calling it again, but she couldn't bring herself to remove her only way of contacting her sister completely.

The phone rang. Each one sounded both long and painful, like something was ripping at her with each shrill tone, but only the voicemail picked up.

"You've reached the cell phone of Eliza Smith. I can't come to the phone right now. Please leave a message." Vee hung up and tried the house phone which was right under Eliza's cell phone number in her contacts list. The phone didn't even ring; it went straight to voicemail, as if they were on the phone, or the line was dead.

"You've reached the Smith Residence. We are unavailable to take your call. Leave a brief message, and we will attempt to return it," came the nasal tone of Frank.

When it beeped, Vee didn't know what to say.

"I—I… Eliza? Tell me… tell me that wasn't… tell me you're okay," was all she managed to choke out, before she ended the call, her eyes welling with tears.

Her head was swimming. Her body was numb. She could feel the humans around her beginning to wake up, moving about their groggy morning rituals. She knew the television was still on. She knew the hard wood floor was going to start hurting her knees. She knew somewhere in her apartment her phone was ringing.

She knew, but she didn't really understand.

The door flew open, shards of wood flying and landing on the futons and floor. She couldn't really comprehend who it was, or what they wanted. She didn't remember the meat tenderizer or the switchblade, which were abandoned on the futon behind her. She couldn't even see through the tears blocking her vision, but suddenly there were arms wrapped around her, strong arms.

She didn't really think of fighting. There was something very comforting about these arms. Something so calming that it nearly took her breath away. She let it out, the sob that had been building in her chest, her breath hitching, and her tears streaming and staining the coat of... who was this again? It didn't matter.

She clutched and pressed, sobbed and screamed. Somewhere in the back of her head she knew her door was probably irreparably broken, and there were very subtle emotions coming from the person holding her, stroking her hair, whispering sweet things.

She quieted, still holding onto them, but catching her breath, slowly calming. Finally, she pulled away, turning her face up to look into the reddish-brown eyes of Durran.

"Durran?" she croaked out softly, confusion flashing across her features.

"I just knew. I—I couldn't wait for Shane. I'm sorry," Durran murmured, brushing Vee's cheek from its tear stains. She felt that small twinge from Durran again. Something Vee would have possibly poked at, had she not been in such a state of shock.

"It's really them, then?" Vee asked, barely able to bring herself to let the words out.

"It is," Durran confirmed, tightening the grip she had on her.

Vee let out a shaky sigh. She was too vulnerable and uncertain of her feelings to care that she was completely tangled in Durran. All she could think of was that her sister was attacked, niece dead.

"It was my fault wasn't it?" Vee asked, her eyes boring into Durran's, which were growing a bit redder with each passing moment.

"We don't know that," she whispered, trying to be reassuring.

Vee glanced at her discarded messenger bag, the large envelope peeking out, still unopened. Thinking about it only made the heartache she was feeling worsen. She glanced back up at Durran's face.

"Who is it? Are they after me?" she asked, determination overwhelming her other emotions. She hated feeling so powerless. She hated the unknown. What could be so tantalizing about her that someone would kill her family?

That feeling of change Vee had felt months ago was taunting her. It had crept into her mind, chilling her and warning her before she had ever crossed paths with Lori or Shane. She never predicted her life would be completely upended when she stepped out of her shop that fateful night, unthinkingly running toward danger to save strangers.

How did she go from being unnoticed and unaccepted for abilities her whole life to being hunted down?

How did she suddenly go from living a single and solitary life to being mated to a leader of a Werewolf pack?

"I'm not sure," Durran said, her face unable at this small distance to completely mask its concern, even though Vee could feel it clearly.

Durran pulled away slightly before Vee felt it; the vibration that she had gotten to recognize as Shane. Just a moment later with Vee still on the floor, but Durran now a good pace away and standing to face the door, Shane burst through the already broken door, which hung crookedly by one hinge.

"You need to come with me now," Shane said, his eyes blazing golden with a rage that she could feel pulsing around her head, infecting her veins.

"Is there an immediate threat?" she asked, standing and now feeling how sore her knees were. There would be bruises.

"Victoria," Shane said, closing his hands into angry fists as he stared her down. "I cannot protect you here. *You* are what they are after. Please come with me, and we will figure something out that may be more suitable for you," he told her through clenched teeth, his voice shaking, trying to hold onto the remaining shreds of calm he had.

CHAPTER 11

"Let me get my things," she said, not pushing him. Right now was not the time to push.

As she turned to go to her room and gather some clothing and various necessities her cell phone rang from its abandoned spot on the floor. Vee's eyes darted to it nervously, not sure if she wanted to know who was calling. Durran, being closer, bent to get it.

"We'll take care of this. Get your things," she said. Vee wandered to her bedroom, but of course, was listening. The distance and the walls between them, meant she could only hear Durran's voice. "She saw the news. She's in shock, and we're going to take her with us. If you need to get in contact with her, she'll be at Shane Keenan's house. I'm not sure how long... Yes. I'll let her know. Thank you," Durran said.

She took a deep breath, trying to ignore the pity that was washing from the two in the other room to her. Instead, she grabbed a small duffle she had stowed in the back of her closet and began filling it with anything and everything in her reach. She went into the bathroom, hastily stuffing her hairbrush and any other necessary hygiene products in before zipping it up. When she returned to the front room only Shane remained, which bothered her. Not that Shane wasn't comforting, but it had been Durran who was there for when she was reeling.

"It will be fine," Shane said, reaching out, now much calmer than before, and taking her duffle.

"What did the person on the phone say? What were you two supposed to tell me?" she asked, putting on her shoes as she waited for the answer. He hesitated, looking at her face, still puffy from crying.

"Eliza…" he trailed off, his face strained, wishing he didn't have to tell her this. It was the last thing she would want to hear. "She died," Shane whispered.

Not that Vee hadn't seen it coming, but the knowledge that the only people she had ever called *hers* were gone was… well, she didn't exactly know how to process it. She stood, not looking him in the eyes as she grabbed her coffee-stained coat and messenger bag and headed out the door.

Shane followed, silently watching her. She was a creature of habit, of solitude. Someone who had never really had much to call hers. She never had a support system. She never had people to rely on. She had always been alone, even in what she was. But the small amount of people that belonged to her, the ones she counted as part of her, were gone.

Shane couldn't fathom if he had lost everyone that had ever meant anything to him. He didn't know how he would cope if suddenly he had no pack, no sons. He had faced all-consuming tragedy before. He had stood by as loved ones aged and died, when Patricia breathed her last breath, but he had been surrounded by people who helped pull him through it. It would take time for her to see the pack as her family, but they were. They counted her as one of them, like they did with the human spouses of pack members.

He put the duffle in the back seat of his car. Vee slumped in the front seat with her messenger bag on her lap, waiting with little emotion on her face, for the car to start moving.

"Have someone fix my door," was all she said for the whole twenty-minute drive, which he had taken in ten when he found out.

It was nerve wracking, to not know who was after her. Usually there were signs, things that would directly point to the source of the attacks, but this attack? He had no idea. Lieb was a suspect, of course, but from what Shane had seen, Lieb was more interested in Vee. He did not seem to be threatened by her. Or at least, not threatened enough to try to kill her. He had sent Thomas and Tommy to the Smith residence to catch the scent of the attacker, but there hadn't been enough time to hear a report back. As far as he knew, it could have been any number of preternatural creatures.

They pulled up to his house, which was teeming with cars and bodies. He knew this was specifically *not* what Vee needed at the moment, but this was what packs did in times of crisis. They gathered together to help, to solve whatever happened and prepare for whatever was being planned.

"Just go up to my room. Go straight there. No one will question you," Shane said as he turned to her. She met his gaze slowly, showing off the shining amber of her eyes, burning with an underlying fury.

Without another word she got out of the car, slamming the door loudly in her wake and storming up to the house. He could see the tension in her body, stiff with rage. She had gone from sad, to numb, to angry. This was going to be interesting.

Vee felt the vibrations and anger of every wolf in the Westport Pack pounding in her head as she walked toward the house. She was too emotionally shot to push their emotions away from hers, or to care, for that matter. She let their anger envelope her, feeling it burn through her was somehow more acceptable than her own grief.

She did as Shane said, going straight through the entry and up the stairs until she reached the second door that led to Shane's room. She didn't even care that she was going to be in his room, again. She moved across the lush carpet, her mind only set on the golden sheets of the bed, those warm, silken sheets that would help her block away the world.

Yes, she wanted to know who had killed her sister.

Of course, she needed to know who could possibly want to kill her.

Yes, she was curious about what she was, and why she was so incredibly controversial.

But now, she needed to sleep.

Despite the angry Weres downstairs pulsing in her mind, despite the fact that she was not in her house, alone, in her bed, and despite the fact that she had to sacrifice everything that her life had been because she decided to help a girl from becoming a monster; she was overwhelmed and tired.

Still in her pajamas from the previous night and without untying her shoes, she fell against the unmade bed and let the oblivion of sleep take her.

CHAPTER 12

Shane sat in the car for a moment after he watched her enter his home. It was a relief she was there, safe and surrounded by his wolves, not alone and vulnerable, but now he had to deal with the findings. His control was temperamental. He had never experienced such huge swings in emotions, or at least not since he had first changed. Not until he met her. For her, his rationality flew out the window. He wanted to kill something to protect her, but he didn't know who to go after. Not yet. With a deep breath, he managed to get out of his car and go to the house. The pack was busy. It was like watching a beehive. Bodies zoomed here and there. People were talking, looking over papers or busily searching on laptops while they argued possibilities. They were protective of her. She had become one of them.

Thomas looked up and noticed Shane, immediately moving through the crowded front rooms to meet him.

"It smelled like a Werewolf."

"Lieb," Shane growled, rubbing his forehead and pinching the bridge of his nose so he wouldn't begin destroying everything around him.

"I'm not so sure. I got Lieb's scent when he visited. It wasn't him, per se. I also smelled..." Thomas hesitated when Shane's eyes snapped up, golden and angry.

"What? What else?"

"A Watcher. It just seemed to be around, like it was observing, but it was never involved in the attack."

This certainly changed things. The only Watcher they knew was Durran, and if she had been the Watcher at the scene, she would not have been able to simply observe. She would have had to do something. Wards would be emotionally distraught if family members were injured or killed. This could lead to any number of complications, such as suicide attempts. Durran would not have been able to just sit by and watch a Were destroy Vee's family, even if she was forbidden from killing them in Shane's territory.

So, the Watcher was someone else, someone who was probably just as curious about Vee as everyone else. The problem for Shane now, was who was interested?

The Fae had yet to make appearances in the mix, so they were most likely indifferent. They were far less organized than any of the other preternatural groups, staying solitary and to themselves. Any Vampire attacks would have been obvious, and they usually were quite straightforward when they wanted information. The Witches in the territory were all White and Grey

Witches. Unless one of the covens took a turn toward Black Craft, they were unlikely to be the culprits. This left only the Watchers and some sector of Weres.

He had to know if Durran knew anything. Doubtful as it was, he had to be sure. With a heaving breath that came out as a growl, he pulled his phone from his pocket and hit Durran's name, perhaps a bit too hastily.

"*She is safe,*" Durran stated as a greeting.

"She's here, with the pack," Shane confirmed, trying to keep himself in check. The way Durran said "she is safe" made it seem like she had been doubtful of Shane's ability to keep her that way up until this point. "It was a Were, but a Watcher was observing," he briefed her, trying and failing to keep his wolf tucked inside. His voice had come out less human than he had intended.

Silence.

Over the phone Shane couldn't tell if it was shocked silence or one of knowing. He waited, his breathing picking up with each passing moment.

"*It can't be…*" Durran murmured so quietly Shane barely caught it.

"It can't be what?" Shane rumbled, trying to hold back from crushing the phone as his fingers fought to change, elongating and curling over.

"*I want to be sure. I'll get back to you when I know more. Keep her safe,*" was all she said before she hung up and left Shane to close his fist; the sound of the phone dying as it crushed beneath his fingers.

"What should we do?" Thomas asked quietly, hunching his body to show submissiveness to his leader. Shane turned his burning golden eyes to his second and let out a guttural sound.

"Follow the scent," was all Shane could say before he marched up the stairs, hands still clenched and body taut with the effort to stop its transformation.

There was one thing he could do that may work to insure no Were, at least, could harm her, but he didn't know if she would agree. He didn't know, if the state he was in, he would let her disagree. He wanted to protect her, and he *wanted* her. She might be safer if she allowed this.

With his hand on the knob, he fought back the urge to rip the door down and tear across the room. It was hard to resist the beast within, gaining control bit by bit. He needed to calm down if he was going to have this work, if she would ever agree, especially with the circumstances being what they were. She was tired, emotionally spent. She had just lost her family.

He looked down at his claw-like hand grasping the knob, deforming it slightly under its strength. He would frighten her if he approached her like this.

He had to be calm to win her.

The beast seemed to agree with those thoughts, allowing him to regain some sense of logic. He stood at the door for a moment, breathing deeply, his form returning fully to human.

He couldn't do this.

She was in no state for him to be pushing this on her, even when he knew the protection it provided would keep her safe from other Weres within his territory. A Were could not kill a leader's bonded mate within his territory. There were magics that prevented it.

He turned the knob and walked into his room and let Vee's scent surround him. As he softly closed the door, he let his eyes fall on her limp form on top of the bed. Her shoes where still on her feet and dangling over the side of the bed. He moved slowly, trying to control his emotions, to block them, as not to wake her. He moved closer and began quietly untying and removing them from her feet.

Next, he slipped his own shoes and shirt off before he climbed onto the bed and pulled her closer. She turned and nuzzled into his chest, sighing softly without a bat of her eyes. The bit of rage that had still been lingering there faded as he held her. Having her close, touching her, had a calming effect. If only he had been there when she found out. If he had come to her when he called her initially, she wouldn't have been alone when she found out. His heart ached, knowing he couldn't take that back. He'd let Ethan's presence push her away. He wouldn't make that mistake again.

The feel of her in his arms was intoxicating; the smell of her, the touch of her skin, the way her dark, silky hair brushed and fanned around her head and his arm. It had been irresistible the other night to not cuddle against her. He knew she wouldn't like it when she woke, but he wanted to hold her, even if it was just for a little while. She had relaxed against him as soon as he pressed himself to her and placed an arm around her waist. Her body knew what her mind didn't want to admit, and here she was relaxing into him again.

Never had he come across someone so completely perfect for him. Her fire was unquenchable, even when she was completely torn down. She was not afraid of him. She did not shy away from him, except for how she felt toward him. She asked for fairness. She would let him in, if he did the same for her. She was his equal.

Hours had passed of simply holding her. It was a bit surprising that no one had come to get him. Either there was no new information, or they were giving the two of them space. He knew he should have been part of the action below, searching for the culprits of her family's demise, but holding her was all he cared to do. Her arm unconsciously snaked over his chest, settling on his stomach. Feeling her skin against his, he thought about what he was going to say to her at dinner the night before. What he wanted her to know so badly but didn't want to risk scaring her away.

He wasn't sure how much she was consciously aware of while she slept, but for once, he wasn't trying to hold back. He closed his eyes, pressing his lips to her forehead briefly.

"I love you," he whispered, letting her feel it. He hoped it would bring her comfort in her dreams. She was safe. Safe with him, always.

He heard her heartbeat pick up a moment later. This was not the slow beat of someone sleeping anymore. She was awake now.

Vee was trying very hard not to open her eyes. She was so close to him. He was all around her. Every sense was immersed in Shane, and she didn't know how … she couldn't think of how … no, she didn't *want* to get away. She wanted to be held by him, to smell him, to touch him. She could feel his devotion, his passion, his…

This wasn't a flicker. She had tried to ignore this growing foreign emotion. She began to realize what that feeling was, though. That feeling that she, within herself, had tried to tamp down.

Love.

Now that she recognized it, it flared within her. A burn that seared through her body.

She wanted his lips on hers again. She was done fighting herself. In her tiny kitchen, when he had stolen a kiss, a passionate, breathtaking kiss, she had wanted him. And she hadn't just wanted him in that moment. Thoughts of him would invade her mind at random times. She would try to justify them, reason that the thoughts meant nothing, but even though she fought against admitting it, after being alone for so long, she didn't want to allow herself the pain of rejection. Alone was safe, but Shane had done anything but reject her. They fought, yes, but for the better part of a year he had been inviting her into his life. He wanted her to be part of his pack; he gave up the ability to find a partner within the preternatural community for her. Shane had practically given his life to her on a silver platter, and *she* had been the one to reject him.

She opened her eyes slightly and let them settle on his. They were gold, but not angry or ready to fight. These eyes were burning for her.

"Vee, I—"

"Kiss me," she said, interrupting him. She didn't want to hear explanations or apologies or anything really. She wanted to feel him. He didn't hesitate as he leaned forward, his mouth soft as he brushed it against hers.

As their lips touched for the third time, she felt that overwhelming, intense connection again. Her hand slipped up his chest to his face, fingers brushing the rough stubble on his cheeks before wrapping around to thread through his hair. His arms tightened around her body, pulling her even closer to him than she already had been. She slipped her leg over his hip.

She had been kissed before, the feelings from her attempts at squashing her loneliness with humans were nothing in comparison to the feeling she got when kissing him. Their lips molded together, moving seamlessly. Teeth scraping and fingers grasping. The way his emotions felt in her mind echoed her own; it was like they were finally in sync, instead of disjointed or overwhelming. The lust she felt from him didn't feel forceful or disconnected in comparison to hers. They were in tune with each other.

As the kiss intensified, it took everything in him to hold back from tearing at her clothes. He knew she could feel everything he was. She knew how he felt, and she was kissing him back, holding him just as tightly. His wolf was begging for control, begging to be released to rip away the last bit of offensive material between them, but he held it back. He had to talk to her first. He had to tell her what might happen if they took this further.

It was with great effort, that he pulled himself away from her lips, their bodies still tangled together, breathing heavily.

"Wait, wait," he whispered, reaching up to push the bangs from her eyes.

"Why?" she whispered back, sliding her hand back around to touch his face.

"I have to tell you something," he said, his eyes showing the worry that was bubbling through to her. He was worried how she would react once she knew the bond was a possibility. That was an awful lot to commit to when they were just now considering more from their relationship.

The worry and the look in his eyes were enough to pull her a bit back to reality. She didn't completely pull away from him but moved her head back a little to get a better look at his expression.

"What is it?" she murmured, wondering what else there could possibly be. Her sister was dead, she was being targeted. Did he know who it was?

But as usual, there was no time for him to explain. A knock came at the door to his room, ending their conversation. Shane sighed and closed his eyes as Vee pulled away from him.

"Yes?" Shane asked loudly toward the door, not moving from where he had flopped onto his back on what seemed to be his side of the bed, now.

"Vee should eat," came Margaret's voice from the other side of the door. Both of their eyes darted to the alarm clock that sat on the dresser catty-corner from the bed. It was a little after noon. They both were equally shocked at the time.

The sound of Margaret's voice brought reality crashing back down on Vee. The comfort of being in Shane's arms moments ago had faded. Fear, anxiety, and shock settled back in.

"We'll be down in a minute," Shane said as Vee slipped off the bed, heading into the bathroom. He listened to Margaret walk toward the stairs and away

from them, before he sat up. Vee closed the bath-room door, and leaned against it, taking a moment to breathe shakily. She wasn't sure what to do. Normally, she would simply throw herself into her work, use it as a distraction from her invasive thoughts, but there was no escape here.

She realized, then, that she had to think of this like a puzzle, a lock that had to be fixed. Yes, the pack was searching for answers, and undoubtedly Durran was too. But she was very good at finding the broken pieces. She needed to think about this logically.

Shane listened, eyeing the door, not sure if the fear he sensed from her was from him or not. He pulled out a t-shirt from one of his dressers and put it on slowly, waiting for her to come back out to him. He was pacing a little as the knob to the bathroom door started turning, making him stop to watch her come back out. Her fear wasn't gone, but her eyes showed a bit more determination.

CHAPTER 13

Vee discarded her stained coat at the foot of his bed, feeling a little chilled without it but not wanting to wander around with it still on. She smelled the food below and could hear the chatter of the pack. She wasn't feeling particularly hungry, but she knew it was not only well past her normal eating times, she also should give her body fuel after dealing with such a shock to her system. Shane stood in the middle of his room, looking at her, waiting for her.

"My bag?" she asked, hoping she would be able to grab a sweater. Hoping she had packed a sweater, now that she thought about it. She honestly didn't remember what she put in that bag.

"I left it downstairs," he said a bit sheepishly.

"I'm just cold," she said, trying to dispel his slight embarrassment. His eyebrows shot up at that, getting into the bottom drawer of one of his dressers and pulling out a grey sweatshirt. It was huge. but it was warm. As an added bonus, it also still had the faint scent of him. "Thank you," she said, slipping it over her head.

Shane was about to hold out his hand to her, but she came up to him, slipping her fingers through his and looking up at him. She was determined, but still shaky, and the comfort of his hand in hers would keep her grounded. They left the room without another word. There were plenty of words to be said, but first she needed to eat.

They descended the stairs, hand in hand once again. Patrick stood in the entry at the bottom of the stairs pacing, while groups of Weres were either talking amongst themselves or looking pensive. Werewolves did best in action, so waiting for something to happen made them tense.

"Thomas wanted to talk to you," Patrick said to Shane as soon as they made it to the bottom.

"Where is he?" Shane asked.

"In the living room," Patrick told him, nodding toward that room. Shane gave Vee's hand a small squeeze.

"Make sure she eats?" Shane asked, tilting his head a little toward her. She rolled her eyes.

"I'll eat," she grumbled as he reluctantly pulled his hand from hers.

"You seem to have an aversion to it sometimes," he said, mild humor in his voice.

Shane headed into the living room with Thomas, while Vee and Patrick looked at each other for a moment.

"There's a bunch of stuff to eat in there," Patrick said with a smile, gesturing toward the kitchen. It wasn't a very convincing smile, especially given the fact that his emotions told the exact opposite. He was incredibly worried, anxious.

"Is there coffee?" she decided to ask, instead of "What the hell is going on?"

"I... let's go look," he said, heading toward the kitchen with Vee in toe. They wandered through, passing the pack members who filled the dining room and headed straight to the elaborate coffee maker. It may have had a half a cup left in the bottom, and by the coolness of the outside, had been there for several hours. "I'll make some more," Patrick assured her, gesturing for her to sit on one of the bar stools and wait. She looked at the vast array of food that was spread across the kitchen island. She had no idea what to start with, so she plucked a strawberry from the dish closest to her and decided to eat that.

"Why aren't you in school?" she asked Patrick as he pressed the button to brew the coffee.

"Spring Break," was all he said, without turning to look at her. Ah, yes. She remembered now that they had discussed him working at the shop this week.

She examined Patrick. He looked nearly as bad as she felt. His shirt was rumpled and on inside out, his pants had mud on them, and his hair was a mess. His appearance would have stood out to her more in a normal situation, but her brain was not functioning well enough to have noticed until now.

"You look like you dressed in a rush," she commented, feeling the defensiveness come off him quite suddenly with her words.

"I went with Thomas to catch the scents at your sister's house," he whispered, turning only enough for her to see the tears that had welled in his eyes.

Concern. Pity. Kinship. Protectiveness.

She shook not only because of the feelings she felt from him, but the realization that he cared for her. He went there for her. This was not simply interest or the mild feelings of mere acquaintances. He was genuinely concerned for her.

"Why?" she choked out in a whisper. They had developed a bond over these nine months, separate from his father. He would say she "rescued him" when she put him to work at the shop updating her digital inventory that he had created, or moving heavy boxes, instead of whatever punishment Shane had in mind for Patrick's various teenage transgressions. He turned to face her completely, leaning against the island across from her.

"Because you are one of ours and what they did to your family would make me a raving animal, while you ... you are hurt, tired, but determined ... brave. Because you have been more of a mother to me than anyone ever has. I wanted to help," he whispered, low, but so full of feeling that it made her quake.

Shane's own son felt as though she was a mother figure? She could see a cool aunt, maybe, but a mother?

A tear escaped before she could catch it, running down her cheek as she looked into his brown eyes.

"Thank you," she whispered, trying to smile even just a little. He smiled in return bending to kiss her on the cheek before he returned to the coffee pot, which had just finished brewing, and poured her a cup.

"Cream and sweetener?" he asked.

"Yes," she said in a half sob, half chuckle, wiping the tears from her cheeks.

The back door opened, revealing a head full of curls that bounced their way into the kitchen. Lori was dressed in what Vee assumed was a track uniform, her gym bag so full it looked like it would break at the seams. Her mood radiated irritation. She noticed Vee as Patrick placed the steaming cup in front of her and went to pour himself one.

Without a word, Lori dropped the bag against the wall and sunk into the chair next to Vee. Vee could tell she was trying to pull back her irritation, most likely out of courtesy to her friend, but teenagers often had a hard time pushing their own emotions aside for others. They were egotistical little things.

"What's got you irritated?" Vee asked after a sip of coffee to regain her former composure. She was certain her eyes were still wet and red from the tears moments before, but she didn't want to dwell on the fact she had been crying over being cared for. Ridiculous.

"Doesn't matter," Lori grumbled, her eyes glancing toward Patrick momentarily, but it was long enough for Vee to see it. Tommy marched in moments later. He too, seemed a bit frazzled and rough around the edges.

"Lori, I don't want to have to fight with you today. I volunteered to stay behind and take care of you instead of going on the search with Dad," he said, nostrils flaring and his blue wolf eyes shining with anger.

"Offered to babysit a practically grown pack member!" Lori scoffed. "I'm a sophomore for god's sake! Nearly sixteen! You don't see anyone watching over Patrick!" Lori growled, gesturing to Patrick, whose eyes narrowed at the quarreling siblings.

"Patrick is seventeen, and he's different. He doesn't need watching unless his father deems it necessary. *Your* father told me to watch you," Tommy grumbled, visibly trying to calm himself. The entire ride home from track practice had consisted of Lori switching between angrily text messaging someone and getting no response to snapping at Tommy every chance she got.

He sniffled too loudly. His voice was annoying. The radio station he selected sounded ridiculous. He was taking the long way to Shane's.

"I don't want to be involved in this," Patrick said, sipping his coffee and averting his gaze.

"Of course, you don't," Lori hissed, pushing herself off the stool and snatching her bag before she stormed out of the room, presumably to another part of the house.

Tommy glared after her for a moment before he moved to sit where she had been. His feelings turned from annoyed and aggravated to embarrassed.

"Sorry about that, Vee," he said, turning slightly to look at her. She kept her face indifferent, even though she eyed Patrick speculatively. She could tell Patrick was involved in Lori's state somehow, what with the guilt rolling off him as he too, had watched Lori leave.

"Better that than thinking about other things," Vee murmured into her cup.

She picked up another strawberry and took a bite just as Shane came through, making Patrick and Tommy straighten up. He didn't say anything, but his mood was clearly tense. Thomas had given him unsettling news. He poured his coffee and leaned against the sink for a moment, rubbing his forehead.

"What is it?" Tommy asked for everyone in the room.

"We're going to have to leave," Shane said, looking at Vee apologetically. Patrick and Tommy stiffened at those words.

"Leave?" she asked, her brow furrowing with confusion. Where on earth would they go?

"We have a property, easier to defend, more private," he said.

"I'll get the others making the calls," Patrick said, heading to the dining room.

"Call Ethan first. He needs to either leave the territory or come with us," Shane said, not particularly liking the idea of Ethan being in the same place as Vee, but also not wanting to risk his safety. He may not have been a member of the pack, but he was Shane's son, and was at risk remaining in the city without the rest of them. Patrick nodded, leaving the room.

"I'll take Lori to get supplies," Tommy said, standing up from the stool he had perched on and followed Patrick out the door, leaving Shane and Vee.

"Eat," he said, gesturing to the food in front of her.

"Where are we going?" she asked, raising her eyebrow at him, disregarding his order.

"Pleasant Hill," he said, face wary as he looked at her cringe.

"Why?"

"It's secluded, private, easier to guard, and protect than being in the middle of the city," he told her, honestly. It was also less likely to draw attention from the humans if they had to fight someone off.

"And what made you feel that was necessary?" she asked, now alluding to what Thomas told him. He sighed, pointing at the food. "Fine," she grumbled, pulling a plate off the stack beside her and scooping some eggs onto it.

"I sent a few people to smell around your sister's house."

"Patrick told me," she said, mouth full of eggs, nodding as if to tell him to go on.

"There was the smell of a Were and a Watcher but also a hint of magic," he told her. Vee's eyes widened a bit. At first, she assumed that her sister had been attacked by another wolf pack, but a Watcher? Her mind instantly flashed to the red headed Watcher she had met months ago at a client's house. Mac. His absolute hatred for her, when she had only just met him, had unsettled her so much. She wasn't sure about sharing that information just yet. She would, eventually. She had wanted to talk to Durran about it at some point first. Why had she waited so long to say anything?

"Magic?" she decided to ask, since that seemed to be the biggest thing troubling him at that moment.

"It might mean Witches, or the Fae, are involved," he said, his feelings turning a little suspicious having watched her face change a few times while she mulled over what he had told her.

Witches or the Fae. That was interesting addition to mystery. What could either of them possibly want with her?

"Why would…?" she started but trailed off. Shane was just as confused about it as she was.

"Markus and I are going to head down to Pleasant Hill with some of the others to get things prepared. I think the Meyers family used it last. Who knows what we're going to walk into down there," Margaret said as she entered the kitchen, not bothering to check if she was interrupting anything before she began talking. "Oh good, you're eating," Margaret said happily, watching Vee take another bite of eggs. Vee turned to the door to give her a strained smile with full cheeks.

"Good. We'll need to gather a few things before we head that way," Shane said approvingly.

"My shop," Vee suddenly said, after forcefully swallowing the bite of eggs. She began patting herself down as if her phone with somehow be on her in her pajama pants and borrowed sweatshirt. "Where's my phone?" she asked, panicked.

Without another word, she slipped off the stool and raced back up to Shane's bedroom, finding her discarded messenger bag on the side of the bed she seemed to gravitate toward and rifled through it until her hand brushed against the phone. The battery was nearly dead but still functioning for now. Only a few missed calls from customers but quite a few text messages from Durran.

CHAPTER 14

Durran had started at Vee's apartment, once Shane had taken her with him, looking over the building for any sort of clue that someone had been watching her. Durran would have noticed in most cases. She often stayed in the tree across from Vee's apartment, keeping guard. But now that Vee had accepted Shane's claim, she had been staying away a little more than usual.

Regret sat prominently in Durran's mind about that. She had allowed her own jealousy to get in the way of her duty. She was supposed to protect Vee no matter her choices. What was wrong with her?

She didn't see or smell anything particularly out of the ordinary at the apartment building. Other than the pack members busily trying to replace Vee's door. They managed to hang it, and at least her things were mostly secure for the time being. Much better than the ragged pieces that would have let anyone trespass. Durran imagined Vee would not want to field the questions of why her door was nearly ripped off its hinges, and she had disappeared to her neighbors. That would have been asking far too much of Vee at the present.

Durran made her way over to Vee's shop. She could smell the slight residual smell of Eliza and Mary from the other day, as well as Vee, of course, but there was another smell…

Durran's nostrils flared with anger, eyes turning red as she stood on the sidewalk outside of *The Missing Key*.

Cormac.

Why had Cormac been there?

Durran hadn't heard from him in months. She had assumed he was still digging for information on Vee's past for her, happy that he was away from Vee physically after their last conversation. The strange mania behind his eyes while he talked about Vee brought him back to the way he looked in the past when wars between the preternaturals raged, and he relished in the kill.

A sick feeling came over her as she got in her car, rushing over to Eliza's house to inspect the crime scene. Her mind raced thinking about what Cormac had said to her.

He was using Frank for information.

What else? What else had he said?

She got there in record time, parking down the street, far from the police vehicles. She had to be careful not to alert them as she moved her way around the property. She was still racking her brain, trying to remember what Cormac's intentions were as she scaled the wall. Once she made it to a bedroom window, she froze. There, very clearly, was the scent of him. Right where Durran was, half in the window, Cormac had been there too.

She looked inside, realizing that this was Frank's home office. This room, because it wasn't the actual crime scene, had been left untouched by the police. She crept around smelling the potent scent of Cormac, which was everywhere. She could almost see the actions playing out. Cormac and Frank sitting in his office, plotting and searching for Vee's unknown past, trying to ruin her. Durran was disgusted as she stood there, eyes looking over the room where Cormac, her longest and dearest friend, had betrayed her.

The sound of clumsy human footsteps coming up the stairs broke her from her rage. She ducked into the small closet just to the right of the desk and listened as the two police officers entered the room.

"I don't know why we're even looking here," one said, his tone bored.

"We don't know what kind of maniac would have killed these people this way, so they want us to look around," the other one said. They simply walked the room for a minute, peering at the papers on the desk and not seeing anything of interest.

"I bet the wife was cheating or something."

"I feel like it was just some lunatic. Did you see how much blood there was?"

"I heard the bodies are unrecognizable..."

Their voices trailed off as they made their way through the other rooms on the second floor, giving Durran a chance to escape.

She slipped back out the window, now heading to search the expansive backyard. These homes off Ward Parkway either had barely any yard at all, or ones that seemed to go on forever, with gardens, pools, and tennis courts. No one was searching these or at least no human had been.

Durran could smell Werewolves all over the area, Shane's wolves. They had been quite thorough in their search. She reached a gazebo off toward the back end of the yard. It was centered in the space, not huge, but large enough to hold two rattan love seats on either side. There was a strange metallic sting of magic in the air there. It wasn't distinguishable what kind of magic; that had dissipated too much by then, but it was there, sending chills down Durran's spine.

What had Cormac gotten into? What had he brought down on Vee?

"I know, Cora, but it's not safe for anyone right now," Thomas said into the phone as he drove Vee to her shop. He had called her to tell her to meet them at the Pleasant Hill property after the rest of the pack dispersed from Shane's house to get ready for the stay. Shane, who had been severely neglecting his financial advisor duties the last few days, had to relinquish Vee's care to Thomas for her errands, so he could catch up before they left.

"I can't do it, Thomas. You know I hate being down there with the whole pack. It's too chaotic," Cora said, her voice strained. Vee had never been down there, obviously, but she could imagine what it could be like with the whole pack loose on private property. Chaotic didn't even seem like an adequate word for what Vee was envisioning.

"We don't have a choice. I would never forgive myself if something happened to you," he murmured sweetly into the phone. Vee heard Cora sigh.

"Okay. I'll head there in a few hours. Love you," Cora said, making Thomas's heart flutter a little and devotion took over his other emotions.

"I love you," he said before he hung up the phone as they pulled up to her shop. "Sorry you had to hear that," he murmured, only faintly embarrassed, to Vee as he shut off the car. She smiled at him. Thomas was a good man; she didn't think she would ever tire of hearing him speak to his wife or children the way he did.

"No problem," she said, getting out of the car. She had haphazardly changed at Shane's house with the odd pieces she had thrown into her bag, but she wanted to call her clients who had pick up orders scheduled for later in the week. There was no way she would be able to fulfill them now, and she had no idea when she would be able to. There was no timeframe on this threat.

She went inside to grab her calendar from under the counter and found the customer information to call. It was fortunate it had been so slow lately. She would be losing out on a lot more business otherwise. She made her calls, explaining truthfully and with an unusually strained voice, that she had just lost her sister and would not be able to work for some time. Both customers seemed to be understanding, but she couldn't help apologizing profusely. She had a little fear that she had permanently lost their business.

Thomas had gone to the inventory room, making a sign to go on the door for her that explained the shop was closed due to a family emergency. He came out, taping it to the glass next to the "closed" sign, just has she finished creating a new voicemail message with a brief explanation. Thomas had packed her laptop and tablet in the bag she usually used to bring fixtures on house calls, while she gathered her road tools she had taken from her car before it had been towed the other day.

She sighed heavily as they left the shop, locking the door felt like it was going to be the last time she ever stepped foot in there for some reason.

"Your apartment, next?" Thomas asked, as they got back in the car.

"Yeah," she said, not completely sure what to expect when she got there, nor did she even know what she should be gathering to bring with her. She had packed essentials for a few days in her duffle that still sat in Shane's entry hall but not knowing how long she would be at this property could mean she practically had to pack everything.

Thomas and Vee wandered up the stairs to her apartment. She had been expecting the door to still be hanging in shards, but a pristine new door was already installed. She hesitated as she put her key to the lock. It looked like her old lock, but she wasn't so sure it

would work. Being a locksmith made her distrust the hasty work of others.

"It's the same one," Thomas confirmed, seeing her look questioningly at the fixture. She unlocked the door, jostling it a little since it stuck, but it was better than what she had been expecting. She pushed the new door aside and looked at her apartment. There was sawdust on the floor with large footprints tracked through it, some pieces of the old door were still littered on her futon, and her switchblade and meat tenderizer were still where she had left them on the floor and other futon. "I sent a few people over to get this replaced while you were sleeping."

She looked at him, thanking him with her eyes and took in a deep breath, deciding she couldn't really concern herself with cleaning it up, even if she wanted to. There wasn't time.

"I'm going to get more clothes," she murmured, not looking back at Thomas as she headed to her bedroom. She pulled a larger bag from her closet, the one she had used when she came back to Kansas City to carry all her worldly possessions. Somehow using it again filled her with a sense of dread. Using this bag meant she was running. It was just as true now as it had been when she ran away and then came back to Kansas City. She could hear Thomas moving around, picking things up from in the front room. She tried not to concern herself with what he was doing. That gentle giant out there was doing nothing other than trying to help her.

She felt annoyed with herself for the lack of clean clothes she had. Her monthly trips to the laundromat were not kind on her when things like this came up.

She only had a few more days of clothes left that were clean to pack away. There were plenty of pajamas and jackets though. Her phone buzzed in her pocket with a new text message. She sat on her bed to look at it.

[Durran: When are you leaving?]

Durran had not been very pleased with the idea of Vee heading out to the Westport Pack's secluded property, but she understood Shane's rationale. The short and uncomfortable phone call on speaker phone between the three of them earlier had helped develop a begrudging alliance between Vee's two protectors.

Durran had confirmed that she also sensed the magic and told them she would discuss the Watcher that had been present at Eliza's house in person when she arrived in Pleasant Hill. Somehow the idea of Durran being there too made Vee uneasy. Shane and Durran may have been okay when they were working to protect Vee together, but Vee hoped there was enough room for everyone to stay a fair distance from one another while they waited and speculated. Too much idle time between them might lead to bad blood.

[Vee: 30 minutes to an hour. I just got to my apartment.]

With a sigh, she stuffed her phone in her back pocket, knowing Durran wouldn't be texting back. Her texts were very concise, never adding more than what was absolutely needed to be conveyed. Vee pulled the bag over her shoulder, doing one final sweep of her bathroom and grabbing a few more toiletries, before heading back into the main room. She stopped short when she saw Thomas was sweeping. He was already done, just gathering it all in the dustpan when she walked back in.

"I thought you might not like coming home to a dirty house when we get back," he said, going to dump the contents into the trash. The way he said it with such confidence made her feel a little better. Thomas was certain she was coming back home, He just wasn't quite sure when. The whole journey here felt like a goodbye to the life Vee had made for herself. She supposed it still was, but maybe not with as much finality as she had made it seem.

"Thank you," she said quietly, moving to set her bag on the table.

"You want to take some food with you? I know Tommy and Lori went to get some to stock us up, but I'm not sure how long we'll be out there. It might all be bad when we get back." She hadn't thought about that, eyebrows rising on her forehead.

"I'm glad you came with me. I would have come back to a fridge full of rotten food," she said with a small smile, taking the two steps from where she stood at the card table into the kitchen. She didn't have much in there, but she grabbed her dairy items and the produce she had stored. The freezer items would keep, and her dry goods would be fine.

Thomas helped Vee carry everything to his car, placing her food items in a cooler he must have always kept in the trunk, then they made their way back to Shane's.

It was odd stepping back into the house without all the others there. She could pinpoint the number of people left in the building. Shane and Patrick. Even though it was much more extravagant than anything she was accustomed to, the house didn't bother her so much with just the two of them there. The energy felt much more relaxed than usual without the loud vibrations of other pack members in her head.

Patrick was already in the entry, his bag packed and over his shoulder, while Shane was descending the stairs carrying his own laptop bag.

"I already packed my car," Shane said to everyone present.

"I guess we'll see you there," Patrick told Vee, smiling brightly. She could tell he was excited to go. He almost quivered with anticipation. Thomas would take Patrick down with him, giving Vee and Shane the much needed fifty-minute drive to talk. It was necessary but daunting.

CHAPTER 15

At first the drive had been silent. They had stopped for gas, and while Shane went in to grab some drinks for the road, Vee texted Durran to tell her they were on their way. It was dark at that point, a little after 9 p.m., but the afternoon and evening had been a whirlwind of activity. Shane had made the decision to leave the city, and everyone jumped into action.

She looked up, glancing into the convenience store to see if Shane was coming out yet, racking her brain as she picked at the strap of her bag. She tried to anxiously anticipate what kind of conversation they would be having on this journey, but her nervousness fell away when she felt the low throb and hum of a Witch.

Her eyes darted around, looking for the source, settling on a woman filling up her own car with gas a few cars away. The woman had a strange, more intense, throb than Witches usually gave off. It almost reminded her of the thumping she could feel when a Fae was around. This woman didn't have a glamor, though. She was most certainly a Witch. Vee watched her for a moment, trying to determine if this was merely a coincidence, or if she should be worried. She was a powerful Witch. Vee could see the magic swirling around her, clinging to her and shimmering with every movement. She was older, gray hair tumbling down to her waist and over her shoulders, but not so old seeming that her movements were stiff.

The way the magic surrounded her made Vee think she had recently done a spell on herself or some sort of enchantment. Not every Witch Vee had come across seemed to glow with magic. It was at these times that Vee was thankful she could see and feel things others couldn't. The humans around them took no more notice of the woman than anyone else at the gas station. Vee took note of the car, taking down the part of the license plate she could see that read "GT7," just in case she felt like they were being followed.

Shane climbed back in the car, breaking Vee out of the anxious trance she had put herself into, watching the woman.

"What is it?" he asked, noticing her heart had an uncomfortable rhythm and speed to it.

"I… there's a Witch over there," Vee said, shifting her eyes back to her. Shane looked over too, watching her for a moment as she set the pump back. It was then that Vee and the Witch met eyes. There was a cold intensity to the brief look they shared, like prey and hunter seeing each other before the chase. Vee's heart started pounding in her chest.

That was all the explanation Shane needed to start the car and gun it. If they were following them, he would make certain they would lose them before they got on the highway. The tension in the car continued for about twenty minutes. Vee kept looking behind them for some time, paranoid that she would spot their pursuer, despite Shane's skillful driving.

"I think it's safe," Shane finally said, reaching over to take her hand, hoping it would calm her a little. It helped enough, letting her settle more in her seat.

"That was just so…" she struggled to find the words. Oddly coincidental?

"I know," he said, agreeing wholeheartedly to her unspoken words.

A few quiet minutes passed where they just simply breathed, trying to relax. That bit of a rush helped make time go by faster, their trip was nearly halfway over. Vee could feel Shane's internal struggle, the worry he had felt earlier in the morning resurfacing. It wasn't the same kind of worry over her safety, that was usually coupled with protectiveness. This had a twinge of loss tangled with it. She looked at him; his eyes trained on the road ahead.

"What else has got you worried?" she asked, continuing to monitor his expression. He glanced at her for a moment, her eyes earnest.

"I want you to know what might happen if we…" he trailed off, taking his hand out of hers to better grip the steering wheel with both hands. He had to keep grounded if he was potentially going to scare her away from him.

"If we?" she prompted, not completely certain where he was going with this, but getting a slight feeling it had to do with the more physical side of their still unlabeled relationship. This was not exactly what she thought they would be talking about. She figured this conversation would be full of declarations, but there was something more here that he had to get off his chest. She wasn't sure if it was better. The air felt heavy with his concern.

Shane cleared his throat.

"If we have sex," he said, having to force the words out. Not out of discomfort for the subject matter, but her reaction when he finally told her the potentially problematic bit. Her eyebrow raised questioningly, even though he wasn't watching her face.

"What might happen, Shane?" she asked, her tone taking on her newly acquired irritation, realizing there was a *reason* why he stopped them earlier in the day. He glanced at her again, noting her expression, which only made his unease more intense.

"The claim only does so much. Many Weres don't have a claim with their partners. It's the beginning of binding magic," he began, giving her a moment to process that.

"Right. You said were mated now in the eyes of the Weres," she said slowly, taking it in.

"The completion of the bond is ... consummation."

Vee's eyes narrowed, now looking at the road instead of him as she considered his words. They were a couple, technically speaking, but if they had sex…

"We will be married?" she half asked, half gasped. Shane's foot hit the accelerator a little harder with his fear, his knuckles white as they gripped the steering wheel hard enough it whined as if he was about to break it.

"It's a bit more than that, but yes."

"A bit more? What do you mean 'a bit more'?" she choked out, eyes wide as she stared at him.

"I'm not even sure if we *can* bond. It usually only happens between Weres, but the claim worked. It was sealed with the magic, not just words. Logically, if that worked between us the bond would too." He felt like he was babbling, everything he had been going over in his mind silently was suddenly tumbling out at her. "If it does, we would be bound emotionally. Able to feel each other's stronger emotions, even at a distance. There are also magics that prevent you from being harmed within my territory, since I'm a Pack Leader," he told her, wishing he could look at her face to at least have some idea of what was going on in her head.

She was quiet. Too quiet. The silence stretched for a few long minutes.

"I have to get out. Pull over please," she said suddenly, gasping, her hand already at the handle of the door as if she were going to jump out of the moving vehicle.

"Okay, hold on," he said, glancing around him to make sure there weren't cars before he started to slow and pull off to the deserted side of the highway. As soon as the car was stopped, she got out, walking a little further from the road, and paced around. He followed her a moment later, stopping just short of the little circle she was making in the grass there.

"You obviously knew this when you made the decision to claim me," she started, not looking at him but at the ground as she stomped.

"I did," he said regretfully.

"And I'm just now finding out about this, why?"

"I've been trying. I needed to know if you felt the same way I did before I made it something to concern you with. Why bother if it wasn't even a possibility?" he told her. She stopped suddenly at that, looking up at him, eyes glowing with fury as they burned into his.

"Feel what way, Shane?" she asked, crossing her arms and glaring at him. He looked at her shocked. She knew how he felt. He had finally let her in that morning, let her feel the full force of his emotions. She was going to make him say it again, but not to her still sleeping form. It needed to be here with her wide awake and at full attention. He raised his chin, looking at her provokingly, meeting the challenge she had given him with his own smoldering stare.

"Victoria Malone, I love you. I have loved you for months," he said with no trepidation in his voice, no block on his emotions. Vee's anger subsided a little, and she gasped at the tidal wave he sent her. He walked to her quickly, taking her face in his hands much the same way he did before their first kiss, but his wolf was not in control here. "I love you, but I worry because I don't want you to feel trapped. I want you to be happy. I don't want you to run," he whispered, pleading with his eyes for her to say something, anything. She stared back, their eyes mirroring each other.

The power of his words broke what little remained of that careful wall she had built up within herself. The

fear of change melted away with his admission, his emotions, his touch. She took a deep breath, letting her trepidation go on the exhale. He was not going to reject her.

"I love you too," she whispered, finally saying what she had been pushing away in her mind for months. It went against everything she had told herself for years, so she had distanced herself from it. But here he was, laying himself bare to her, and she couldn't deny it.

She loved him. Even if he drove her crazy with his overprotectiveness. Even if he was sometimes pushy. She loved him for who he was. The strong, caring man, who treated everyone under his care like they were his family. The man who drank his coffee black, but still stocked his house with things for others. The man who appeared as though he would kill someone if they looked at him the wrong way but would drop everything to go to his sons. The man who would upend his own life to protect hers.

Shane's whole being tingled with elation at her words. There was no thought as he bent his head and kissed her, his fingers raking through her hair. Somehow this kiss was more than it had been in the past with them both fully letting themselves feel everything. They were lost in the passion of it, teeth scraping at lips, hands gripping tightly as they tried to get impossibly closer.

It wasn't until Vee's body couldn't deny the cold anymore, and she began to shake that Shane managed to pull away from her.

"We have to keep moving," he said, a bit out of breath but still holding her close. She nodded, taking his hand as they trudged up the hill back to the car.

Shane immediately blasted the heat once he pulled back onto the highway, and then his phone started ringing. He answered it over the Bluetooth.

"We saw your car back there. Is everything okay?" Thomas asked.

"We just had to pull over for a minute. We're back on the road now," Shane said, glancing at Vee who smirked a little, rubbing her arms as she continued to shake a bit.

"A minute? You had to have been pulled over for twenty minutes at least for us to have caught up to you," came Patrick's voice. Vee and Shane were a bit surprised at that, having thought only a few minutes had passed since they stopped the car.

"We're right behind you now," Shane said, ending the call and pulling up behind Thomas's SUV.

Vee had finally stopped shaking but still put her fingers to the vent. She was far from angry now and was using the bit of clarity from not being touched by Shane to think about the strange arrangement that was coming together here. Shane loved her. She loved Shane. They were "official" to the Were community but might be bound together even more deeply with magic if they were to ever have sex. Something that would be unavoidable the way things were going if they were around each other long enough without interruption.

"So, if we were to have this bond…" Vee started, a bit worried at what his reaction to this line of questioning would be, "What exactly does that mean?"

"We would be mates. Well, we already are, but we would be married in the preternatural community, essentially," he said, having a hard time figuring out how to fully explain it. It was much more than that. They would be connected on such a deep level, given that he knew already that she was his True Mate, he imagined that connection would be even stronger than a normal bonded pair.

Vee nodded her head, sucking in a breath. She had somehow gone from single, to begrudgingly coupled, to almost married in a few short days. Things seemed to happen quite quickly with these Werewolves around.

"That's a big commitment," she murmured, thinking about her life, her routine. It wouldn't be so bad to have Shane more regularly in her little world, in fact, she would welcome it, but to completely give up her home... that was something she wasn't sure she was ready to part with. At least not yet.

"You would have that protection within the territory. You could... you could go back to your home once we get through all of this. If you wanted to..." Shane said, a little hesitant and a bit of sadness coloring his feelings. He clearly knew her, if his thoughts were mirroring her own. His admission made her feel a bit relieved, even if she could tell by the hesitation and sadness coming from him, he did not want that. It warmed her to know he wanted her fully in his life, by his side, a true partner. But she needed to ease into things a bit more.

"Don't be upset by this question. I'm not planning for anything, I just want to know." she prefaced, placing a hand on the side of his face. He glanced at her, concern taking a stronger hold. She hated doing this to him, but she had to know. "Can the bond be broken?"

Shane tightened his grip on the steering wheel again, to keep him from succumbing to the dread from hearing those words. Even the idea of breaking the claim was heart wrenching.

"There are a few ways it can happen, yes," he said very quietly. He glanced at her again, wishing he could block her from what he was feeling, but she was still touching his face. Her eyes sympathetic and almost tearful, feeling what he felt. He understood her need to know. She didn't want to slip into this lightly, but she was making it clear to him she wasn't pushing him away, either.

She decided to leave it there, not wanting to upset him anymore than she already had with her line of questioning. If there was a way to break it once it was formed, and she needed to know, she would find out. Simple as that. The timing was good to end the conversation, as they turned off the highway onto a country road. Her hand slipped from his face as the road became a bit less smooth and he turned his focus onto the directions to get there instead of their conversation. There had been signs for Pleasant Hill, but they didn't go through any major thoroughfares. They had close access to the highway without alerting the town. It was much better for doing secret pack related activities.

It wasn't long before they took a turn off the road into some trees. At first Vee thought they had just turned into some woods but realized it was a very well-covered driveway. The thick trees flanked it on either side for several minutes of the journey until it opened to a wide clearing. It was hard for her to see. The darkness was much more complete here with so little light pollution, but she could make out the silhouettes of several buildings dotted here and there, like a small village unto itself, with one large house located at the center.

Shane glanced over at her to see her reaction as they approached the big house, letting his previous feelings from their conversation melt away, excitement taking its place. She had let her mouth fall open at it. The houses were spaced far enough apart for privacy but close enough to the main house for convenience. Several of the smaller buildings were lit, but the main house was the one teeming with activity.

They seemed to be the last ones to arrive. Thomas's car was already parked, and several pack members were helping them unload things and take them into the house. Shane shut off the car and turned to her once they had found a spot in the gravel beside the house.

"They're all just getting the main house set up. They'll go to the smaller houses later," he assured her, sensing her tense a little at the sight, feeling of the whole pack in the house.

"We're staying in *that* house?" she asked, face not changing from the awed expression she had when they approached it. Shane tried to look at it from her perspective. Her whole apartment building would have easily fit inside the large house. He knew she had thought his house was large and extravagant in the city, so seeing this one, knowing it was also his, was quite overwhelming.

"We are," he confirmed, smiling a bit as he opened his door to come around to hers. She let him help her out, briefly thinking how old fashioned it was that he opened her car door and offered her a hand. He didn't release her hand as they headed toward the house. This hand holding business was becoming rather commonplace now.

They took the steps to the expansive porch that seemed to wrap around the whole first floor. The waves of Were minds and a few human minds grew more intense as they got closer to the door. Vee took in a breath, steeling herself the chaos within.

She hadn't been wrong. It was chaotic when they walked through the door, but it was an organized chaos. Many bodies, all moving about with purpose. The front room that they walked into was huge. A massive living room with a fireplace and large couches covered in blankets and pillows was on her right. In front of her was a wide hall that stretched to the back of the house. She could see the stairs, though they faced the back rather than the front of the house. To the left was an even larger solid wood table than the one at Shane's house in the city. She imagined most, if not all, of the pack members could sit at that table together. There were several people already sitting and eating at it.

"Do you want to eat something?" Shane asked, steering her past the table and toward the kitchen, which she could now see was where most of the people were. Tommy and Lori were divvying up groceries from bags that were strewn across the counter to various people.

"I can take that half gallon to our house," one woman said, pointing to the little array of things on the counter by the refrigerator.

"That's Vee's, so it stays. Just take the full gallon, Susan," Lori said, her voice had an edge to it. Vee suspected corralling and passing out things to all these families was quite the task.

"It's Vee's," came John Meyers' voice behind Susan. "Of course... Let's just go get unpacked," he said, his voice laced with annoyance. Shane let a small growl come from his chest, glaring toward John, whose eyes snapped up to meet his leader's. Vee felt the tension between them. John's annoyance and slight hostility toward her was understandable, given the circumstances. They all had to uproot their families and come out to this property to defend her. She could imagine some of them felt a bit frustrated about the situation.

"I think I can wait until tomorrow," Vee finally said in response to Shane's previous question. She was an outsider in this situation but could feel intense vibrations from their minds in the enclosed space. She could also feel the rising tensions amongst the pack and knew she needed to get away. She would eventually get used to them being there but walking into this after having just been alone with Shane for the past hour or so made it all the more difficult.

"Let me show you the rest of the house," Shane said, seeing the tightness in her body and feeling how her fingers had clamped down on his hand.

They walked away from the kitchen and down the main hall. There were several doors that lined it, but he didn't show her what was behind them. Instead, he walked her right up the stairs. Again, there were many doors, and she suspected they were all bedrooms. It made her feel even worse that the rest of the pack was staying in the smaller houses, probably because of her.

Patrick came out of the door toward the front of the house as they made their way down the upstairs hall.

"I just put your bags in there, Vee," he said happily, his face changing instantly from tired to elated once he saw them. She smiled back a bit, unable to hide how exhausted she was, but appreciative, nonetheless.

"Did Ethan come?" Shane asked as they got a bit closer to the door.

"I haven't seen him yet. He didn't say what his plan was," Patrick told him, a bit of guilt slipping through as he glanced at Vee.

"Mm…" Shane murmured, nodding. His emotions waffled between disappointment and relief. She wasn't sure what was there, but clearly Shane and Ethan were having a hard time with one another at the moment. Not terribly unusual from what she gathered about their past. There was a reason Ethan was a lone wolf.

"I'm going to help Thomas unload your car. I think that's the last of it, at least until Cora gets here," Patrick told them, touching Vee's shoulder lightly as he headed past them down the stairs.

They entered the room which was obviously Shane's. Large wooden furniture dominated the space. It was just about as big as his room in Kansas City but laid out slightly differently with the bed facing the door, set against the windows. She imagined the bed was just as comfortable, and she ached to lay in it and cocoon herself to block out the world. She would need to process

everything from the last twenty-four hours, but she couldn't do it right now.

"Can the rest of the tour wait until tomorrow?" she asked, sagging a little and leaning into him.

"Of course," he said, releasing her hand, but only to cup her face and put a small kiss on her lips. "I need to go corral the others. You rest," he said, before he pulled away from her, rather reluctantly, and left the room.

Vee noticed her bags were placed next to a dresser on the left. She opened the larger bag, knowing her vast selection of pajamas were stashed in there. She grabbed a pair and then looked at the two doors on either side of the dresser. One of these had to be the bathroom. She opened the first door only to find it was a closet.

There wasn't much in it. Some boxes were stacked in the corner and a few clothing bags hung from the rack, but otherwise it was quite barren. She went to the other door, opening it to finally find a bathroom. It had a huge bathtub that might as well have been a jacuzzi, as well as a massive shower stall. The idea of a shower sounded wonderful, since she hadn't showered that day, but she was too tired to put in the effort. She used the restroom, changed her clothes, then returned to cocoon herself within the bed's warmth and comfort.

CHAPTER 16

Durran had been calling. She called and called with no answer to Cormac's phone, while she raced around the city, trying to find him in his usual haunts. He hadn't been to any of them recently given that his scent was nowhere to be found. It was on her way back to Vee's when she noticed it. The faint scent of magic in the air, coming through her open car windows.

She slowed near the source, pulling up to an old Victorian style house in midtown. It was three stories high with scaffolding on one side, as it was clearly being repainted. Most of the house was dark, except for a warm glow coming from behind the heavy curtains on the main floor. As she smelled it more intensely, she knew this was the scent of that magic she had found on Eliza's property.

Without an ounce of hesitation, she quickly texted the address to Shane's phone.

[Durran: The source of the magic.]
[Shane: We'll do some digging.]

Shane's text back was immediate, which Durran appreciated. In fact, there were quite a few things she appreciated and respected about the pack leader. She just didn't like that he was encroaching on Vee.

Durran looked at the house, knowing she would have to tell the Elders about this now that her ward was being targeted by more than one group of preternaturals, and apparently Cormac. What other explanation would there be to murder Vee's only family? It was either a message or a threat to her life.

She wanted to go up to the house, to peer in the windows, and see the faces of the Witches that were hunting for Vee, but there were wards in place, spells to keep out unwanted or uninvited guests. She wondered if she would come upon Cormac's scent if she got closer. Would she see him within those windows?

Durran felt odd not being near Vee. Not that she was always beside her, but she usually knew where Vee was and was merely a stone's throw from her at any given time. Being almost an hour away from her hadn't happened since early on into her assignment. Vee's previous solitude had afforded Durran more freedom. Now that Vee was tangled in this mess with the Werewolves, she stayed close.

[Shane: What of your Watcher friend?]

The text came through as Durran decided to move on to Vee's apartment again.

[Durran: No word yet.]

Durran turned down Vee's street, the same metallic scent of the Witches' magic lingering in the air the entire way there. Her eyes glowed red as she realized they had been there recently, most likely while she had been hunting down Cormac. She got out of her car, eyes on Vee's apartment windows, which should have been dark. Vee never left lights on when she was away, but the lights in her living room where on, casting an eerie glow to the ground below.

She moved so quickly to Vee's apartment, she didn't even recall parking or getting out of the car. She went around the building to the fire escape. The whole building was encased in magic. Her skin tingled as she touched the ladder and began to climb. This wasn't a spell to repel, otherwise it would have been far more difficult for her to break through it to even touch the building. It must have been a spell to keep others from noticing a coven of Witches as they entered.

She got to the third-floor window, easily lifting it to climb in. The new windows that had been installed since Downing's final attempt to attack Vee were easy to push up and they barely made a sound. She walked slowly down the hall to Vee's door, stepping carefully to make sure the wood beneath her feet did not creak. The door was slightly ajar, as if someone had just stepped out to grab something and didn't latch it all the way.

She stood for a moment, listening to the rooms within. There was no breathing or heartbeats, no indication that anyone was in there now. Of course, they wouldn't be. She pushed the door open fully to look at the wreckage. Vee's entire apartment was in shambles. It was like they were looking for something in particular. What could Vee possibly have that these Witches would want?

No, there was no way around it. In order to protect Vee, Durran would have to appeal to the Elders. Otherwise, they would all be starting a war.

Shane sighed as he looked at his phone, rereading the text messages that he had received from Durran. Witches were definitely involved, based on what Durran had told him. He was trying to piece everything together. What on earth could a Werewolf, Witches, and a Watcher all have in common with Vee to want to hurt her? He had seen Vee's life for the last nine months. She had previously wanted nothing to do with other preternaturals, so why would so many of them band together to pursue her?

Thomas sat with him at the dining room table. He was straining to stay awake while he waited for Cora's arrival. Everyone else had made their way to the various houses they would be staying in. Normally, Shane would have more of the single pack members staying in the big house with him to give more privacy to the families, but with Vee there, he had wanted her to feel a little more comfortable, at least on the first few nights they were there.

Patrick was up in his room, snoring lightly, and with so few people in the house, Shane could hear the soft beat of Vee's relaxed heart from where he sat. The two of them safely under his roof made him feel a bit better, but the reality of why they were there in the first place dampened it.

"I still don't understand why Witches would try to attack Vee," Thomas murmured, hitting his phone with his fingertip to keep it from going black as he watched Cora's progression toward the property.

"Me either," Shane murmured back.

"So, we just wait this out?"

"I imagine it will come to us at some point." As unfortunate as that sounded, he knew they were hunting her. The Witch they had seen at the gas station only solidified his assumption that they were gathering their forces and would find them eventually. "Tomorrow we'll need to research the address Durran sent," Shane said, part of him wanting to push off much needed sleep to dig into finding out who they were facing but also knowing he would be utterly useless if he didn't rest.

"I know we couldn't leave the families at home, but the idea of Cora being anywhere near a battle is..." Thomas trailed off, his eyes forming that same worry Shane saw on his face the night of Lori's change. Their pack hadn't fought as a group for so many years. Long before Thomas had met his sweet, delicate wife. Cora had, of course, seen the pack changed, but she had never seen a Werewolf *truly* fight.

"The barns still have the Sha's wards. If it comes to that, even the Witches won't be able to penetrate them. They'll be safe in there," Shane said, trying to be comforting but also feeling that same despair. The Sha had placed protective wards over certain buildings for each pack to provide safety from attacks for the vulnerable during the time of the great wars; they were practically impenetrable to nearly every type of physical and magical attack. Shane never had a reason to use them during his time as a leader, but he hoped they would hold still. He didn't want to think about what it would mean if they didn't.

"What of the bond?" Thomas asked, curious if it was still Shane's plan to complete it. Shane shook his head with uncertainty. They may have discussed it, but he was still not sure what her true thoughts on the matter were. He still wasn't completely convinced it would work between them.

The bond would keep her safe from Weres. There was still some uncertainty about how involved they were. Was it a lone wolf joining with the Witches and planning this attack? Or was there a pack teaming up with them for some other sinister reason? The magic of the bond would keep her safe from the Weres harming her, and the magic was strong enough to hold some Witch magics at bay for a time.

Shane thought back to their conversation in the car. Vee loved him. She trusted him. He understood her trepidation on committing to this. It was quite a lot to say yes to, magically binding and essentially marrying him after only recently giving into her feelings for him.

It was a lot of change for her. If he knew nothing else about her, it was she didn't do well with change.

A quiet howl rang out in the distance toward the front of the property from one of the wolves that were on guard for the night. Thomas lit up his phone again to see that Cora had arrived, just as faint headlights could be seen peeking through the thick trees surrounding the property.

"I'm going to get her settled," Thomas said, standing from the table. Shane smiled at him and nodded, watching as he hurriedly headed out the door to greet his wife.

Shane looked at the time on his phone, realizing it was well into the early morning hours. He needed to sleep. Who knew what the coming days would bring? He walked up the stairs and went into his bedroom, finding Vee peacefully sleeping on *her* side of the bed. He smiled a little at the small gesture. She was making new routines, in a way, with him.

Quietly, he delved into his own bags to change into sweatpants, slipping off his shoes and clothes, laying them on the chair beside the bed. It was not quietly enough, since Vee began to stir. He pulled on the pants, just as her eyes began to open.

"Go back to sleep," he whispered, climbing into the bed with her and reaching to encase her in his arms.

"What time is it?" she whispered back, cuddling up against him, her hand resting on his chest.

"Too early in the morning for you to be awake," he replied, kissing her on her head. His hand had slipped under her shirt, touching the small of her back's bare skin. For just a moment he recalled feeling her skin

there as they had kissed in her kitchen, giving him the briefest twinge of desire, but it was enough for her to notice.

She looked up at him in the dark, the moonlight washing over them through the window. There was something magical about being basked in moonlight as they looked into each other's eyes. She was still worn out as she could tell he was, but that little hint of desire ignited her own. There they were, practically alone in this enormous house together. She felt safe or at least safer than she had felt in the last few days. He was looking into her eyes with only love for her as she felt it pulsing through him.

She didn't want anything but him in that moment. She slowly moved her body up so she could reach his lips. The kiss started as a slow but strong burn. Their lips brushing gently against one another. Shane's other hand cupped her face while he gripped slightly at the skin on her back. She could tell he was trying to hold back from the desire he felt, trying so hard to maintain calm despite the passion building inside of him.

She was losing herself in it, feeling so oddly in tune with him that her own desire was becoming overwhelming. She sat up slightly, not breaking their kiss, as she shifted herself on top of him, straddling his lap. A low growl rumbled in his chest at that action, and he broke the kiss, breathing heavily and looking up at her. She sat up, unintentionally pressing herself a little harder into him.

"Vee, if we don't stop now... I..." he said, his voice gravelly as his wolf was surfacing. She leaned back down to his face, her eyes starting to change as she was giving herself over.

"I don't want to stop," she whispered.

"The bond," he said, trying to hold onto the last shreds of his control to remind her, to warn her. She touched his face with both her hands, eyes never leaving his.

"I love you," she whispered, touching her lips to his before he could say anything more.

Shane's control was gone with those words and her searing kiss. His fingers gripped her sides. In an instant, she found herself flipped, her back to the mattress, and him settled between her legs. Their kiss became more intense, not the sweet, slow burn it had been, but now a raging fire. Tongues and teeth. Lips bruising from the force. Their hands gripped and pulled, anything to be closer.

His wolf was now in charge, hands starting to tear at her clothes as he ground himself into her. Her hips unconsciously moved to meet his. He pulled away from her for a moment, to look her over. He had ripped her shirt, exposing her breasts. Her chest heaved as she breathed raggedly, watching his eyes move over her skin hungrily.

He bent over her, eyes back on hers, as his lips lightly brushed over the skin on her chest. He moved down slowly, his fingers hooking on the sides of her pants to pull them down as his lips traveled. She shivered at the contact, having never been touched this way, with a sort of reverence. He sat up to pull her pants off her feet, throwing them to the floor as he slipped off the bed, never breaking eye contact with her.

She watched him, eyes eager, as he slipped his own pants off, climbing back onto the bed and over her. He hovered there for a moment, looking into her eyes, searching with the last bit of control. He had to be sure this was what she wanted. The scent of her was absolutely intoxicating. If she was in any way unsure of this, he wasn't sure he would be able to stop himself if their lips met once more.

He didn't have to say anything. She could feel his internal struggle. She reached her hands up, touching his face and pulling it back to hers to lock them in yet another kiss. Her hips moved up to his again, but this time there was nothing in their way. That was all it took for him to thrust into her, already being lined up with the tilt of her hips.

They both gasped uncontrollably. The sensation of their joining was more than either of them had ever felt before. If the feeling of their kiss had been strangely powerful in its intensity, it paled in comparison to this. He could sense her, not just physically, but the very essence of her. Every emotion, every thought, and worry that sat at the back of her mind was there but not at the forefront. Not dampening to the pleasure and passion of the union. She could feel all of him too, and not in the unpleasant way she had felt other partners from the past. It was as if a puzzle piece had found its perfect spot within her. She felt the powerful weight of his love for her and shook with the ecstasy of it.

With each thrust of his hips, they could feel more and more of one another. They could see each other in their entirety. In that moment, knowing the other better than they knew themselves. Vee looked into his glowing golden eyes, wide with awe as she suspected hers were. They were moaning, touching. Joining over and over. Their joined minds and the overwhelming feeling of pleasure was all consuming. It was the most anything had ever been for either of them. And then, somehow it began to build.

How could it grow?

What else was there?

The pleasure was insurmountable.

Their eyes met again as they began to reach their peak, both unable to hold back from the screams of pleasure that ripped from their lips as stars exploded behind their eyes and tremors racked their bodies. Shane fell to the side, taking her with him, so they were still joined. They just looked at each other, breathing heavily, as they slowly came down from their bliss. There was nothing they needed to say, and if there were, they couldn't bring themselves to words. They simply looked within each other's eyes for a time.

They laid like that, feeling what the other one was. Being separate yet one at the same time and in awe of it. Perhaps being bonded was not such a bad thing, Vee decided, feeling so complete in that moment. Comfort and exhaustion soon took them both, however, and they fell asleep, still tangled together.

CHAPTER 17

Durran's heart stopped for a moment, her mind swirling and eyes unfocused. She could feel the magic, the connection, the *bond*. When a Watcher is assigned a new ward, a small, shallow bond is created by the Elders' magic, to help the Watchers be better attuned to their ward's needs. It is only a one-way connection. The ward is unaware of its presence. This bond only grows stronger with time and trust.

Durran had become more bonded with Vee than she ever had with another ward. It may have had something to do with Vee's abilities, or it may have been the love Durran had formed for her. But regardless of the reason, Durran felt it. She felt it the moment the bond between Vee and Shane formed. She let out a small, pained sound as she drove down the highway, gripping the steering wheel to keep her focus. It went on and on. Each moment like a knife was ripping through her chest, knowing what each agonizing twinge meant.

She was headed to the Pleasant Hill property. Her plan had been to go to the Elder Realm from just outside it. For a moment, she felt like her heart was being torn from her chest, feeling the complete love that Vee felt for someone else. She considered not appealing to the Elders, but she would be abandoning her duty. Her own jealously couldn't get in the way of protecting her ward.

She blindly made it to the country road just outside of the property, taking in a shaky breath as she parked the car just as she felt the climax. She felt sick and utterly torn apart. Her eyes glowed an intense red. She wanted to tear the car apart, to launch it as far from her as possible without care for where it landed. Instead, she kept herself perfectly still, trying to breathe through the intense emotions. Her chest heaved with the effort. It took her longer to calm down than it did for Vee to fall asleep, their connection falling away and the intense emotions dissipating.

She gathered herself, taking in a deep breath, as she stepped out of the car. She had to be calm and collected to face the Elders. They were old and powerful. They were far removed from human interactions, and the emotions Durran was feeling would not be looked at kindly. Her eyes still glowing fiercely, she let the glamor of her coat fall away, revealing her wings to the night. Her hands and wings lifted together in a single movement, and then she shot through the sky, disappearing into the Elder realm.

It was a place between worlds, cold and dark. No natural light touched this place, only the Elder magic gave it a faint glow, just enough for Watcher eyes to see. Durran changed into her true form. Her features became more androgynous, more of the asexual beings they were meant to be. Any glamor that had been in place, stripped away, revealing odd yet beautiful perfection.

They walked through the space. It was a wide hall with black stone walls and floors, which sucked in the little bit of light there was. They could only see just far enough to take each step. The walk seemed like an eternity, but it was one Durran had taken many times before. The subtle scent of other Watchers started to build the further they got until finally, a figure appeared.

"Durran, we've been expecting you," came the sultry voice of the older Watcher before them.

"Turien," Durran said, nodding their head in respect. Turien was tall and lean, like Durran. Their skin was ghostly white, especially against the eerie glow, eyes red, but not glowing. Those who stayed in the realm too long often succumbed to a less human-like state and appearance.

"Come, Mical will see you now," Turien said, gesturing for Durran to follow.

Together they turned, continuing the long walk into seemingly unending corridors; however, now Durran passed other younger Watchers like themself. Durran hadn't spent as much time in the Elder realm, usually being sent off on their next assignment immediately. They barely had a moment to grieve the loss of their ward before they had to form a relationship with the next. For some, that was not the case. Watchers, like Cormac, often had a cooling off period in the Realm before they were given another ward.

"I heard you are watching a woman who isn't human. Curious," Turien said, not giving anything away in their tone other than interest.

"We have not yet determined what she is, but she does show interesting capabilities," Durran told them, trying not to add any sort of additional feelings they may feel for Vee to the surface. This was not the place for that.

"Here we are. You are reminded that it is not the Elders' place to intervene, despite your reasoning for being here," Turien said as a final warning. Durran knew this was asking more than they should of the Elders, but the threat to the preternatural world, and therefore the human world, was very real.

"I know this," Durran said in response, eyes showing red for a moment. Turien stepped aside, ushering Durran into a much larger open space.

The floor was still beneath their feet, but the walls were no longer visible, appearing more like an endless void they had stepped into, rather than a large room. Durran continued forward until they came upon seven figures, standing on platforms. Mical was in the center, Galieb and Rapha at Mical's flanks, Zazol, Uric, Azrin, and Biel filling the spots on either side.

"Durran, what brings you to the realm when your ward still lives?" Azrin said, their voice booming over the space, echoing off unseen surfaces. Durran stood for a moment, the weight of all their eyes bearing down on them.

"My ward is being threatened by more than one preternatural sect. The remaining members of her family were slaughtered yesterday, the culprit an unknown Werewolf, but there is evidence Witches and a Watcher are involved," Durran said, trying not to show how much the idea of Cormac as part of this plot twisted at their heart.

For a moment Durran could see the surprise cross some of their faces. Their eyes looking over each face as they turned to one another.

"Which Watcher?" came Galieb's voice, their red eyes growing bright as the others began whispering unintelligibly.

"Cormac," Durran said, voice flat. The whispering from the others intensified with this admission. All seven sets of eyes glowed with angry intensity as they turned back to Durran and the murmuring ceased.

"Cormac is not to meddle. They are currently being punished for their misdeeds against their previous wards," Rapha said.

"Yes, but Cormac has been wandering aimless. They…" Durran hesitated, the embarrassment for their blunder making their throat thick. "They tricked me," Durran said, turning their eyes to the bit of black stone at the Elders' feet and away from their prying eyes.

"How did this happen?" Biel asked. Durran stood there for a moment, knowing that it would very likely bring the wrath of the Elders down on them with what they were about to say.

"My assignment to Victoria Malone was to watch, protect as any other ward, but also discover what she is. My duty to her safety was keeping me from pursuing her past. I felt the upheaval could unbalance her. Cormac offered to help," Durran finally said after several quiet moments.

"Cormac offered to look into her past for you, and this somehow led them to…" Uric reiterated, wanting Durran to continue.

"I smelled and sensed him at Victoria's family's home after their murders. His involvement with them came to my attention some months ago, but I never thought…" Durran trailed off as their voice wavered, struggling to not show emotion as they thought about the brutal destruction of Eliza, Frank, and Mary.

"And why would you? It is not in our nature to harm humans. There was no reason for you to believe Cormac would," Mical said, their voice echoed oddly, louder than all the others. It seemed to linger around the hall long after their words had left. Durran stayed silent, eyes downcast as Mical stepped from their platform.

Mical, like the other Elders, was lean and graceful. Their hair cascaded in long blond tendrils around their shoulders, eyes glowing red, not from intense emotion, but from power. They were taller than the others, shoulders broad for a more masculine appearance, but their facial features still held the beautiful androgyny the others had. Mical exuded power and grace. Dangerous and breathtaking.

"Cormac's punishment was clearly not enough. They have become corrupted, selfish. Much like the Nezilim sect. I thought we had purged them," Mical continued, turning their head ever so slightly toward Zazol, who also cast their eyes downward.

Long ago, many of the Elder Watchers had mated with humans, creating hybrids. Their offspring, though powerful like the Watchers, grew to have the corruptible hearts of humans. They wrought havoc, leading the Elders to dispatch their own descendants. Zazol's line, managed to avoid the slaughter, proving to not have been as far gone as the rest. Durran's eyes lit up in realization. Cormac had been one of them.

"What else is there, Durran?" Mical asked, sensing there was more that wasn't being said. Durran swallowed, trying to rid themselves of the lump that had formed in their throat, knowing this question was coming. Knowing what they had to admit.

"Victoria has bonded with a Werewolf," Durran whispered, but the whisper reached all their ears. They all shook a little at those words, eyes widening in surprise.

Werewolf bonds were incredibly rare. Bonds between a Werewolf and a human or otherwise, were unheard of. The bonding magic was very specific to the descendants of the Sha, and therefore even other preternaturals usually couldn't bond to a Were.

"You know this without doubt?" Galieb asked, also stepping forward off the platform so they stood to be beside Mical.

"I felt it happen just before I came to be in the Realm," Durran whispered, willing their heart not to break further before them.

"How? How could this be?" Uric asked the other Elders, no longer questioning Durran, inciting hushed, anxious chatter amongst the rest of them. Mical raised their hand to silence them, looking down upon Durran.

"Her purpose has yet to be determined, but you may no longer shy away from your other task. Finding out what she is, is now of the utmost importance. It seems we are not the only ones who deem her of interest," Mical told Durran.

"And what of Cormac? How do I protect Vee from them?" Durran asked, meeting Mical's eyes. There was a long silent moment where they all stood, waiting for what Mical had to say. It was clear from the way their eyes glowed, they were angry.

"Cormac has chosen to stray from our purpose. We will no longer offer our protection to them. Let the wolves take them," Mical said, their voice low with malice and disgust.

"But this could mean war between the Witches and the Werewolves. Can we not intervene?" Durran asked, eyes pleading, as they looked into Mical's.

"And bring the Watchers into that war? We would never again risk such a thing."

Durran took in a shaky breath at those words. The Elders would stay away. They would sentence Cormac to his demise but remain free from the conflict. This was not the solution Durran had wanted, but they understood the reasoning. At least Vee's protectors would not have to worry about bringing the wrath of the Elders down upon them for killing a Watcher.

CHAPTER 18

V ee woke still surrounded by Shane. Her cheek was pressed to his chest, one leg hitched over his hip. It was rather amazing she could sleep so peacefully touching another person. How did his emotions and the buzz of his presence not wake her over and over? He was still asleep, breathing deeply and evenly. The thought of waking him to move sounded terrible, but she desperately needed to pee. The sun was making its way above the trees, and she knew it was far later in the morning than she normally would be waking. She felt around with her mind, noticing there were more people in the house than there had been and the distinct smell of coffee wafting from below.

She couldn't wait any longer. She tried to carefully sit up and slip her leg off him, but it didn't matter.

Shane took in a deep breath, his eyes opening just as she was trying to slip off the bed.

"Don't go," he murmured sleepily, reaching for her.

"I'm just going to the bathroom, I'll be right back," she told him in a whisper, smiling a little to herself.

She finished, glancing at the large shower and wishing she could hop in there. She'd skipped showering the day before but did not want to leave him waiting for her. When she came back in the bedroom Shane was still lying in the bed but had his hands behind his head against the pillow, staring at the ceiling, deep in thought. He was feeling hopeful comfort, surrounded by the warm glow of devotion. She climbed in the bed beside him, stretched on her side with her head propped up on her hand to look at his face.

"So, we're married, huh?" she asked quietly, her eyes watching as he turned to her. The question made his heart skip a beat in his chest.

"In the preternatural world, yes," he said honestly, trying to stay focused on her face, but struggling with it a bit, as she was just lying naked before him.

"Hmm…" she said, having felt the bit of desire within him.

"Hmm?" he questioned, not being able to find the words he needed. She was quite distracting.

Vee smiled a little, before turning her eyes toward the ceiling like his had been moments before, flipping onto her back. Shane could now feel the little twinge of desire from her as well and turned, bracing himself with one arm to place a hand on her stomach, fingers trailing over the faint scars from Downing's attack.

"I won't be changing my name," she said quietly but playfully, turning her eyes back to his. He let out a small chuckle at that, gripping her sides and pulling her onto him. Their lips met again then, humor, love, and desire all culminating together. Their kiss became more passionate, the humor sliding away as their bare skin touched. Vee's breath caught as his hands moved down from her waist, stopping and holding her still right as she was going to slide onto him.

There was a knock at the door.

"Dad…? Um… Ethan is here, and Margaret said she found something," Patrick said from the door. The reality of everything came crashing down on them with those words. There were many other things to think about, to do right now, other than get lost in their little blissful bubble. Vee was grateful Shane stopped her, she hadn't been listening at all for the sounds around her, completely lost in passion.

"Give me a minute," Shane said, trying to make his voice sound normal. The sound of Patrick's descent back down the stairs prompted them into action. Vee climbed off him, pulling the blankets around her as Shane got up. He rifled through his bag on the floor, pulling out clothes, and began to get dressed. "Come down when you're ready," he said to her, coming around the bed to kiss her once more before leaving the room. They both struggled to part from it, but they managed.

She let out a breath she didn't realize she had been holding in as she looked around the room. She thought back to the shower, realizing she needed to wash the smell of sex from her if she was going to show her face to the rest of the pack today. Shane may have been fine walking around with everyone smelling it on him, but the idea of all of them, especially Patrick, smelling her that way made her blush.

She hopped back out of the bed, gathering her shower necessities from her bag, and wandered back into the bathroom. She set her things beside his on the little cut out in the tile and turned the water on. As soon as she did, hot water immediately poured out of the dual shower heads on either side of the stall. It amazed her to not have to wait for hot water. She stepped into the spray, relishing the feel of it. She took her time, partially because she was enjoying it immensely, and partially because she knew once she stepped out she would have to deal with the things she had been blissfully forgetting to worry about.

When she got out, drying herself and pulling clothes from her bag on the floor, she glanced at the window. She noticed people greeting someone just outside the house. He was tall and built like Shane, but his hair was more auburn than the nearly black locks of Shane and Patrick. She hadn't seen him before, so she assumed that must be Ethan. She turned her eyes away, hiding back in the bathroom to pull her clothes on. If she could see out, they most certainly could see in. Naked in the window was not the first impression she wanted with Shane's oldest son.

Once dressed, she went to the door, bracing herself before she went out there. The sounds of conversation and the buzz of many Weres hummed in her head as she went down to find coffee. Exposure seemed to be the key to becoming used to it. She sighed at herself as she stood at the top of the stairs, allowing the feelings from those below wash through her for a moment, letting their presence settle over her.

After a moment, she began to descend. She realized there was a second way into the kitchen from the back where the stairs let off. She hadn't noticed it last night, mostly because she was whisked upstairs by Shane. She turned the corner into the large room to see Patrick, Lori and Tommy all sitting together at the island. Other pack members were in the dining room beyond. Her favorite little trio was happily sitting and eating breakfast.

"Morning," she said, trying not to seem too awkward as she walked past them to get to the coffee.

"Good morning!" Lori said cheerfully, eyes alight and vibrating with anticipation. Vee tried not to look at her as she rummaged around the cabinets, trying to find the mugs. Patrick got up from his stool beside Tommy and opened the cabinet that had them hidden away.

"Thank you," she said, forcing a smile as she took one from his hands. Somewhere in the back of her mind she knew he heard them in those early morning hours, being the only other person in the house. She fought a cringe at the thought.

"Do you want me to make you something to eat?" he asked, looking around and realizing the food that had been made nearly an hour ago was either gone or cold by now. She noticed her yogurt sitting next to the half gallon of milk Lori had so gallantly saved for her the night before in the refrigerator.

"I'll just have some yogurt," she said, grabbing them both from the shelf and setting them on the counter next to her mug.

"What's it like?" Lori asked, her voice eager, the energy coming off her was fierce.

"What's what like?" Vee asked, stirring the milk in her coffee, deciding to not bother Patrick with asking where the sugar or sweetener was at the present moment, as he had just sat back down.

"The bond," Lori said, her eyebrows up expectantly. Vee glanced at Tommy and Patrick, neither seeming particularly bothered by the topic, in fact they were also looking at her curiously.

"It's... fine..." she said, trying to think if she felt any different. She did have a sense of where Shane was and how much distance was between them. She felt like she had an unconscious pull toward him. She was able to resist it, but it was still mildly lingering there, just under the surface. His emotions very clearly stood out from everyone else as he spoke with Margaret and Thomas in the other room, a room she felt oddly familiar with, despite it being one of the closed doors they had passed last night in their hasty tour of the house.

"Just fine? What do you feel like? Do you feel different? Was it amazing?" Lori asked, her questions coming out one after another with no pause in between. Vee gave her a startled expression. Her mouth opened a bit, unsure of what to say to any of that.

"Calm down, Lori! She's just come down here. Let her have her coffee before you start interrogating her," Patrick said, coming to Vee's defense, irritation overriding his previous feelings of intrigue. She hunched a little sheepishly, giving Vee a mournful expression as an apology.

"You're fully fledged pack now, Vee," Tommy said with a smirk.

"I guess it's a good thing I'm used to all of you already," she said, faking the grumble in her voice. They all smiled at that.

Vee's imitation of a grumble also hid a sudden realization. Tommy's words stuck at the back of her mind.

She *was* pack now. She wasn't alone. A strange warmth spread through her. A feeling of belonging she hadn't felt since she ran with her odd little foursome in St. Louis as a teenager.

Shane came in the kitchen a moment later, eyeing the three sitting on the stools suspiciously as he went to grab his own mug for coffee.

"Your emotions were all over the place for a minute there. They aren't bothering you, are they?" Shane asked her, turning to glare at them once he filled his mug. For Shane, the insight into her emotions gave him a whole new perspective of her. She was constantly working to moderate her own emotions; the ones she let others see were only the tip of the iceberg on what she was really feeling. He imagined at some point she would learn to better shelter her emotions from him, but for now he had a full view to all her feelings. He was grappling with the scope and depth at which she felt everything. If this was how she felt everyone else, it was no wonder she shied away from others.

"They're just curious," Vee said to him, taking her own sip. Her nonchalance as she said it hid her internal panic well, he noted.

"Are you going to get human-married too?" Lori asked, this time her question directed at Shane. Vee spit a bit of her coffee back into her mug, as Shane felt just as flabbergasted as she had moments before. He narrowed his eyes at Lori, deciding to avoid that question, as he turned his attention back to Vee.

"There are some new developments I want to tell you about, but you should eat first," he told her.

"Have *you* eaten?" she asked, raising an eyebrow, knowing he hadn't. He narrowed his eyes at her, but she saw the corner of his mouth twitch with amusement.

"I'll make some more," Patrick said, getting back up from his stool and heading toward the stove.

Lori and Tommy watched Vee and Shane with amusement as they stared happily at each other. A strange sight to have them both seem content, but the warm bubble burst as the back door opened suddenly and Ethan walked through. He stopped in the doorway, his nostrils flaring as he took in the scent. Shane's eyes snapped up to look at Ethan as soon as he entered the room. Vee felt him stiffen at the way Ethan sharply took in air through his nose. Vee sensed how protective Shane became as all of his other emotions melted away while he looked at his oldest son. It wasn't for Ethan though it was for her. She furrowed her brow, confused. She had no idea what that was about. Shane hadn't really talked to her about Ethan much. In fact, they hadn't really discussed Ethan since the Downing incident last summer.

"You did it, didn't you? You completed the bond," Ethan growled, his eyes already golden with rage. Shane set his mug on the island in front of him and stood at his full height.

"We're not doing this here," Shane said calmly, even though Vee could feel his wolf's rage building to match Ethan's.

"This is her?" Ethan asked, eyes falling on Vee as he took a step forward. Tommy stood from his stool and faced Ethan as well. Obviously, whatever Ethan's feelings toward Vee were the whole pack knew about it.

"Outside," Shane growled, stepping in front of Vee to shield her. The whole house quieted. Vee felt Thomas and Margaret coming from the other side of the stairs to the kitchen as well.

"No, this is insane! You bonded with this... this..." Ethan's golden eyes looked at Vee with absolute disgust, unable to get the words out, because he had no idea what she was.

"Your dad said outside," Tommy barked. Ethan laughed as he turned his searing gaze to Tommy, who stood at his full, dominating height.

"Are you all really defending his decision? You are all okay with this? What happened to this pack?" he snapped, looking at all the pack members who were slowly moving toward the back door, toward him.

"Go outside, and we'll have this conversation," Shane said, his wolf at the forefront. His voice barely holding in the growl that threatened to escape. Ethan glared at his father, feeling the intensity of the pack surrounding him. He turned abruptly, going out the door and pacing in the dead winter grass, waiting for his father to meet him.

Vee stood shocked as she watched Shane walk out after a beat. It was as though he was making sure Ethan was safely away from her before he left her side. He silently signaled for Tommy and Patrick to stay with her. She realized it was the bond that made her understand the soundless communication between them.

The whole pack watched Shane. Tension of the inevitable fight pulsed in the air as Shane stepped off the back porch. He seemed unfazed by his bare feet crunching the rough, cold grass. His body posture held power. He exuded alpha energy, predatory and protective.

"How could you?" Ethan said, his eyes blazing brighter than the winter sun behind him as Shane approached.

"I love her, Ethan!" Shane yelled, his voice echoing around the clearing. He took in a breath through his nose, trying to steady himself as he looked at his son, who only snarled at him. "I love her. The pack loves her. We're bonded, and there's nothing you can do or say that will make me change it. If this is the final straw for you…" Shane held out his arms. "Well then, I'm sorry, but this is what I choose," Shane said more calmly, but his eyes still held their fiery intensity.

"*She* is exactly why there shouldn't be interbreeding," Ethan hissed, spitting on the ground at Shane's feet. Shane moved in front of Ethan faster than what he had been expecting, catching his throat.

"She is bonded to me, my True Mate. It's not going to change," he said with a low grumble in his throat.

"It will when she's dead," Ethan said, his voice low and deadly. The certainty in his voice was chilling, washing over everyone present.

Shock rocked through Shane at those words. His eyes wide, realization sinking in.

"What did you do?" Shane whispered, his hand still at his son's throat. Ethan smiled, seeing the absolute dread that came over his father's face.

"She's an abomination. She shouldn't even *exist*, let alone be protected. *They* are coming," Ethan said, eyes blazing, before he began to change into a wolf right under Shane's fingers.

CHAPTER 19

Vee's heart pounded loudly in her chest. She was vaguely aware of the coffee mug slipping through her fingers and falling to the floor as she felt Shane's overwhelming shock and betrayal. The words "they're coming," were still echoing in her ears. She felt a surge of power run through her, a spine-tingling flow of magic. Shane was changing into his wolf.

Her feet moved, giving into the pull of the bond as she slipped past the Werewolves standing in her way, at her defense, to go out the open back door. She could feel them trying to hold her back as she walked past them but didn't care as her bare feet hit the freezing cold wood of the back porch, moving to the steps and to watch.

After a few minutes Shane's wolf stood there, more massive than any normal wild wolf. His black coat glistened in the sunlight; his white teeth bared as his eyes looked upon his son's wolf, still finishing his change. Ethan was smaller but not by much. What he lacked in size, Vee could feel he made up for in the absolute malice he felt. His coat was lighter, a deeper brown rather than black, but his eyes were just as golden as his father's, glowing with rage as he snarled and snapped.

The rage was directed at Shane, but he was who stood in the way. Vee's heart pounded as she watched the two wolves staring at one another. The air felt heavy. The whole pack held their breath to see who would make the first move. Would it be father or son who drew first blood?

It was Ethan who attacked first, leaping across the short distance between them, teeth trying to sink into Shane's neck. Shane dodged the attack, turning quickly to face him again. He was not trying to attack his son, only defend himself, despite the rage and anguish flowing within him. Ethan went in for another attack, this time aiming for Shane's back leg. His teeth missed yet again, but his claw managed to catch the skin and tear a large gash causing Shane's wolf to let out an angry, painful sound.

Vee took a step down, preparing to run over to them. Everything in her wanted to protect Shane. Tommy's hand reached out and grasped her shoulder, planting her in the spot.

"It's too dangerous, Vee," he said, struggling to not intervene himself. His body was rigid with the effort not to change as he gazed upon the fight.

The entire pack seemed to file out of the house, their wolf eyes glowing in various shades from their human faces. Their movements were silent as if they were on a hunt, but Vee felt them all waiting and watching.

Shane turned back to Ethan again, his rage growing with his own pain. The power seemed to shimmer and warp the air around him. He braced himself, hackles raised as he growled, staring Ethan down. Ethan dug his claws into the cold earth beneath him, preparing for another attack, disgust and hatred fueling him. He lunged once again, but Shane was ready for him, moving just enough to avoid Ethan's teeth. He then wrapped his own mouth around Ethan's neck.

Vee held her breath as Ethan's wolf strained and struggled to pull from his father's massive mouth. Shane dug his claws into the earth beneath his feet, holding him in place. The pressure of Shane's mouth around Ethan's neck slowly cut off Ethan's oxygen, making him gradually fall unconscious.

Everything was silent for a few rapid heartbeats as they all looked at their leader who was panting and growling, still filled with rage and adrenaline. Thomas, who had made his way just behind Vee stepped forward, descended the few steps of the porch, and slowly walked across the grass toward Shane. Shane's wolf snarled at the approach, releasing Ethan's neck from his mouth, but not stepping away from him. *His.*

"I'm only going to restrain him, Shane," Thomas said, holding his hands up as he approached with caution, understanding exactly what Shane said with nothing but his posture and his eyes. Shane growled again, his wolf struggling. He was filled with pure fury,

disappointment, betrayal, and pain. Shane, the man, was not in control here. The wolf was all that was present. Vee pulled her shoulder from out of Tommy's grasp, stepping forward off the stairs to Shane. Somehow, she just knew both wolf and man had chosen her. Both loved her. Both would never hurt her.

"Shane," Vee said quietly, bringing his eyes to focus on her. "Let Thomas take Ethan," she half pleaded, half demanded, causing his eyes to snap to her at the sound of her voice. She wasn't sure if he fully registered what she said as he growled mildly. "Thomas won't hurt him or let him loose to hurt me, right Thomas?" she asked, but more forcefully, stepping even closer to Shane. She felt the fear and hesitation in every Were present at her closeness to Shane.

"We will restrain him for now," Thomas said, eyes wide with the exchange going on, wondering if Vee would be able to convince him. Worried if what she was doing didn't work, he would have to fight his leader to ensure Shane didn't hurt his own mate. Shane's wolf was fully in control here, and it would be strange if her words had any meaning to him.

But shocking the whole pack, Shane stepped forward after a long, frightening moment, pushing his head under Vee's outstretched hand and signaled her to follow him away. The crowd at the porch parted to let Vee and Shane reenter the house. Shane immediately moving up the stairs to their bedroom with Vee silently following behind. Once inside, Vee closed the door with a snap, turning to face the massive wolf she had just trapped herself with. He was pacing at the foot of the bed, back and forth, breathing still heavy, the occasional low growl coming from his chest.

Vee knelt on the ground to be more level with him. She had questions. They had new developments to discuss, and he needed to be human in order to do this, no matter how beautiful he was as his wolf. No matter how certain she was that he would never hurt her.

"Shane, I need you to turn back now," she whispered, making him stop, eyes turning back to her. The anger he felt still smoldering on the surface. He walked to her, his claws lightly scraping the carpet beneath his feet as he took each tentative step. It surprised him that she wasn't afraid of him, knowing that he was so angry and volatile at that moment, ready to snap. She didn't hesitate as she reached her hands forward slowly, placing them on either side of the thick fur on his face.

His heart began to slow at her touch, the rapid beating calming. He closed his eyes and began to change back. It was slow. Quick changes back and forth were difficult without the moon. Bones and ligaments snapped and shifted back into place. The hair that covered him receded into his skin. She could feel the twinges of pain from him as it happened and the exertion that it took. Slowly, but surely the massive wolf transformed under her hands back into the human Shane, sweating and panting as he crouched naked on the floor before her.

He winced slightly as he moved to sit before her, taking one of her hands as they dropped from his face. Blood from his leg wound was smearing into the carpet, even though it was slowly starting to heal. Vee started to stand, thinking she should get a towel or something for his bleeding wound, but he tightened his grip, keeping her on the floor with him.

"You didn't like my wolf?" he asked quietly, trying to lighten the mood, but his voice was still gruff and strained. She smiled a little.

"*He* can't talk," she said in return. If she wasn't so absorbed in his labored breathing and the blood oozing from his leg, she would have told him his wolf was the most beautiful thing she had ever seen. But perhaps she didn't need words, since his eyes seemed to sparkle as he watched her face.

"Let me get something for that. You're bleeding all over the carpet," she finally said, breaking the eye contact after a moment and glancing down at the long scratches over his thigh. He sighed, releasing her hand and letting her go to the bathroom to grab some supplies. She tried not to show how shaky her hands were as she returned to him, using a wet washcloth to dab and clean the wound before she pressed a fresh, dry towel to it to stop the bleeding. Had she been a wolf, she could have licked his wounds like he did for her before, but as it was, she wasn't able to do that for him.

"It will heal by tomorrow," he mumbled, watching the way her brow furrowed with concern. "It would take less time if it hadn't been a wound from another wolf." She didn't respond, only pressed her lips more firmly together. She didn't like him getting hurt.

"So..." she started, unsure of how to begin the obvious conversation about Ethan that needed to occur. "Seems like Ethan has some strong opinions about me," Vee murmured, not looking at his face but feeling the sadness and betrayal surround him again.

"He has voiced his concerns to me about you before," he said quietly. She couldn't be mad at Ethan's logic. His father, a highly respected leader, old and powerful, was bonded to a woman who was practically human for all the power she had. And now the pack was being targeted because of her.

"I don't blame him," she murmured, still not looking up into his eyes.

"He has a very old-fashioned way of looking at mating and bonding," he said, watching her expression as it changed with her thoughts. He reached his hand to her chin, titling it so their eyes finally met again. "It's not his place to dictate who I love." His eyes were still gold, shimmering with emotion. It was still tainted by the sadness he felt, but his anger was gone.

"But I have brought nothing but a mess onto the pack ... onto you. He's not wrong. We shouldn't have bonded," she murmured, trying to hold back her own sadness from him, but she couldn't. He felt her sadness, and oddly, it made him happy. She wanted this just as much as he did.

"What's yours, is mine. It's my mess now," he whispered, caressing her cheek. Vee let herself lean forward slightly as he pulled her to make their lips meet. It ended just as quickly as it began when she accidentally pressed her hand too hard on his thigh causing him to wince.

"I'm sorry!" she said, pulling her hand away, but making sure the towel was still in pace there. He smiled a little at her, watching her fuss for a moment, making sure she felt that he wasn't upset.

"Do you think it's because of his mother?" she asked after a quiet moment. She knew he had partners and at least one wife before.

"I never bonded with his mother," he told her, pausing for a moment to study her face. There was a lot about his past he hadn't yet told her he realized. "You are the only person I have ever bonded to, actually," Shane said, raising his eyebrows, surprising both of them as he said the words out loud.

"Why?" Vee asked, clearly shocked.

"Ethan's mother was before I became the leader. The man who led us then was…" He sighed slightly, his gaze looking distant while he thought about the unpleasant past. "Well, he wasn't kind. He believed in pure breeding and wanted the pack numbers to grow. Instead of having us try to turn others, he decided to… to have the stronger of us bed the few females of the pack," Shane said, clearly uncomfortable recalling it. Not that he would have liked the idea of attacking humans in the hope they would change, either. Both options were reprehensible.

"He … bred you? Like livestock?" she asked, disgusted. Shane nodded a bit.

"Ethan's mother was not a particularly kind woman. She was quite a bit older than me at the time, but she was a fervent believer in O'Neil, the previous pack leader. After she had Ethan, she was given over to another male in the pack. If a binding would have been offered, I wouldn't have wanted to take it." He shivered slightly at the thought of being bound to that woman. Only his love for Ethan made what happened between them tolerable.

CHAPTER 19

"What happened to her?" Vee asked, unable to quench her curiosity.

"She died in a battle with another pack when Ethan was two. I raised him alone, but some of the old ways seemed to have slipped into him," Shane said, his eyes closing with frustration.

"How often do others bond?" she asked, watching his face change with her question, eyes coming to rest on hers again.

"It's very rare. We can't bond with humans though most Weres claim their human spouses. There are no others bonded in our pack, besides us," Shane told her. The way he said "our pack" gave Vee a strange feeling of happiness. She had felt like such an outsider, not being a Were, not really being anything to them, other than the helpful locksmith. Now the whole pack had rallied for her, everyone coming out of the house to surround and protect her, to be on guard to protect Shane. The warmth that had blossomed with Tommy's words earlier grew ever so slightly as Shane made it even more real. She was one of them now.

"What will you do with Ethan?" she asked, as Shane leaned in to give her a quick kiss before slowly standing and heading to his bag of clothes. He paused. He wasn't quite sure what he was going to do. The idea of hurting his son was viscerally painful, but he felt certain that Ethan had a hand in this plot against her. *Something* had to be done.

"I don't know yet," Shane told her honestly, pulling his clothes on. The bleeding had stopped, but he knew if he moved too much it would resume. Vee stood too, taking the hand that he offered her as he headed downstairs once again.

Margaret stood at the bottom of the steps, her eyes not on them but the commotion in the hall. Vee glanced over the banister as they got far enough down to see Thomas, Tommy, and Emily going through one of those doors, descending to a basement Vee had no idea existed. They were carrying Ethan, who had changed back into his human form. Perhaps she should have gone on that house tour after all.

Shane steered them past the basement door, heading into the room he had been in with Margaret and Thomas before the whole incident began. Of course, he had an office at his getaway property. She couldn't begrudge him that. If she could have lived in her shop, she would have.

"We will eat, I have no doubt about that, but first I wanted to show you what Margaret found," Shane said, pulling open the laptop on his desk and logging in to show her. "Durran texted me last night with an address. She found the source of the magic. It has a distinct scent," he started, pulling up the house on the internet.

Vee knew that house. She had been helping a Witch refurbish the locks there for months. She hadn't been inside the house. The pulse of magic always deterred her, but she had dropped locks off a number of times.

"I've helped that Witch," Vee said, her voice quiet, panic and recognition running through the bond to Shane.

"What do you mean, *helped?*" Shane asked, confusion evident in his tone and expression.

"She… she had me fixing the locks in that house," Vee said, eyes changing between her normal emerald and amber.

"Just her? Or did she have a coven?"

"Every time I dealt with her she was alone, but I never went in that house. Her name is Gwen Tallon," Vee told him, looking away from the screen.

"Well, I guess Margaret dug around finding her name for nothing. I should have just asked you," Shane said, not actually annoyed but irritated with himself. For some reason, even though he knew how capable she was, he still found himself trying to shield her. He should have asked her more questions about who she had been in contact within the preternatural community.

"Yes, you should probably stop hiding things from me," Vee said, both in response to his words and the annoyance she was getting from him. Her tone wasn't accusatory, yet he still took it that way, even feeling what she was feeling.

"And what about you? Do you have anything else to share?" Shane snapped back. Vee looked at him, feeling his frustration, but the underlying cause was concern for her.

"That tone is unnecessary," she started, raising an eyebrow at him. "Just a few days ago we were basically a flirtation as far as each of us knew. Don't act like I've been intentionally keeping things from you. It wasn't your place to know before," she told him, crossing her arms over her chest and turning to face him.

She was right. He knew it before she even said it to him. He was a hair-trigger at the moment, quickly flitting through his emotions in the last few hours, few days. He didn't have to say anything in return. Vee felt his apology as he opened his mouth to try to fix it, but she shook her head at him.

"I came across another Watcher months ago," she said, instead of letting him talk. "I should have mentioned it earlier, but I had wanted to talk to Durran about it first," she confided. Her speaking gave Shane time to collect himself a bit.

"What happened?"

"He was just at a client's house I was replacing locks for. He *hated* me. I was shocked, having only just met him. I still don't understand why he was there. He was playing handyman to the neighborhood," she said, thinking back on that day. She remembered the way his eyes seemed to burn with recognition. He radiated feelings of an eagerness to get to know her that accompanied the burning feeling of hatred. It confused her when she had never come across this creature before. Her anxiety had only increased when she was leaving, as she was trying to avoid being recognized by Eliza's husband, Frank, who lived just a few houses away. "It was Eliza's neighborhood," Vee whispered through a catch in her throat, letting the pieces click into place in her mind as she said it.

"Did you get a name?" Shane asked.

"Mac."

CHAPTER 20

"Cormac, actually," Durran said, leaning on the doorway. Shane and Vee both whipped around to see her.

Vee was shocked she didn't notice Durran's presence, but she assumed it had to do with the buzz of Weres in the house. Durran's void of a mind could easily get lost amongst them. Without a second thought, Vee crossed the room and hugged her. She was flooded with Durran's trepidation. She felt an unease that seemed to be surrounding everyone, but this feeling wasn't just about the threat that loomed over them. Vee could tell there was more hidden under the surface, mirrored by the stiffness of Durran's body at Vee's touch.

Shane couldn't help the jealousy that bubbled up inside of him as he saw Durran's arms circle around Vee, hugging her back after a moment. Their eyes met, and he saw the brief hint of scowl show on Durran's face before it smoothed back to an indifferent expression. Yes, there was good reason for Shane to be cautious of Durran's feelings for Vee.

"So, it's confirmed, then? It's him?" Shane grumbled as Vee and Durran parted.

"It is. I appealed to the Elders, but…"

"But they won't don't anything," Shane said, finishing Durran's sentence with disappointment. He knew that was exactly what the Sha would have said to Shane as well, had he reached out to them. There had been too much going on for him to even try, and he didn't think they would get to the property in time for it to make a difference even if they said yes.

"They have at least washed their hands of him. No ill will should befall the pack if he is killed," Durran said, red eyes staring into Shane's golden ones.

"But we still have no idea how they're all connected. The Witches, Cormac, and…" Vee turned to Shane, her heart sinking to the pit of her stomach as she wondered if it had been Ethan.

"It wasn't Ethan. The others would have known if it was him. They would have noticed his scent," Shane assured her, understanding the conclusion she had just come to by the crestfallen look on her face.

"The Witches could have altered the Were's smell," Durran warned, eyeing Shane warily. "What does your son have to do with this?"

"He said, 'they're coming,'" Vee reminded Shane, her brows pulling together with worry. Shane's hands curled into fists. It was possible, and that glimmer of

CHAPTER 20

possibility was enough to make him want to tear everything around him apart.

"He was in my house the night of the attack. He
couldn't have done it," Shane growled, trying to
remember if he had heard Ethan leaving the house
that night. Had he? Did Shane simply brush it off,
thinking Ethan was headed to a bar?

Vee felt the inner turmoil. This was too much for
him. Their bond, her safety, his own son's possible
betrayal. Not to mention he was now wounded. He
was spiraling.

"Stay here. Do not move, either of you," Vee said,
glancing between the two of them before darting from
the room as quickly as possible, turning to the very
next door and heading directly down to the basement,
slamming the door behind her.

"Vee?" came Shane's voice from the other room a
beat after she left it. She took a deep breath as she
heard him race to the door, but she had locked it. He
would have to break it down, which she was sure he
would do eventually. In fact, he could have torn it
down immediately, but thankfully he was controlled
enough to pause.

"Stay there!" she yelled back, descending the stairs
to see Emily and Tommy still down there with Ethan
tied to a chair. It made sense he would have guards, at
least for the time being.

Ethan was awake again but still groggy, she could
tell. Lack of oxygen to the brain takes a bit more
time to recover from, even for a Werewolf. She took a
moment to study him. Though his coloring was quite a
bit lighter than Shane and Patrick, the bone structure

of his face was the same. Even struggling a little with confusion, he still looked powerful.

"Vee, this isn't a good idea," Tommy said to her, stepping a little forward as if he were about to place himself between her and the bound man. There was no way he could hurt her before she got away or someone else intervened. Vee waved Tommy off, halting him from moving any closer. Her eyes focused only on the man in the middle of the room.

"Ethan," Vee said, bringing his attention to her. He looked at her strangely, like he was confused or unsure of who she was for a moment. She felt out his emotions. He was no longer angry, rather disoriented and astonished. She waited until she saw the recognition in his eyes, however dazed he still seemed. She took in a deep breath, preparing herself for the answer to the question she was about to ask. "Did you kill my sister?"

Ethan grew a bit more coherent at her inquiry, narrowing his eyes as he looked her over. This small woman was intimidating, he admitted to himself now that he looked at her. Her eyes, still holding their emerald color, showed burning emotion. Her body was petite, but he could see she was not without muscle. And most importantly, she was not afraid of him. She wasn't concerned with how his feelings affected her relationship with his father. She stood there, strong and menacing before him, demanding answers. In another situation he might have liked her, but right now she was simply an irritating enigma, a pest invading his father's life.

"No," he said coldly. There was no burn to indicate he was lying. He was being honest. The relief that washed over her made everything seem a bit more achievable.

Shane still had a difficult decision to make regarding Ethan, but death didn't have to be on the table. She couldn't imagine how that would torment him.

She stepped a bit closer now, her eyes turning a blazing amber with each step, and halted a few feet before him. "But you know who did?" she asked. Ethan fought the gasp that threatened to escape as he watched her eyes change.

"I don't know the Were personally," Ethan said, choosing his words carefully. Vee nodded her head and sighed. He wasn't going to make this easy for her. She looked at Tommy and Emily, both confused at her questioning. They quickly registered looks of shock when they realized what his statement meant.

"What *do* you know?" she decided to ask. She would be able to feel each lie he decided to say and would question him from there.

"I know you shouldn't exist. That the very thought of some crossbreed like you is a crime against nature," he spat, snapping back to his original thoughts on her, even though a hint of a lie burned at Vee's eyes. She smirked a little causing him to growl in warning. Even he wasn't sure of his original convictions anymore.

"Ethan, much like you, I didn't choose to be born, but I never had the luxury of knowing where I came from. Answer the question."

"I told them where we are. It doesn't matter if you know who it is or not. They will take what you shouldn't have and rid my father of you," Ethan hissed. The way he said, "take what you shouldn't have," rang in her head. She didn't quite understand how anyone could do that, but she admittedly, wasn't hugely versed in magics. Out of all the potential players they knew of there was only one who would be able to "take" something from her.

"Gwen Tallon?"

"Ah, you've figured that much out," Ethan said, a little concern coloring his amusement. "She's an abomination just as much as you, but at least she's not some simpering weak thing that needs the protection of my father's bond and pack." Vee tried to not let those words bother her. His disdain for her was palpable as he looked at her. At some point, if he survived this, she would have to find a way to remedy how he perceived her. She could already see the little seeds of doubt planting themselves within him, but now wasn't the time. "I can't believe he completed the bond with you. How did you manage to convince him you were his True mate, hmm?"

She furrowed her brow at that. This was the second time she heard the words "True Mate" said, and she wasn't sure what that meant.

"I didn't convince him of anything. If anything, he convinced me," Vee told him honestly, making sure to tuck that information away to ask Shane later. Ethan sneered, not believing her still.

"Margaret where's the key?" Vee heard Shane say faintly from upstairs. She only had a bit longer before he would be down here.

"And what about the Watcher?" she asked.

"I only met him once. Seems you have enemies everywhere. I warned them ... about the bond. I hoped there wouldn't be time, but you found a way to seduce him," Ethan grumbled. Tommy growled beside her. She could tell it was taking all of his willpower to not step in and say something. With each disparaging word Ethan said against Vee, Tommy had grown more and more infuriated. The lines of his body rigid with the effort to not hurt Ethan.

"How is it that I have enemies, and yet I don't even know what I am?" Vee decided to ask aloud to no one in particular. How could so many creatures want to harm her, to *take* what she had, if she wasn't privy to her own origins?

"You've been on their radar for a while. It's your scent, I think. Subtle. Almost ignorable, but there's definitely something *other* about you."

"Witches don't have that ability," Vee said, narrowing her eyes.

"But they can sense magic," he said, smiling eerily.

The door at the top of the stairs finally opened, Shane racing down them despite his injured leg with Durran not far behind.

"I'm done," Vee said, her eyes not leaving Ethan's. "He wasn't the Were," she told them.

"We should prepare," Durran said, as Vee turned to head back up the stairs.

"We should," she agreed. She wasn't quite sure how *she* should prepare. In some respects, Ethan was correct. She was weak in comparison to her counterparts. She might be able to hold herself up in a fight with a human. She took kick boxing lessons for a time when she had come back to the city alone, but preternatural foes were a whole different thing.

Shane stood in front of his son for a moment longer. His eyes golden pools of fire as he looked down at him on the chair.

"When this is over you will be banished," he told him, his voice low and deadly, making everyone stop in their tracks. Vee gripped the railing on the stairs, reeling a little from his disappointment and betrayal. No, he hadn't been the one to kill Eliza and her family, but he had provided information to the enemy.

"I'm only trying to rid you of this parasite!" Ethan yelled back in protest.

"You endangered the whole pack by telling them where we are! I don't care what your motivations were! There are children here, Ethan. Your *brother* is here!" Shane roared. That realization crossed over Ethan's face, filling him with dread.

"There's not time for this," Durran hissed, heading up the stairs behind Vee, prompting her to continue her ascent. Vee glanced one last time down at Ethan, who looked rather distraught and speechless at his father's last words before she turned away.

Vee moved back to the kitchen. Patrick was at the stove, continuing to make the food he had been before Ethan burst through the back door. His emotions were all over the place, and he was clearly trying to focus on something even if it was only making food for his dad and Vee. If he didn't, he would crumble to pieces in front of them. She knew the feeling, needing a bit of a distraction herself. Her broken coffee mug was still shattered across the floor, providing an excellent opportunity to get lost in a mindless but needed

task. She bent to pick it up as Patrick turned around to face her.

"I've got it," she said, waving him off as she picked up the shards of ceramic. Durran sat on one of the stools as Shane reentered the kitchen, eyes still burning.

"Patrick, go find Lori. Take the humans and children to the green barn," Shane ordered. Patrick froze mid-crouch at his father's command.

"I'm not babysitting," Patrick said, looking up at Shane.

"You're going to protect them," Shane reaffirmed.

"I'm not going to just sit there while you risk your life!" Patrick yelled, standing to face his father.

"Patrick, we aren't discussing this. You and Lori will go with them to the barn," Shane said coldly. His icy tone didn't fool anyone. He was trying to keep Patrick safe behind the wards with the human pack members. Shane *needed* Patrick safe. It was the only way he'd be able to focus his energy on protecting the rest of them. Protecting Vee.

"Vee is important to me too. I want to help," Patrick said, his voice a little quieter as he looked back down at Vee. She stood, setting the broken pieces on the counter and turning to him.

"You will be helping. You must keep *them* safe. They are the most vulnerable here, Patrick. I would never forgive myself if something happened to any of them because of me," she whispered, looking up into Patrick's eyes, pleading with him.

"Vee... I..." Patrick murmured, his eyes welling a bit with tears. She could feel it, the warm glow of love. Not romantic, by any means. What he told her before was true. He loved her like she was his mother, and the thought of losing a mother again was tearing at him. He couldn't protect his real mom, but he wanted to protect her.

"Listen to your father, Patrick," she said quietly, touching his shoulder. He stepped forward, pulling her into a tight hug, and let the tears escape from his eyes. It said a lot that he didn't try to hide the tears. Patrick released her, giving his father a respectful nod before roughly rubbing the tears from his eyes and heading out to the front to grab Lori.

Durran had watched the interaction between Vee and Patrick with utter disbelief. She knew Vee had been letting the two younger wolves work at her shop off and on since the previous summer, but she had no idea the level of affection between them. The clear familial way that the young Were felt toward Vee was shocking to Durran. In fact, the way they all seemed to hold her in such high regard was unusual, considering she was nothing like them.

Vee had resumed cleaning the broken mug once she saw through the front dining room window that Patrick and Lori were well on their way to the first house.

"Leave it. You need to eat," Shane said, moving over to help her but immediately cutting his hand on a jagged piece of the broken mug in his haste.

"You're already bleeding from one place. I don't need you to keep getting injured. Go clean that up," she said, waving him off. He begrudgingly stood to wash his hand in the sink, using a kitchen towel to put pressure on his cut thumb. The shallow cut would close in minutes as opposed to the much deeper cuts from Ethan's claws.

"He's right, Vee. You need to eat something before all this begins," Durran piped up, watching Vee dump the shards into the trash and proceed to wipe the remaining coffee mess from the table.

"I'm going to! Will both of you just let me finish this?" she snapped, not looking at either of them. She needed to do this. For just a single moment she needed to do something as normal as pick up broken pieces of mug.

"I'll have most of the pack in the surrounding woods. We need to keep Vee as protected as possible," Shane said, pausing to glance out the back windows. "Maybe you can take her to the other barn, keep her there. The Sha's wards should keep them from being able to get to her, at least for a time. It may buy us the time we need," he continued, looking at Durran, who had followed his gaze out the windows. The idea of relinquishing Vee's protection to the Watcher wasn't ideal to Shane, but she would be safe in her hands. He knew Durran would fight to the death for Vee. If not for her duty, then for love.

"*You* need to eat too, Shane," she said, interrupting his planning and poking him in the chest aggressively as she went to snatch a clean plate from the counter.

"I will," he said back, brow furrowed as he turned to watch her scoop some of the scramble Patrick had made for them.

"Where is this barn?" Durran asked, turning the conversation back to the plan. She did not notice another barn as she glanced where Shane had been looking, but he knew this property well and better than anyone. If he said there was another barn away from the one that would house the humans and children, there would be.

"Southeastern side. It's red. Smaller than the one right here," Shane said, nodding toward it. Durran and Vee looked out, seeing the large green colored barn about seventy-five feet or so from the house. Clearly, they called it the green barn because it had once been painted green; however, most of the paint had been stripped away, leaving mostly bleached wood in its place. Only a few places hinted at the color it had once been.

Vee looked out at it, watching as the families file in through the huge doors. The number of children, most of which she had met to sense if they would turn someday, shook Vee to her core. Her very existence had made them a target. Now, instead of safely at home, they had to take shelter in a barn, preparing for the unknown battle to come. What could these Witches possibly want with her? What could she possess that they couldn't already do themselves?

"Ethan said they wanted to *take* something from me," Vee suddenly said, letting her thoughts flood out into the conversation.

"Take something?" Durran asked.

"Yes, he did say that," Shane murmured, finally filling a plate with food as well.

"What could they possibly take?" Vee whispered, food no longer having any interest. Durran's face twisted as she thought.

"Black Witches have been known to steal power," Durran said, recalling the Witches of the distant past. That knowledge was supposed to have died out. Black Witches still existed. They possessed magic seeped in pain and death, but they hadn't been ripping the essence, the souls, from others since the wars. They had become too powerful back then, stealing from the other preternaturals. It warped and changed them into beings that should not exist. Unnatural. True abominations. What humans described as demons in some instances. It was forbidden magic now.

Durran looked at Vee with horror, realizing what they planned to do. This Witch wanted Vee's magic, and she would rip Vee's soul from her body to get it.

CHAPTER 21

The remaining bit of day went by quickly. The anxiety and commotion of everyone preparing for the unknown made time seem to fly by. Shane had let her wrap his leg, but both of them knew it wouldn't hold if and when he turned back into his wolf. It made her feel better nonetheless, at least for a moment. The idea of Shane already being hurt when the threat was still unknown and imminent troubled her.

They had prepared as much as they could. Only Durran had ever fought against Witches before, and they weren't sure if Gwen had more than one Were at her disposal. Shane had waffled between different ideas of how to deploy the pack. He didn't know if it was better to keep the pack centralized, closer to the houses, or spread out with half remaining nearby. He also wasn't sure if he should keep Ethan guarded. The idea of being down even one of his pack with such uncertainty about their opponents was unfathomable.

"The only advantage we have is we know what she's after," Durran said, looking at Vee who she sat on the couch, pulling on her shoes.

Vee wasn't really dressed well for the cold outside, but that was more a matter of her poor laundry routine. All her warm clothes were still at her apartment dirty on the floor of her bedroom instead of here where she needed them. She mentally admonished herself, vowing she would work the laundromat into her routine a touch more often than once a month from here on out.

She had slipped Shane's sweatshirt back on that she had been worn the day before along with some severely worn jeans that probably should have been thrown out ages ago. The sweatshirt hung down almost to her knees, so that did provide a bit more warmth. Her shoes were heavy boots that she wore every day for work, so they were worn to the point of comfort. They had molded to her feet so much they would be quite good for running if she needed them to be.

"But we shouldn't alert her to where Vee will be," Shane said, pacing the floor in front of the dark fireplace. His movements were fairly normal, despite his injury, except for the falter every now and then that only Vee seemed to notice.

"Will your wolves be able to hold it together with the full moon?" Durran asked, causing both Shane and Vee to freeze.

How had no one realized it was the night of the first full moon?

Vee felt Shane's anxiety creep in. Most of the Weres were seasoned. They would be able to focus their thoughts on the task even with the moon's call, but he wasn't sure what this Witch could do to them. The magic of the pack could withstand a lot, keeping them focused, keeping them in control of their beast, but their experience with Witches was with the more benevolent sort. They had only come across more benign covens throughout the city. The most they had ever had to deal with was fending off other preternaturals from messing with the white or grey covens. They never had to defend from the covens themselves.

Was Gwen manipulating the wolf who killed Eliza and her family, or did this wolf have its own connection to Vee?

"Under normal circumstances, yes. Unfortunately, with the situation as it is we can't count on anything," Shane said with a sigh, rubbing his forehead so vigorously that Vee feared he'd scratch off a patch of skin. She leaned back into the couch with a huff, making Shane stop to look at her anxious face. He immediately stopped pacing, moved to kneel in front of her, and took her hands in his. "We'll get through it," he tried to assure her, but his own lack of confidence was evident. Vee worried for all of them.

"I know you'll try," Vee said quietly.

"We need to get you to the barn," Durran said, trying to hold back her jealousy as Shane and Vee looked longingly into each other's eyes.

"Yes, I need to go be with the pack," Shane whispered, still not pulling his eyes from Vee's. She leaned forward, pressing their foreheads together. The bond between them almost ached, as if they knew this would be their last moment together. Shane tilted his head up, pressing his lips to hers for a final searing kiss before he tore himself away, trying not to give into the despair they both felt. "You'll protect her," Shane said, turning to Durran.

"With my life," Durran said honestly, her eyes bright red with both resentment and anticipation of the battle ahead.

Vee stood as Shane headed out the door. She walked out onto the front porch behind him, looking up at the moon as it came over the treetops. The howls of various members of the pack rang out through the surrounding woods. They were ready. Their wolves eager to fight, to let their bloodthirsty nature free on their enemies and protect their own. There was electricity in the cold crisp air. It was palpable, thick.

Vee could feel it before she saw it. Her eyes watching with fascination at the magic creeping in through the trees. To her, it was like a thick fog, cascading and swirling as it slithered past obstacles, moving over the property once it broke through the tree line. It seemed like it had a mind of its own as it moved. Intelligent. However, she knew the intelligence didn't lie within the smoke-like tendrils.

Shane looked back at her from where he stood on the gravel driveway, his eyes golden, as he rid himself of his clothes. The moonlight seemed to focus on him as the magic of his transformation began. This change with the moon seemed more natural than what it had been when he came back to his human form earlier in the day. The magic pulsed around him as his body smoothly shifted and morphed into his wolf form. His bones and muscles rearranged and fur slid in place of skin.

She had never seen a wolf transform so beautifully before. All of her experiences watching a transformation happen were odd and grotesque with bodies shifting unnaturally. The power of the moon and the power of being the leader of this pack seemed to help his change along. Shane and his wolf were so in sync after years of practice that it looked more natural. It was like his body was supposed to be a wolf. She felt the power and strength surging within him through the bond. She felt almost like she could have changed into a wolf herself had she been given enough time.

She could have watched him forever. The transformation's beauty and grace took up her whole view, but she was suddenly torn out of her trance watching him. Her head snapped up as she heard horrible, gut-wrenching noises and howls from the wolves in the woods. Shane's eyes, which had been trained on her for the whole of his transformation, tore from hers to the tree line as he waited, shaking off the last pangs of pain from his change, and listening for them.

They watched in united horror as a dozen wolves raced out of the trees, faster than Vee had ever seen a wolf run, back toward the houses and Shane, escaping the magic that was now creeping ever closer.

Vee was expecting a figure to come out of the mist from the woods, or maybe even many, since they weren't sure if Gwen had a coven or not, but no one emerged. Minutes passed like hours, the magic moving over the grass through the clearing, seeming to gain speed.

"Vee, we need to go," Durran hissed from behind her.

It all became eerily silent. The sound of her own breathing was all Vee could hear.

"*Victoria*," came a whisper from somewhere behind her.

Vee turned around on the porch, hoping it was Durran, but it was like time froze for a moment. Durran stood half in the doorway, eyes wide with fear, hand reaching out to Vee, but like a statue. Goosebumps covered Vee's skin as she turned back toward the entrance of the property. Shane was also frozen there. His wolf looking back at her, hackles raised.

"*Victoria*," the voice said again. This time it was less a whisper, but it echoed around her as if she weren't in the open air of the outside but in a cathedral instead.

Vee's eyes were still planted firmly on Shane. She could see the magic was now engulfing him. He was frozen, unable to move, as it overtook him. She felt the sting of the magic through the bond, as if it were on her own skin. It burned, and she was certain if he could have, he would have made the same horrible sounds they had just heard from his other wolves before they fled the trees. She felt the throb and hum of the Witch. Gwen was close now. Close enough for Vee to feel her presence, her mind, but she still couldn't see her.

"*He can't protect you anymore*," the voice said sinisterly. Vee's eyes scrutinized the space that surrounded Shane. He was at least a hundred feet away from her, but she could see the faint glimmer of something more there than the magic mist. She concentrated on the shimmering spot harder, and a figure began materializing into her view, standing at Shane's wolf.

Gwen stood there, eyes alight with madness as she looked at Vee. She was just as Vee remembered her. A wild mane of curly blond hair, pale skin, but her eyes were never as wide and sinister as Vee saw them now. Her pupils were dilated to the size of saucers; Vee could barely see the blue of her irises. Gwen grasped Shane's fur, her head bent at an odd angle as she watched Vee.

Gwen seemed to somehow know as soon as Vee could see her. In the hand that wasn't touching Shane she held a dagger of glistening silver with intricate designs carved and welded into it. Vee watched, paralyzed with fear, as the Witch bent to Shane's leg, and cut the wound that was already there more deeply, blood dripping over the blade, coating it.

More figures came from the trees, a few more than half a dozen. Their bodies shadowed in dark cloaks. Vee could hear the whispers of their spell through the magic that was now closing in on her.

"Can't have that pesky bond ruining all our fun," Gwen said as she spread the blood over her hand from the blade.

Before Vee could even move, Gwen's lips began to move, the haunting whispers of her incantation echoing all around. She could feel the bond, Shane's pain, his horror, as the unintelligible words created an orb of magic in Gwen's hand that moved to hover between them. Its color was deep crimson like the blood that she had stolen from Shane. It hung there for a moment before split in two, one heading toward Vee, the other toward Shane. Somehow, she knew the moment the orb touched her the bond would be broken.

CHAPTER 21

Vee didn't question how she knew, finally finding her feet and stepping off the porch to run. She realized she was the only one who could move in this space. Every other person and wolf was trapped, frozen. Their eyes watched as Vee passed them, heading to the red barn, which now seemed so much further away. The orb pursued her. The magic was not hindered by things like gravity. She could feel it getting closer, the air growing hot. Her feet moved, eyes trained on the red barn. It was still so far from her reach.

Vee felt it as it hit her back, sending her flying through the air from the force of it. The cold, hard ground hitting her body was painful, but it was nothing in comparison to what she felt as the spell surrounded her. The pain was excruciating. Every inch of her body was on fire as the spell spread out from its impact on her back, ripping and destroying any place the bond might hide within her. It snaked through and wrenched at her viciously, making her writhe on the ground uncontrollably. It was like she was being torn apart. The force of the bond being pulled from her was agonizing.

Vee had been choking and gasping but was finally able to let out a scream. Her voice echoed oddly as it came out of her. It was like a tidal wave, pushing the strange mist back away from her much faster than it had rolled in. The hold the witches had over all of them released. Gwen seemed to falter her stance, feeling her magic fall away in a rush, and was shocked that the torturous mist had been thrown back. The inhuman, devastating roar of Shane broke through the near silence of the property as the pieces of Vee ripped from him just as they were being torn from her.

She managed to stand up, despite the horrific pain, Shane's presence within her was slipping away with each torturous moment. She tried to keep running, but she stumbled as each new wave of the bond's magic being pulled away felt like her heart was being yanked from her chest. Suddenly, she was no longer standing. Strong arms were now holding her, and a small bit of reassurance came through to her. She looked up through blurred, teary eyes and saw Durran's determined face. She had scooped Vee from the ground, making it to the red barn in nearly an instant.

They went inside, and Durran placed Vee on a beat-up couch that sat in the middle of the open space. The old barn was essentially a shack. Dirt, broken pieces of wood, and other debris littered the floors. Trash, presumably belonging to various youngsters of the pack over the years, dotted the floor.

The pain began to subside, leaving Vee gasping through uncontrollable sobs. Where the bond once resided there was now an awful emptiness. She had never felt so alone before. She didn't feel like she was suddenly back to herself. She felt lesser. The bond being taken away took a piece of her with it. Her mind and body ached for what she had. Even for the short time they were bound, it had melded into her, settling in her bones as if it was meant to be there. He was gone. Her breath hitched as she clutched her chest like she would somehow be able to fill that missing piece with her own hand.

Shane's claws griped into the earth beneath him. It was a massive, sheer amount of will power that it took him to not succumb to the absolute agony he felt as their bond stripped away. The pain only amplified his rage. He went to lunge at the Witch, who had moved away from him, his blood still dripping from the dagger in her hands. He was then struck out of nowhere by another body. A Were. It hadn't gotten ahold of Shane, so once they both recovered from the blow, scrambling back to their feet, he set his eyes upon the wolf. It was a brown wolf, with eyes that he could tell were normally a vibrant green but were slightly obscured by a haze. It was as if a film were covering them.

This wolf was entranced.

There was a small bit of relief that Shane felt, knowing this wasn't a Were attacking on its own free-will, but it was dashed quickly when it went for him again, snarling with ravenous foam dripping from its mouth. Emily's wolf, small but mighty in its silvery coat, came just as it was about to get to Shane. She clamped her jaws onto its back and sent them tumbling away from him. He used the opportunity to try to run toward Gwen again, but his leg, now deeply injured, prevented his usual speed.

Snarling, growling, and roaring could be heard echoing all over the clearing, Shane could see many wolves breaking through from the tree line around them, eyes aglow with the same haze as the wolf that had just attacked Shane. As he got closer to Gwen, his wolves began to attack the enchanted ones at full force. He hadn't seen them in any sort of battle like this since the last leader of his pack took them to war with neighboring packs. Many of these wolves were too young or too new to the pack for that battle and had never fought like this before. The bone-chilling recollection of his packmates dead in the aftermath of that war sent his hackles rising.

Gwen had made it around the house. Her bare feet were unfazed by the freezing ground she walked on as she went closer to the green barn that held the humans and children. The wards from the Sha seemed to repel her back, as he clearly saw her trying to push closer and then stumble backward. It provided him enough time to get close to her, but just as he was about to jump, going for her arm, she raised the blade that was coated in his blood, halting him in his tracks.

"You will not touch me, wolf," she hissed, turning to face him. "This blood and the pain I gained from it is all I need to make you my slave, Shane Keenan. Your wolves would fall prey to mine in an instant. Give me Victoria and all of this will go away. Like she never was," she said, twisting the knife in her hands.

Shane stood not halted by the magic she possessed, but in contemplation. She and her coven could overtake the minds of Weres, but with every spell it took some type of ritual. An incantation was needed to put its effects in place. He thought he might have time and speed on his side, but just as he put those pieces together, they had begun.

Take us to her, came many voices now, flooding his mind.

Take us to her, they continued, making him cringe as their words echoed and throbbed like spidery tendrils clawing their way through his memories. Shane tried holding it back, pushing his knowledge of where Vee was away from his mind, but it only brought it more to the forefront. Gwen's eyes snapped up, making her turn toward the red barn that was much further away, barely a smudge against the dark landscape of the property.

"She's there, Cormac," Gwen said, pointing to the red barn where Vee had made her escape. It was then that Shane noticed the tall red-haired watcher on the roof of the house. His coat glamor was gone, showing of his expansive black wings in the glow of the moon. His eyes shined a vibrant red as he turned to look upon the darkened and seemingly abandoned barn.

Shane could feel his control slipping. The Witches' chanting words were still ringing through his head. Now the words were unintelligible, voices overlapping and cascading over him and, he assumed, the rest of his pack. The fighting ceased, growling and howling going quiet as they slowly took control of each member. Shane steeled himself. He had no choice, no power to push away the effects of the spell that were overtaking them all. In his last moments of control, he was thankful. He knew Patrick and Lori were protected from it, safely within the warded barn with the others. They may have changed into their wolves with the moon, but within those walls they would still be in control of themselves.

With one final howl breaking from his lips, Shane was no longer his own wolf.

CHAPTER 22

Vee's heart beat wildly in her chest. The pain of loss still burning there. She heard the fighting in the distance. The regret she felt for any members who were injured or killed because of her tore at her even more. She looked at Durran who stood at the door, her wings' glamor gone, in fact all her glamor had dissolved. Vee finally saw their true form.

Durran stood tall, lean, and graceful toward the front of the barn, their wings cascading at their back like a fountain of beautiful, glistening black feathers. Their hair was the same, short and messy black locks that contrasted to the pale white of their skin, which seemed to have a slight glow to it in the darkened space. The only clothes they wore were leather-like strips crossing across their chest and pants with a long silver sword at their right hip. They were beautiful.

CHAPTER 22

"It's gone… he's gone…" Vee whimpered hoarsely, tears escaping her eyes. Durran turned to her, red eyes taking in her disheveled appearance. The knees of her pants were muddy, her hands scraped and bleeding from the force of being thrown by the bond-breaking spell. The tortured look on her face was only made more haunting by the glow of her amber eyes.

"I know," Durran murmured, trying not to feel pleased about the bond being broken. Any pain that Vee felt made Durran unhappy, and the bond being broken only put her in greater jeopardy. They should have known that the Witch would break the bond immediately with Ethan's tip off. Gwen had to have known it was the only way to get to Vee. The bond would have prevented the dark magic of the ritual that Gwen was planning.

The only thing Durran could think to do was move closer, kneeling before Vee and wrapping their arms around her. Vee hugged them back tightly, her breath hitching as she tried to get ahold of herself. She couldn't fall apart. This wasn't over yet.

After a moment, Vee managed to calm herself. They both remained still and silent, listening to the commotion outside in the distance. Vee wished she could go out and help them, but she felt powerless in this body. She had the source of magic this Witch wanted to possess, yet she had nothing of value to offer to even protect herself, let alone the Weres that she felt certain were dying for her.

But the fighting seemed to quiet, making Vee look at Durran with an odd sort of intensity. Were they all dead? Why had the fighting stopped?

"Durran!" came Cormac's singsong voice from outside of the barn. They both stiffened at the sound. Vee could feel the void of his presence getting closer. "I know you're in there, protecting your little pet."

Vee and Durran both stood. Vee remained firmly planted, but Durran moved a few paces closer to the door. Vee could tell the idea of Cormac being Durran's enemy was troublesome to them. The mark of broken trust. An agony of loss. She should have talked to Durran about Cormac sooner.

"Can he breach the ward?" Vee asked in a whisper quiet enough that only Durran would be able to hear. Durran's face grew grim.

"I don't know," Durran said honestly, fear penetrating the other feelings swirling through them.

"Just bring her out. You can tell by now, there's no use. Gwen will get what she wants from her one way or another. I'd rather not have to hurt you," Cormac said, so close now his voice seemed to be right outside the barn doors.

"Why are you doing this, Cormac?" Durran asked, quietly and pained. Cormac clicked his tongue audibly; they could hear his footfalls outside as he paced before the door.

"You sent me digging into what she is. Didn't want to overwhelm your poor sweet Vee, with the unknown *pain* of her past, did you?" Cormac asked tersely, but it was more of a statement.

"I wouldn't have, had I known..." Durran started.

"If you would have known, what? That your love for this creature would disgust me this way?" Cormac snapped, his voice little more than a growl as he said it.

"It's normal for us to develop a close bond with our wards, Cormac. You should know that!" Durran yelled back.

"What you feel for her is more than just a *close bond*. I could see it in your eyes. You *love* her," Cormac said with disgust.

Vee's eyes widened as Durran turned their red ones to look upon her. What Cormac was saying was true. Durran loved her. She could feel it now, radiating off of them. The revelation sent Vee spiraling.

How many times had she felt that twinge from Durran? How many times had they hugged or looked into each other's eyes, and she saw it there? She had dismissed it every time. Vee had dismissed her. No wonder she felt the jealousy oozing from Durran each time Vee even spoke of Shane. And yet, despite Vee choosing Shane, loving Shane, Durran was still there. They were still fighting for her.

"I do," Durran said, their voice heavy. "But that still doesn't explain why you'd do this. What does my love for her have to do with *you*?" Durran questioned, tearing their eyes from Vee's and glaring at the door of the barn.

"Because *I love you*," Cormac hissed. Vee felt the jealously coming from the Watcher outside before he had said it. "I decided, when you set me on that little task for you—no, for *her*—that I would use what I found to win you. To take you away from her. I realized that it would take more than that, especially when I came across a Were who had known her before."

A shiver ran down Vee's spine as he said those words. There were only two Weres who had known her and what she could do from her past.

"What did you do with them?" Vee asked in a hoarse whisper, unable to keep the words from escaping her lips.

"Oh, they're here with us tonight, along with the whole St. Louis pack. They've all come to help us, Vee," Cormac said, chuckling sinisterly. That meant it had to be Jack. Bea had been a Werecougar.

"How did you meet Gwen Tallon?" Durran asked, eyes narrowing.

"She had been curious about Vee for years. Her daughter had also known Vee, funny enough. She regretted killing her daughter so hastily years ago without fully discovering more," Cormac told them, resuming his pacing. Vee's breath caught. Talia, her White Witch friend from years ago was dead. What she and the other two had suspected when she disappeared was true; she was captured and killed by her own mother.

"But how did you meet her?" Durran repeated, hands curling into fists.

"She sought me out, actually. Like she knew what I was searching for," Cormac told them.

As Cormac said those words, Vee could feel Gwen's presence getting closer. She could feel a hundred minds moving toward them, including Shane's. His presence was different. The buzz she felt in her mind from him was more disjointed than it normally was. She knew, feeling his internal struggle, how hard he was fighting.

Despite moving calmly, ever closer, she knew he was trapped within his own body. He was in Gwen's control.

"Enough story time, Cormac," came Gwen's voice as she approached, Shane at her side. "I think it's all very simple. Victoria, you have power that I want. You will give it to me, or they all die."

"What good would it do you? It's rarely worth-while," Vee said, staring at the door as if she could see the Witch on the other side.

"It doesn't matter what I want with it. You don't deserve to have that magic coursing through your veins," Gwen hissed. "I'll say it again. Come out and give yourself over, or they all die."

As she said those words, every Were there, Westport pack or not, was suddenly in overwhelming pain. The pain flowed from them, crashing into her with such force she nearly fell back. Shane's pain was the worst. She heard a howl rip from him so intensely, she sobbed. She turned her eyes to Durran. Durran knew what she planned the moment they looked at her.

"No, Vee. You can't go out there!" they said, eyes blazing with anger and sadness.

"I can't let them die," she said, walking painfully to the door. She couldn't let her friends, the pack, Shane, die for her. The struggle to let the whole pack go to battle for her had been hard enough to cope with, but the feeling of their torment within her head solidified what she needed to do.

With only a brief moment of hesitation as she touched the handle of the barn door, she pulled it open to see the strange scene before her. There stood Cormac. They were in their true form, wings outstretched and

eyes deadly. Their red locks seemed more vibrant, matching the glow of their eyes. A little semi-circle had formed around the entrance of the barn. Gwen was directly in the center with Shane writhing in pain at her feet. His powerful wolf form reduced to a twitching, shaking creature on the ground as she inflicted this curse upon him.

Other Witches were strategically placed evenly around the circle as well. The wolves beside and behind them were also writhing in the insurmountable pain being inflicted upon them. Vee set her eyes across from her at Gwen. She looked so much like Talia had. Her hair was wild and curly as it framed her upper half, like a mane, but her eyes were murderous as they looked into Vee's. Now that she knew she was Talia's mother, she was shocked she hadn't seen it before. Perhaps that was part of the reason she had been more apt to help this woman instead of shying away from her the moment she realized she was a Witch. Gwen had been hiding in plain sight, watching, waiting, and pursuing Vee for the better part of nine months. Or almost eleven years, if Cormac's words held any truth.

"What could I possibly have that would be of use to you, Gwen?" Vee asked, stepping out of the threshold of the barn. Durran followed her out, knowing there was no way to stop her. They knew there was no way to convince Vee to remain protected. They had seen the determination on her face. Options were spent. The barn was surrounded.

Gwen laughed, high and manically.

"You *still* don't know what you are? You are a cross breed. I could tell by what Talia said about you all those

years ago, but I wasn't sure until I met you. It's the only way you could possibly possess the abilities you have. The magic within you is in perfect harmony. More perfect than mine and more powerful if you knew how to wield it. You don't *deserve* it," she said, her lips curling.

"And you do?" Vee asked, causing Gwen's face to twist into a sinister scowl.

"I've worked for years to hone my craft, perfecting my skills. I built my power. You don't even know what you have within you. You haven't even *tried* to wield the power you possess."

Before Vee could even fully comprehend what Gwen had said the other Witches surrounding them began chanting, their voices low and rough, speaking ancient words fueled by greed and hatred. Vee chanced looking away from Gwen to glance over at all of them. Some were young with wide naive eyes that showed more fear than confidence, while others were older, their own sick greed seeping from them as they glared at Vee hungrily. She recognized the Witch she had seen at the gas pump on the way to the property. At least Vee hadn't overreacted when she and Shane raced away and lost her.

Gwen stepped forward, bringing Vee's attention back to her. Her chest rising and falling in time with the other Witches' rhythmic chanting. She wiped the blade in her hand on her skirt, ridding it of Shane's blood, as she moved more toward the empty center, closer to Vee. Vee could feel the crackling energy of the magic as it started spilling from the Witches' mouths, heading not to her but to Gwen. They were imbuing her with the magic. It was the power she needed to steal Vee's.

Durran had heard this chant before, seen this ritual play out. Their stomach lurched, knowing what was about to happen. They began to reach out to pull Vee away. If they could just get her far enough from the coven, from Gwen, Vee would be safe. They knew Vee would hate them forever if they did it, since it would mean a death sentence to all who were left in their wake, but they couldn't sit idly and watch as her soul was ripped from her body.

Just as they were about to grab her, Cormac's blade swung down, nearly cutting off Durran's hand. Durran stepped back, shocked, looking over at their friend, whose eyes burned with greed.

"Just stay out of it, Durran. Everyone will be better off when she's gone," Cormac said, brandishing their sword toward them. Durran pulled their own sword from the sheath.

"You know I can't," Durran said coldly. Cormac flew into the air, prompting Durran to follow, their swords clashed in the night sky, silhouetting them in the light of the full moon.

"No one to protect you now," Gwen said, grinning widely as she stepped closer to Vee.

The chanting continued, echoing off the barn and seemed to surround her as the magic continued to funnel into Gwen, a strange ethereal glow pulsing around her. She took in a deep breath, letting the power settle into her. Raising her hand with the dagger, she brought it down and seemed to puncture the air between them.

The point of the dagger's blade stopped suddenly with her stabbing stroke as if it hit an invisible wall. Vee felt a tearing at her chest like the flesh was being torn open just above her sternum, though when she looked down there was nothing there. No exposed flesh, no blood. It was almost as excruciating as when the bond was been torn from her body. So many emotions were buzzing. Humming. Throbbing. Eliza... the magic... the moon... pain. Vee's head might have exploded at the pressure of it all, but her eyes fell on Shane's writhing body once again. His eyes were hazy with the spell that held him captive there, and she knew she couldn't just *let* this Witch have what she wanted.

Vee took everything she was feeling. She took her own pain and the emotions of everyone around her, bringing it all within herself, tears falling from her eyes with the force of it. Gwen looked confused as the tear in the air seemed to shrink a little as Vee's body pulsed and throbbed, the magic within her growing. Gwen pushed harder with the dagger, trying to slash the air open so she could reach her hand in. As soon as she did, Vee's eyes snapped open, her body lifting just slightly off the ground as everything seemed to stop.

"What are you..." Gwen started to ask, having no idea how Vee was managing to resist this, but she was cut short when Vee opened her mouth and started to scream.

Her voice was like a sonic boom, rippling from her lips and sending everyone in the vicinity flying backward. It didn't sound like any noise Vee had ever made before. It was like a mix between an inhuman roar and ear-splitting ringing. Every hint of the magic

surrounding Gwen shattered around her and dissipated like dust in the wind. For a moment, everything was quiet and still. Durran and Cormac had been thrown to the ground with the force of Vee's voice, and every Witch was several hundred feet further away from where they had been, crumpled on the ground.

CHAPTER 23

Vee fell the few feet she had risen into the air. Her knees buckled and gave out, causing her to go down onto her hands and knees. She was shaking, her breath coming in unevenly as she tried to steady herself. The feeling around them seemed almost normal again. The magic that had permeated the air dissipated with the force of Vee's scream.

Shane was the first to move, slowly pulling himself up, his injured back leg dragging slightly as he hobbled over to Vee. He pushed his nose under her chin causing her to lift her head and look into his eyes. Even without the bond he could see what she felt; fear, shock, amazement, relief. Her eyes glistened with tears as she struggled, exhausted, to lift her hands from the ground and touch the fur on his cheek.

"No!" Cormac screamed, scrambling to their feet and taking only moments to dash the hundred feet or so to where Vee and Shane were in the grass before the barn.

Cormac raised the sword over their head, preparing to bring it down on Vee's neck to finally rid themself of her, when they heard the unmistakable sound of a blade running through flesh. There was no flash of movement to indicate what had happened, only that Durran was suddenly there, their own sword stretched out in their hand, now dripping with deep purple tinged blood. Cormac's mouth opened and closed for a moment, eyes wide with shock. A strange gurgling sound came from their lips as they stumbled back, turning their body to take one final look at Durran's face.

Durran looked frightening. Eyes cold and deadly as they burned bright red, glaring at Cormac. Their mouth was set in a grim line. There were no words to say as they looked upon their former friend with an expression that was complete and utter hatred. Cormac tried to say something, lips moving soundlessly as their hand outstretched to graze Durran's cheek, before their head slid from their neck, tumbling to the ground followed shortly by their limp body.

The other Werewolves finally began to stir, both Westport and the other pack's members seeming to shake themselves of the spell they had been under. Menacing growls and fighting started to ring out as Shane's wolves took the upper hand on both the bewildered Witches and the other Weres.

Durran knelt beside Vee and Shane. Their eyes bright as they looked both of them over; it was as if a mask slid perfectly in place of the frightening one Vee had seen just moments before. A mask also trying to restrain the pain of just beheading their oldest friend.

"We should get her out of here," Durran said to Shane, moving to pick Vee up from where she remained. She couldn't move. She had spent the last of her energy. Shane stared at the Watcher as she lifted Vee from the ground. He wasn't happy about it, but he knew even in his human form he would have difficulty taking her with the state of his leg. Thomas's wolf approached him. His coat looked fully black with dirt, hiding the red patches and the lack of light. His blue wolf eyes meeting Shane's golden ones as if to ask permission to lick the wound that was still bleeding rather profusely.

Thomas had barely started when Gwen managed to begin stirring. Her appearance had a much less ethereal look to it, now that she had been stripped of her power. Vee's scream had completely obliterated all the magic she had ever stolen from any other being. This left her older looking and quite a bit weaker. Thomas's wolf immediately jumped on her, his paw breaking the arm that held the dagger, causing her to scream out in pain.

Shane began to change back into his human form, pulling on the power of the moon to make it smooth and quick, despite his exhaustion. He stood tall and brooding over her after a few minutes, his second in command still pinning her to the ground. He stretched his neck, vertebrae cracking, before he took in a deep breath and moved over to Gwen's sprawled form. He showed no outward signs of pain or weakness, his strong body moving smoothly, his breath even and slow.

"You've committed crimes against the preternatural community for what you've done, Gwen Tallon," Shane said, his voice booming and echoing over the clearing. Some of the fighting wolves stopped at the authority in his voice.

"Breaking a bond isn't a crime against the whole community," she hissed painfully, her eyes still menacing.

"Hunting and intending to kill a preternatural is. Using your abilities to cause harm and death to others is. You are a disgrace," he spat.

"*She* is a disgrace! She doesn't deserve to wield such power!" she screamed, writhing under Thomas's claws. He sank them into her, the smell of her blood hitting the air, causing Shane to growl. His wolf wanted to rip her apart, to taste her blood on his tongue until he knew with satisfaction, that she was cold and dead by his fangs. He couldn't give in to those desires, not the man, the leader, or Vee's mate.

"You are quite the hypocrite, Miss Tallon. I can smell the Fae in your blood," he whispered instead, leaning down to look more closely in her eyes. She winced slightly at the wolf that looked back at her, eyes glowing with golden rage.

"The Fae in us brings us closer to the magics. Passed through blood, just as the Witch was. It *gave* me the ability to take from the undeserving." Shane looked at her with a mixture of hatred and pity. She truly believed what she said.

"You don't deserve to live," Shane growled. His words were all it took for Thomas to attack her throat, ripping it out with his teeth and leaving her trying to gasp and breathe. Her blood pooled around her head, saturating her mane of hair. He clenched his fists, unsatisfied it hadn't been him, but content the deed was done. This Witch was no more, and the world was better for it.

Durran still stood, holding Vee only a few paces away. Shane limped over to them, taking her hand in his.

"It's over now. Take her in the house?" Shane asked, looking at Durran, his eyes pleading. They both had her best interests at heart. Their animosity could wait until things were more settled. For now, Shane could again relinquish her care to Durran, so he could deal with the remaining intruders. Durran nodded, taking two steps before extending their wings and flying back to the house in the distance.

Another wolf began to change to its human form a good twenty feet from Shane. The power surged, pulling from the moon and the air around him like only another leader could. Shane recognized him. The St. Louis pack leader. A few of the wolves from both packs were still fighting amongst themselves, the sounds of deep growls and howls of pain as they fought ringing out around them.

"Shane!" he called, his voice strained as he dodged wolves, trying to get to the cleared place where Shane stood.

"What is this, Dante?" Shane spat, his fury emanating from him as he glared at the other pack leader approaching him.

"Where are we?" Dante asked, slowing his approach as he realized how angry Shane was.

"You came with this Witch," Shane said, gesturing to the corpse beside him that was once Gwen Tallon.

Dante stared down at the pale form of Gwen, his eyes wide with recognition, before he collected himself. His eyes darted back to Shane's who had been watching him intently.

"Wolves!" Dante yelled, getting the attention of every St. Louis pack member, causing the fighting to cease, the occasional growl still here and there. Shane glared at him, still signaling for his wolves to be ready. He didn't trust this pack leader as far as he could throw him in normal times, let alone after what had occurred here.

"What are you doing getting involved with Black Witches like this?" Shane growled, eyes burning as they bore into Dante's. Not for one moment did Shane believe he was truly ignorant of this entire plot. In fact, it reeked of him. Dante's wolves may have been entranced by the coven's spell, but Shane imagined they drove themselves here on *his* orders.

"Other than knowing she's the most prominent coven leader in Missouri, I didn't know of her before tonight," Dante said, trying his best to be sincere. Shane knew that those words were lies. Gwen had come from St. Louis, after all. There was no way Dante wouldn't have known her before this.

Shane stood before him, glowering. Both leaders' power was equally matched, but only because Shane was injured for the time being. If Dante wanted to, he could have taken Shane in battle for territory. They both knew it, but Shane saw the flash of realization come over him as he recalled the little that he could about Vee's abilities behind the enchantment they had been under. Shane had Vee at his disposal on top of being more powerful and having a larger pack.

"I want you off my property before sunrise. Collect yourselves and leave," Shane told him, his voice unwavering as he stared the other pack leader down. Dante nodded his head, backing away and quickly beginning to herd his pack back toward the entrance of the property. The sounds of their run through the property thundered until it faded into the distance, but one wolf remained, eyes on Shane.

He began to change. It was more laborious than it should have been for a wolf as old as this one clearly was. He was not a new wolf. As the minutes ticked by Shane could see the abundant scars that littered his skin. It was very hard to permanently scar a Were. These scars were from torture.

"Is Vee..." He paused to gasp, still cringing through the last of his change. "Will she be okay?" the man asked, his eyes showing the pain and regret he felt for everything that had transpired. The croak of his voice was not just from strain but concern. Shane looked at him quizzically for a moment, trying to determine how this person would know Vee. Why would he be so concerned for her?

"You're one of the Weres from when she was young?" Shane asked, taking a stab in the dark.

"Jack," he said, nodding. He was the one. The one who had given up information on Vee, but it wasn't out of hatred or distain. He was tortured for it, most likely by his own leader. Shane's heart ached to see the scars, to see how broken this man was that stood before him.

"She will be fine. I'll make sure of it," Shane told him. Jack seemed to gasp and shudder in relief, nodding again as a silent 'thank you' to Shane before he slowly turned back into his wolf, following where his pack had left moments before. Had there been more time, Shane would have inquired more, perhaps tried to convince Jack to join them, but there were other things to take care of now.

That just left the remaining Witches, all of whom were frozen, frightened on the ground where they had been thrown. It was clear by the looks on their faces that none of them had expected to fail. Shane walked to the one nearest to him. His limp, which he no longer cared or had energy to hide, not taking away from the impressive dominance that radiated from him.

"Do you know the penalty for what you have all done, Witch?" Shane growled, glaring down at the woman before him. She was older than most of the others, but he could smell the Fae in her too. She was the closest to Gwen, the most powerful other than Gwen had been herself, and he recognized her from the gas pump the evening before. Her eyes fell to her former leader's body, whose face was turned toward her, a silent scream stuck on her frozen, lifeless face.

"We were just following orders! She would have killed us if we didn't comply!" the woman screamed, tears falling from her face as she looked up at Shane. That was certainly true of some of these young Witches but not her. He could tell she was very willing to participate. There had been hunger in her eyes, and her heart was beating erratically as the lie spewed from her lips. He sighed as his eyes grazed over the other crying Witches, all of whom reeked of fear and anguish.

"If you want to live, you'll do a blood oath between one another now. None of you will practice these forbidden magics again. They have been banned for a reason." The Witch before him gulped loudly as she sat up, looking around at her counterparts and silently begging them all to do as the pack leader said.

They all crawled toward one another, each of them drained of their magic and exhausted but desperate to escape this situation with their lives. The dagger that Gwen had used was collected, and one by one they all cut their palms, hissing with pain as their blood started flowing freely. The pack watched silently as they all spoke the words of the oath, vowing as their hands met together that they would never touch forbidden magics again.

Even with the oath in place, Shane still had them followed off the property by a few of the wolves who hadn't been injured. It was time to assess the damage of what this night wrought. It seemed like no one was dead. There were a few major broken bones that were being set by the Weres who had already changed back before being carried off to the building where they were staying. Thomas went to the green barn as soon as they got close to the house again, hastily changing into his human form as quickly as he could and ripping the doors open. Cora was immediately there, embracing him and crying.

"Is everyone okay in here?" he asked, his voice hoarse with emotion and the quick change, as he clung to his wife. Normally Cora shied away from the dirt and filth that came along with them running as wolves, but she didn't hesitate to embrace him back, the blood still coating him from his chin to his chest, sticking to her blond hair.

"We're all fine. Lori and Patrick were ready," Cora said tearfully, pulling away to look at the two young wolves flanking the entrance of the barn. Not only had they protected the families, but they had controlled their own wolves throughout the whole crisis.

The rest of the families of the pack members came flooding out around them, rushing to their wolves who eagerly awaited them, injured or not. Several ran past everyone to go to their designated houses for their more injured kin. Patrick ran to Shane, giving a brief lick to his father's still injured leg, and then glanced around. He was looking for Vee.

"She's already in the house," Shane told him, gesturing for them to go inside to see her. Patrick's eagerness was only surpassed by Shane's, as he still felt the painful void where the bond once was within him. It was well into the early morning hours, not long from when he and Vee had formed the bond just the night before. He went to snatch his clothes from where he had left them in the gravel driveway, putting them on before he went inside.

Durran was sitting on the coffee table, still unglamored, but with their wings folded against their back. Their eyes were strictly trained on Vee with a measure of deep concern. Vee was lying on one of the couches, awake, but utterly exhausted. Her eyes did light up a bit when Shane and Patrick came in. Patrick's wolf excitedly came up to Vee, licking her face. She could feel Patrick's concern but also relief to see her alive.

"I'll be okay, Patrick," she whispered, her voice nearly gone as she batted him away and tried to wipe her face. He looked briefly at his dad, a wolfish grin on his face, before racing through the house, she assumed to change and get dressed again. Vee turned her attention to Shane. "How's your leg?" she asked, eyes grazing over where she knew his wound was, obscured by his pant leg which was now soaked with blood. He limped over to her, sitting beside her on the couch.

"Thomas cleaned it a little for me. I'll be okay soon," he told her, reaching to touch her face. The skin contact felt comforting, in lieu of the bond.

"She should sleep," Durran said, still feeling uncomfortable as they watched the exchange between the two on the couch.

"Yes," Shane said, pulling her into his arms. "If you sleep, Watcher, there are plenty of rooms here," Shane told Durran as he stood, cradling Vee.

"I'll keep watch," Durran told him, nodding in thanks as she changed back into her female form. The changes shimmering and smoothly sliding over their body until it was as if nothing had changed about her at all. Durran nodded once more, locking eyes with Vee who smiled weakly at her, before heading back out the door to stand guard on the porch.

Shane didn't wait for Durran to exit before he moved through the house. Patrick, even though he had changed back into his human form and dressed, knew that now wasn't the time to interrupt his dad, as he watched him come up the stairs, eyes only on Vee.

They went into the room, and Shane slowly set Vee on the bed, the sheets and blanket still disheveled from earlier that morning. She slowly sat up, trying to pull Shane's sweatshirt over her head, but it was a struggle. Who would have thought that using so much of her ability would make her physically ache?

Shane continued, untying and pulling off her shoes just before removing his own clothes and replacing them with his discarded sweatpants from the night before. All he wanted to do was hold her. He had to slow every movement to keep himself from accidentally hurting her. He crawled into the bed, pulling her closer to him, pressing their noses together.

"I thought I lost you," Vee whispered as her eyes drifted closed.

"You didn't. I'm here. Sleep," he whispered back, kissing her forehead.

CHAPTER 24

S hane woke with a start, having heard a crashing
sound from somewhere in the house. It was still
early morning. The sun was just barely coming up,
but they had all gone to bed in the wee hours of the
morning. He unfurled himself from Vee carefully, so
as not to wake her. He left the room and was con-
fronted by Patrick, who seemed to have also woken
to the sound.

"It's Ethan," Patrick said quietly. Shane nodded,
having come to that realization too. They made their
way down together, Durran coming through the front
door as they got to the basement door.

"It seems to be clear now," Durran said, eyeing the
father and son with skepticism as they opened the door
to the basement.

"We have to deal with Ethan," Shane murmured. Durran's eyebrows shot up, not expecting Ethan to still be on the property. It had been chaotic, and she assumed Ethan had used the fight to escape. Apparently not.

The three descended the stairs together, finding Ethan still partially strapped to the chair, which was now on its side. He looked up at them, eyes burning with anger.

"You must have forgotten about me," he said, a scowl coming over his face as he tried to untie the last thing binding him to the furniture.

"Didn't forget. Just couldn't deal with you until we had some rest. Now you've rudely interrupted my sleep," Shane said, moving closer to help him get free from the knot.

"So, I suppose everything has worked out for you, then?" Ethan grumbled.

Shane paused, eyes narrowing as he ripped the rope from Ethan and the chair roughly, not caring if he left rope burns. Ethan hissed mildly at the momentary pain.

"She's alive, if that's what you mean," Shane growled, stepping back to be next to Patrick once again.

"You know this is wrong, don't you Patrick?" Ethan asked, snatching his clothes from the ground and glaring at Shane as he started to put them on.

"What? That Dad might finally be happy? Or that a woman, who isn't a Werewolf, probably just saved the whole pack?" Patrick asked, his anger evident by his tone and stance. A little pride bubbled in Shane as Patrick snapped back at his brother. Ethan's eyebrows shot up in surprise. For whatever reason, he thought Patrick would be on his side.

"Really, brother?" Ethan whispered in question, his voice letting on his shock.

"She's pack," Patrick said definitively, crossing his arms.

"And you have made it very clear that you don't want to be," Shane said in a gruff voice, mixed with sadness and anger.

"I don't understand you," Ethan said coldly to Shane. "You allow yourself to align with other preternaturals and humans. This pack was better off when O'Neil was the leader," he continued, gesturing to Durran who stood silently by the stairs. Shane's eyes glowed a bit more vibrantly at those words.

"O'Neil betrayed this pack and its members, time and time again. He's the reason your mother is dead," Shane growled.

"O'Neil had principles."

"And what of the Sha? They have worked tirelessly for harmony amongst the preternaturals. You don't think that warrants building alliances?" Shane asked. Durran was surprised. Shane wasn't just talking about Vee; he considered Durran an ally now too.

"It will never amount to real harmony. Mixing preternaturals will never work," Ethan said, lacing up his shoes. They all were quiet as Ethan finished putting on his boots and headed up the stairs. "So, am I banished?" he asked, pausing halfway up, his heart aching a little. He was a lone wolf, but the pack was his home. This pack. The idea of being banished wounded him deeper than he showed on the surface. His previous punishment from the Sha last summer meant this was

the only place he could go if he were to run with other Werewolves on the full moon.

Shane sighed, looking at his son. He had made mistakes with his firstborn, things he now regretted deeply, but he had done the best he could at the time. His love for him would never leave him, no matter how flawed his opinions were. He walked to meet Ethan on the stairs, looking up at him with a mournful expression.

"I won't banish you, despite what you've done, but I want you to really *think* about why you feel this way. Your punishment from the Sha still holds. I don't want you back for a run for six months. You run alone until then," Shane told him.

Shane, Patrick, and Durran followed him outside, watching as he climbed on his motorcycle that was parked against the porch, revving it loudly, before driving down the gravel road, into the trees, and out of sight.

Vee woke to the sound of the shower running. She kept her eyes closed for a moment, trying to see if she could recall the previous night's events clearly. Had it all really happened? She opened her eyes to stare at the ceiling above her, the wood beams casting shadows as the sunlight poured in from the windows behind her. She could feel the buzz of quite a few Weres on the floor below, something that, much to her surprise, no longer felt like an irritation at all.

She could tell by the way the sun was coming in it was well past eleven. She went to sit up, becoming aware of the soreness that was still lingering over her body more acutely with the movements. It wasn't nearly as bad as the night before, but a hindrance, nonetheless. She glanced toward the bathroom, noticing there was a mug full of coffee set on the bedside table for her, still steaming as if Shane had placed it there moments before. She moved to sit up, her body protesting it, but she pushed through, determined to get to the delicious roasted elixir.

The water shut off in the bathroom, just as she took her first sip. The door opened a moment later, Shane walking out into the bedroom in a towel.

"You're awake," he said with a smile.

"You brought me coffee," she murmured back, lips still settled on the mug, ready to take another sip.

"I didn't want to wake you, and I thought you might need a little time before you were surrounded by people again," Shane said, moving over to his bags on the floor.

"I appreciate that," she said, watching him as he nonchalantly pulled the towel from his waist, moving to dress himself. She had seen this man naked more times than she ever thought she would in the last few days, and somehow it still made her titillated. She tried to push the feeling aside, considering she was disgustingly filthy and sore all over. Shane, of course, noticed her change in heartbeat and glanced over at her as he pulled up his pants. She tore her eyes from him, taking another sip as she moved to stand up.

"I think I'll take a shower, unless you used all the hot water," she murmured.

"There's still plenty," he said, deciding to move back over to her instead of don his shirt. He went to pull her into his arms, but she held up her hand.

"You just got clean and I'm…" she gestured down to her dirt-streaked clothes.

"I can help you," he said, watching her wince as she moved toward the bathroom door.

"I'll manage," she said, giving him a small smile before she ducked into the room, closing the door with a snap.

She felt him move about the room a bit, pacing as she stepped into the water. He was worried, that was evident, but he was also feeling the same anxiousness he felt before when they were trying to discuss their feelings for one another.

It wasn't that Vee didn't want him because she most certainly did. It was more that the claim had previously been made from necessity, for her protection, and less out of his actual desire for her. She knew he wanted it again. She still felt painfully lacking without the bond there, only feeling slightly better when they touched. It was quite the predicament she found herself in. She now had to face if she was ready to make that commitment with Shane but fully of her own volition. Not out of a need for protection, but because she wanted to be with him, and him with her.

She stepped out of the warm water, her muscles feeling more soothed from the heat than they previously had been, and she wrapped herself in a towel, much like Shane had. She moved back out to the bedroom where he still stood, having stopped his pacing when she turned the water off.

"Would you mind grabbing my bag?" she asked, still not feeling quite strong enough to lift it from the ground. He did, putting it on the bed before her.

"Vee, I…" he started, but as usual, there was a knock at the door, interrupting him. He sighed, closing his eyes and rubbing his forehead.

"Yes?"

"Um… is Vee awake?" came Lori's voice from the other side of the door. Vee smiled a little, looking down at her bag. The timing of these intrusions always seemed impeccable.

"We'll be down in a minute, Lori," Shane said, also unable to hide the smirk from his lips.

"Our track record remains unchanged," she said, pulling out a wrinkled grey shirt and pants from the bag.

"We don't seem to have much uninterrupted time," he agreed, turning away to grab his own coffee, which he had set on top of one of the unused dressers. Vee let the towel drop, being certain not to look at Shane as she pulled her clothes on. Her hands were still scraped and her body bruised from when she had been thrown to the ground from the blast of the bond-breaking spell. She was sure she looked horrendous and not at all appealing as his body had looked to her.

Shane looked at her with a mixture of desire and pain. Her naked body made his pulse immediately quicken but seeing it covered in bruises made him realize how fragile her form was. Seeing the signs of how much less resilient she was than him both made him worry about how she would survive now that she was out to the preternatural community and brought out a deep need to protect her.

She finally let their eyes meet across the room once she had finished dressing. "Let's not keep them waiting," Vee said, moving to the foot of the bed and reaching her hand out to him. The small bit of reassurance she felt from him at the gesture warmed her.

They made their way down, moving into the kitchen which was flooded with activity. Vee briefly wondered where Durran had gone but realized once the Witches and the St. Louis pack had left, Durran would have made their exit. They also weren't one for crowds. Cora was busily ordering people around, sending off dishes of food to be passed for serving. Vee had always known she liked this woman but was even more impressed with her as she watched her snapping and barking orders at a bunch of Werewolves.

"Oh good! Vee's awake," Cora said, her eyes sparkling excitedly when they fell upon the two of them in the doorway of the kitchen.

A chorus of "Vee!" rang out through the house causing her to blush.

"I couldn't sway them. They insisted on a celebration," Shane whispered in her ear, noticing the redness flooding her cheeks and the way her hand tightened in his.

"You couldn't have warned me?" she grumbled.

"Lori was very insistent on it being a surprise," he said, chuckling a little.

Vee was ushered into the dining room by Lori and was forced to let go of Shane's hand as they squeezed through the sea of bodies that had all somehow packed into the house. She supposed the house was designed for this, to hold the whole pack and their families, but to have so many people in one place was quite a bit more than Vee ever thought she'd have to deal with. She seemed to quickly get over it, enjoying herself as she talked and ate with the pack.

"Tell me everything that happened. No one's given us the full story yet," Lori finally said after a few hours. Vee looked at Shane, who was far at the other side of the table as the whole house seemed to quiet at Lori's question. No one present but her really knew exactly what happened, she figured, not having been enchanted or cursed.

"How much do you know?" Vee decided to ask, watching Shane's eyes, trying to see how he felt before she told the whole pack they were no longer bonded. He looked back at her, longing settling in his dark brown orbs.

Several of them piped up, mentioning the mist, being frozen in place, the feeling of being enslaved by Gwen's spell, and the horrific pain that she inflicted on them.

"It was so strange. I was moving my body, but not able to control where it was going or what I was doing. I could see, but I could barely remember what happened until…"Tommy trailed off, the human companions and children all leaning forward, engrossed in the tale as it had been told so far. Vee sighed and leaned back in her chair, bringing all the eyes on her.

"Well, first I have to tell you what happened when you were all frozen, how Shane's leg was so badly injured," she said, looking over at him again. She told them about the spell and the bond being broken. They all collectively shivered at the way she described it being ripped from her, leaving her feeling as though there was a void where it should have been. Shane merely nodded solemnly as some of them turned to see if that's how it felt for him too.

"But you can get it back, right?" Lori asked, her voice strangled with empathetic sorrow. Vee's eyebrows shot up. For some reason she never even considered it not being possible to put back in place, but now that Lori mentioned it, her fear that it couldn't took over any previous trepidation she felt. All eyes fell on Shane, who rubbed his forehead anxiously.

"I don't know," he murmured honestly. A gasp went through the room, deep sadness surrounding Vee from all sides. They were all silent, taking that in. The unknown of it, far more disheartening to Vee than it had been to simply be conflicted.

"So, what happened after that?" Emily asked, pulling them all from that moment of despair.

"The Watcher, Cormac, found the barn, but he couldn't get in. Then Gwen came with all of you enslaved." Vee sucked in a breath, thinking back to these moments with absolute clarity. "I assume she couldn't penetrate the wards on the barn either. Otherwise she wouldn't have started to... to torture all of you," she said, her voice ending in a whisper.

"She did that to draw you out?" Tommy asked, horrified, the napkin he had been twisting anxiously in his hands ripping slightly.

"She did. I couldn't let you all die for me," she said, eyes welling with the memory of the pain. Margaret reached over and took Vee's hand, increasing the flow of gratefulness Vee felt from all of them. "You all would have done the same for me. You *were* doing the same for me. I couldn't let you die," Vee said, looking into Margaret's eyes.

"But she didn't take it. Your soul," Lori said, confusion coming over her face.

"I-I don't know how to explain it," Vee said, looking down at her hands. She was trying think of how to describe something that had felt so instinctual to her somehow. The need to protect, to save the pack, her family. "I took it all in. The pain, the anger, everything I was feeling, and I somehow…"

"Pushed it back at her," Shane finished for her, eyes having turned golden.

"Yes, but it wasn't just that. I stripped her of that magic," she whispered, shocked by her own admission as she met those eyes with equal parts confusion and fear. She had no idea how she did it. She thought back to Gwen's words. She was more powerful than she knew, and she realized she had no idea what she was truly capable of.

"You saved all of us," Patrick said, pride surrounding him as he leaned against the wall behind his father.

"You did," Shane confirmed, his own pride in her welling within him.

Somehow the conversation turned back to more jovial topics, allowing Vee to slip away for a moment, heading out to the porch to breathe in some cold air. She leaned against the railing, her gaze fixed up at the setting sun as Shane joined her, closing the door on the ruckus inside.

"They've all already packed, so they'll head back once they get a good run in," Shane told her, following her eyes to look at the color-changing sky.

"Ah, yes… second night. That makes sense," Vee said with a nod, looking up at the full moon that was starting to show despite the sun's light still on the horizon. They were both quiet, taking in the last of the sunset side by side for a moment. "And are we heading back?" she decided to ask, eyes turning to look at him.

"We can, if that's what you want," he said quietly, meeting her gaze. He was holding back again, blocking her like he had been before their bond.

"What are you blocking me from, Shane?" she asked, fully turning her body to face him now. He sat against the railing, crossing his arms, and just staring at her for a moment.

"If I were to do the claim again, right now, would you take it?" he asked, not answering her question. He didn't know if it would work, but he wanted to try again. He had proposed it all to protect her, yes, but now he knew she loved him. He had revealed that he loved her, and he wanted it back more than anything.

"We don't know if that will work, do we?" she asked, her heart aching with the thought of it.

"Well, the claim should work again."

"But the bond?"

"We don't, no. But say it did. Would you want it?" He was holding his breath as he waited for the answer, watching the emotions flicker across her face too fast for him to fully read.

She took a shaky breath, realizing what he was asking her, even if he didn't seem completely sure of the implications of his question.

"Don't ask me this way," she whispered, eyes turning amber.

"What?" he asked, confused at the sad look that had settled on her face.

"Figure out a better way to ask me. A better time, a better place. Ask me then," she said, turning away from him to walk back in the house. Shane sat confounded, staring after her.

CHAPTER 25

The car ride back to the city had been strangely quiet. They had left a little after midnight, giving the Weres time to run with the moon, and have all the families get back to their homes before the morning came. Shane, Vee, and Patrick were the last ones to leave. When they arrived in Kansas City Shane pulled up to his house, making Vee anxious for a moment. Not that she wanted to be away from Shane, but she wanted to recuperate from the past few days. She needed her things, her space, to be able to do that. He shocked her when he turned to the back seat, shaking Patrick's knee to wake him.

"I'm going to take Vee home. Why don't you head up to bed," Shane said quietly, as Patrick yawned and stretched in the back of the car.

"Okay... 'night, Vee," he murmured sleepily, climbing out of the back seat of the car and trudging up to the front door.

Vee didn't say anything, despite how surprised she was as Shane drove her back to her apartment. She felt a little from him, even though he continued to block her, indicating his continued confusion about her earlier statement. She hoped he would come to the conclusion on his own. The idea of spelling it out to him was embarrassing, to say the least. Never before had she wished she could sic Lori on someone, but her blunt, blatant way of approaching things was just what Shane needed.

He parked in the spot she usually did when he pulled up to her building, turning to look at her, his brow furrowed. He was clearly still overthinking what she had said. She looked back at him, feeling like she couldn't just *tell* him what she meant.

"Did you want to come in for a minute?" she asked him, only proving to deepen his confusion. This was not something she would have suggested just days ago.

"Yes," he said, shutting the car off. They both trekked up the stairs, Vee a bit stiff with soreness and not being able to move much the last hour as they drove.

When they reached her apartment, Shane stopped her from entering after she unlocked the door and pushed it open. He smelled Witch, a little belatedly, perhaps due to his own thoughts distracting him, but he caught it before they actually entered. They both stood aghast, looking at the wreckage of her apartment from her open door. That was *not* how she and Thomas had left it when she came to grab those last few things before heading out to Pleasant Hill.

"What… I…" Vee muttered in shock, stepping in behind Shane, who moved quickly, checking around to be sure no one was lurking there.

"They must have been searching for something," Shane said, once he ensured her bedroom and bathroom were empty. Vee looked at the destruction, even her futons were torn to shreds.

"Who?" Vee shrieked, gesturing around at all her worldly possessions, demolished.

"Gwen's coven. I can smell them. They must have come here after we left," Shane said, stopping to look at her. Vee's face was twisted between anger and anguish. She had held it together for this long, but the weight of it all came crashing down on her as she looked at the destruction.

There was no way she could stay here.

No going back to her life.

She had no car. No apartment. No way to make her living.

No sister. No bond.

Nothing.

Her careful control of her own emotions had been cracked and battered over the last few days, but now it was gone. Ground to dust and blown away.

"I-I have nothing… I have nothing, now!" she choked out, eyes welling with angry tears. Shane crossed the distance between them in an instant, taking her into his arms.

"You have me," he whispered into her hair, letting her sob into his chest. Her fingers clutching and scraping across his coat.

They stood there for a long time, the two of them, just holding one another. Her crying died out, and her fingers relaxed as she listened to the thrum of his steady heart beating, feeling his love and understanding. She pulled away from him slightly, glancing up at him apologetically.

"I'm sorry," she murmured, taking a hand from his coat to wipe the tears from her cheeks.

"You don't have to be sorry, Vee," Shane said, lifting one of his hands to hold her face.

"I'm just…" She took in a ragged breath. "I'm such a mess, aren't I?" she whispered, chuckling slightly, embarrassed at her outburst.

"I told you, it's my mess now," he whispered back. Tears welled in her eyes again. The knowledge that the bond may never come back, burning in the place where it once was within her.

"Not anymore," she said before she could stop herself.

Shane looked deeply in her eyes, thinking about what she had said to him earlier that evening. She hadn't told him "no," when he asked her about the claim. She had said to do it differently. The way she said, "not anymore," so full of sorrow, clicked the pieces together for him. He wasn't sure if this was the time or place, but it didn't matter to him. He had the right words this time. He gathered her face in both his hands, thumbs swiping away the new tears that had fallen there.

"Vee, will you marry me?"

Her breath hitched in her chest; her eyes wide as she took in those words. A bit of mild amusement sprinkled over her emotions, happy that he figured out what she had meant earlier. She looked into his golden eyes and felt his unwavering love. This man would have died for her, and she for him. The commitment, though scary and different from the life she had thought she'd have, was not as frightening as not having him.

"Yes," she whispered.

Shane's face lit up with joy. He bent his head to kiss her, their lips touching, sparking between them. They hadn't kissed since their bond had been broken. It felt like the first time all over again. Their passion was building between them as they stood in the middle of the destruction of her former life. This time it was Vee to pull away, breathless.

"Wait," she murmured against his lips.

"Why?" he whispered back, not letting go of her waist.

"Claim me," she said.

Shane pulled back to look at her more fully. Her eyes were glowing with determination. He took in a deep breath, watching her. Holding her made this feel much more intimate than the first time he had claimed her. He felt the magic within him building up as he prepared to say the words.

"I claim you, Victoria Malone, as mine. My mate. All those who dare touch you shall pay penalty as dictated by me or the Sha. You are mine," Shane said. Vee watched the magic snake from his lips swirling around them as it waited for her to complete it.

"I accept your claim," Vee whispered back, the magic seeping into them for the second time. This time it felt stronger, as if the fact that they had done this, not out of necessity but out of love, made the magic more powerful.

Shane lifted her up, her legs easily circling his hips and her fingers threading through his hair. This time their kiss was not only filled with passion and love but need. They needed to touch each other. They needed the bond that had felt so right back. Shane walked them into her bedroom, not caring that her mattress was torn, and everything that had been on her dressers and nightstand littered the floor. He placed her on the bed, standing to take off his clothes.

She sat up, pulling her own off with haste, eager to have the feel of his skin on her. She had barely unzipped her pants when he was on her again, his lips kissing her bare chest as he tore the pants from her body. His hands travelled up over her hips as his mouth made its way to her neck. He breathed in her scent as she tilted her hips, her own hands running down his back, making him shiver. Shane looked into her eyes just as he pushed forward, joining them for the second time.

This, too, was somehow more. More than it was the first time. They could feel the bond forming again. The essence of each other flowed freely through them, settling back into place. The void they felt before, the emptiness, was completely obliterated as they feverishly joined over and over. Nothing else mattered as they clung to one another, the feeling of ecstasy building. Shane pulled her up, so she was straddling his hips, their faces aligned, eyes locked as she moved over him, her hips grinding into his. It grew, coming to the peak, Vee's hands clutching onto him as they both cried out with trembling completion.

Shane looked at her, brushing the hair from her face as their breathing slowed, and their hearts began to beat normally again. They didn't have to say anything. They could feel it all through the renewed bond. It took them a while to return to reality. The full moon shined brightly through her bedroom windows, basking them in its glow.

"I love you," she whispered, tracing his face lightly with her fingers as she stared at him.

"I love you," he whispered back, pure awe in his voice.

They finally looked away from each other, seeing the destruction around her. Vee raised her eyebrows, not really wanting to climb off him but knowing they couldn't stay there. They had somehow managed to avoid cutting themselves on the pieces of mattress springs poking out a few inches away, and her futons were even more uncomfortable even when they weren't torn to pieces as they were now.

"Let's go home," Shane said, the word "home" coming from his lips so naturally.

"Yes, let's," she said, pressing her lips to his lightly.

Vee moved off of him, bending over to grab her clothes from the floor. Shane, leaned back a little, watching her. She was back to moving a little stiffly, her body just as bruised as it had been that morning, but it was still beautiful to him. She glanced at him briefly before she put her loose shirt back over her head. The look in his eyes matched the reverence she felt from him. She let a tiny smile breach her lips at the look as she picked up her pants, which she realized were irreparably torn.

Shane burst out laughing at the shock that came over her, and the look on her face as she moved them in her hands, trying to figure out what exactly went wrong.

"You owe me a pair of jeans," she said, tossing them playfully at him.

"It was worth it," he said, still smiling, but his desire had come back, just remembering how satisfying it had been to simply rip them from her body.

She felt that way too, but chose to ignore it, grabbing a pair of sweatpants that sat in the bottom of the dresser drawer that had been ripped out from its slot. Shane began getting dressed as well, pulling his shirt back over his head as Vee began parsing though her scattered things.

"We don't have to do this tonight, Vee," Shane said as Vee stood with a few small items in her hands.

"Just this, for now," she murmured, walking back into the living room and placing them into her bag. The little flash of that yellow envelope caught her eye as she tossed the small objects in. She sucked the air through her teeth, realizing what the coven had been searching for.

Shane joined her in the living room, donning his coat once more, feeling her realization through the bond.

"What is it?" he asked, looking at her as she stared into her messenger bag.

"They were looking for this," she said, pulling the thick envelope from it and standing to show him. His confusion at the crumpled yellow thing in her hands only deepened. "Eliza brought it to me, right before

she…" Vee swallowed, trying to not feel guilty about the way their last conversation ended. "They're my adoption papers," Vee admitted, staring down at it like it would jump out and bite her.

Shane reached out to take it from her grasp, tucking it under his arm, feeling her fear at what was hidden under the paper enclosure.

"We'll look at it tomorrow," he said confidently, reaching out with his other hand to take hers. They walked out, after locking her apartment, to head home.

CHAPTER 26

[Vee: I'm going to look at the adoption papers today.]

Vee was texting Durran, sitting at the kitchen island of Shane's house with her first cup of coffee for the day. The house was so strangely quiet with Patrick still asleep upstairs, and Shane having woken her with a kiss to tell her he had to run an errand. It felt odd to be practically alone in his house.

[Durran: Do you want me to be there?]

Vee furrowed her brow at the message. Why wouldn't she want Durran there?

[Vee: Yes…?]

She felt Patrick stirring upstairs, prompting her to glance at the clock. It was well past noon.

[Durran: When?]

Vee wasn't sure how long Shane would be. She didn't really want Durran to be at the house with her without Shane there. Somehow that felt like it would be pushing him too far.

[Vee: I'll let you know.]

Vee set her phone on the counter as Patrick wandered into the kitchen, bleary eyed.

"'Morning, Vee," he said, not even batting an eye that she was there. She was expecting some kind of surprise given that he went to bed thinking Vee had slept at her apartment, but he just moseyed on over to the coffee pot, pouring his own and sitting in the stool beside her.

"'Morning," she said back, grasping her own cup between her hands. They both sat there for a few brief moments, sipping their coffee against the quiet house, when she felt Patrick's amusement bubble within him.

"I thought you were going to your place last night," Patrick said, a little smirk forming on his lips as he took another sip of coffee. Vee raised her eyebrows, turning to him. He *had* noticed.

"That had been the plan," she said quietly, turning her gaze ahead of her, hearing Shane's car pull up in the driveway.

"Are you moving in?" he asked, trying to maintain his cool, but she could feel his excitement. She felt Shane coming through the back door in that moment. She was a little unsure what to say. Her apartment was unlivable, she would be staying there indefinitely, and she realized she *had* agreed to marry Shane the night before. It would be a bit strange to have her own apartment.

"I guess so," she said, turning back to see his eyes light up.

"What changed?" Patrick asked, unable to hide his elation as he grinned at her.

"She agreed to marry me," Shane said, walking into the room. Any sleepiness Patrick may have been feeling seemed to evaporate with those words.

"When?" Patrick asked, looking between Vee and his father, who had moved to pour his own coffee.

"We haven't gotten that far yet," Vee said quietly, a small smile on her lips at the way Patrick was reacting with such excitement, and Shane's emotions seemed to glow with happiness even saying the words.

"We will have to go to Vee's and pick up some things later," Shane said, his brow now furrowing as he thought about where all of her things would go. He had plenty of space for everything, of course, but this house was *his* style. He was certain she would want to change a few things to make it more her own. Not that the idea of her changing anything within his home was troubling. It was more that *she* might have difficulty with that.

"I'll help," Patrick said, seeming to sit up even more, like he was already ready to go.

"I'm going to finish my coffee first," Vee told him with a smile.

"Fair enough," Patrick said, remaining in his seat, but seeming to hum with energy.

"So, what were your errands?" Vee asked, turning to Shane.

"Oh, just met a client for coffee, then I made a few calls," he murmured, turning to look in the refrigerator. Anticipation and excitement were running through the bond. Had the bond been gone, she could tell he would be trying to block her, since they were not nearly as pronounced. It wasn't something malicious he was hiding, more like a surprise for her. She wasn't exactly someone who liked surprises, but she decided she wouldn't question him for now. Not enough coffee to try to dig to find out what he was hiding there.

"I really need to go back to the shop at some point, too," she murmured, looking at her phone. No missed calls, but she had changed her shop message, so that wasn't really shocking. It was the idea that she had lost so much in potential customers. She had nearly gotten back to where she had been with her savings before her inventory was demolished nine months ago by Lori's wolf. But with days of lost income, and her alternator needing to be replaced on the Lumina, she was practically back where she started.

"Whenever you'd like, but I do have one little thing I want to do with you first," Shane said, turning back to her. She narrowed her eyes suspiciously at him.

"And what's that?"

"We have to take a quick drive, that's all," he said, brown eyes sparking with amusement at the dubious look on her face.

"I can go to your apartment and start packing some things. I bet Lori would come with me," Patrick said, fishing his phone from his sweatpants and going to text her.

"But—"

"She's been there before, right? She'll make sure I don't mess anything up," Patrick said, still not looking at her as his thumbs moved over his phone with urgency. The idea he could mess anything up in the wreckage that once was her home was laughable.

"I suppose…" Vee grumbled, standing from the stool. "I'm going to get dressed, since the day seems to be planned out already," she told them, glancing at the two men in the kitchen with wariness before heading back up the stairs, coffee in hand to get dressed.

When she returned, Patrick had already gone to get dressed himself, and Shane was now alone in the kitchen, sipping on his own coffee. He had been dressed in his customary slacks and button up shirt, which she assumed was for the meeting with his client. After days of seeing him dressed more casually, it seemed rather odd for him to be dressed that way. She blushed a little recognizing how nice he looked. After all, this was the type of clothes he normally wore around her. The clothes she apparently fell in love with him wearing, while she remained in her rumpled t-shirt and jeans that she had worn days earlier.

"Are you ready?" he asked, grinning as she walked back into the room.

"Patrick will need my key," Vee said, glancing around.

"Just leave it on the counter," Shane told her, as he grabbed his coat from the stool he had slung it over and slipped it back on. She pulled her keys from her messenger bag and removed her apartment key, setting it on the counter, when she noticed another key sitting there. "What's that?"

"A key to the house," he said. She picked it up, scrutinizing it for imperfections. Had he gone to another locksmith for this? No, she realized this was one of the many spare keys she had made for him within the last few months. She looked over at him, past the key before her face, and saw him smile.

"What am I going to do without the pack paying me?" she wondered aloud.

"You'll get a flat rate as a retainer. No one will have to pay for your services. The security company will just have you on payroll. Well, we'll have *The Missing Key* on payroll," he told her. Her eyebrows shot up as she quickly slipped the key onto her ring where the apartment key once sat. It seemed he had already thought of everything.

"That's awfully presumptuous of you," she said, raising an eyebrow at him as she headed toward the back door.

"We need your services often enough. It just makes sense," he said, following her out as they headed to his car.

She wasn't sure where they were going, only that he was certainly pleased with himself for whatever this surprise was going to be. She remained skeptical the entire time, switching between trying to figure out

where they were headed to eying him. They had only travelled about twenty minutes or so, moving steadily down to the Westbottoms, the warehouse district for the city. Shane pulled up in front of an unlabeled brick building and got out without a word. She followed, even more skeptical now that they had apparently arrived.

"What are we doing here?" she asked, walking beside Shane up to the door.

"This is the security company headquarters," Shane told her, opening the already unlocked door. They walked into the front office. It seemed small in comparison to the big exterior building. There were a few nice couches on one side with a glass coffee table between them and a counter. There was one door beside the counter and a set of double doors with small windows at the top directly behind it. Thomas and Tommy were already there, obviously expecting them.

"We pulled a few out for her," Thomas said, grinning at Vee but talking to Shane.

"Good," Shane said, taking her hand and walking around the counter to the double doors beyond.

"What are we doing here?" she hissed as he opened the doors.

"Getting you a new car," he said as they walked through.

The ceiling was high, ending about halfway up the building's height. The room itself was huge, spanning the whole width of the block. Huge loading doors meant to fit semi-trucks sat on one side, while floor to ceiling windows let the light cascade into the space. And sitting in the massive open room were rows and rows of black cars with tinted windows, all varying shapes, sizes, and models. Vee looked at it all in shock.

"How much do you own?" she choked out, realizing that she seemed to have downplayed how wealthy he was. Or perhaps it wasn't him downplaying anything. It had just been her own attempt to push the thought out of her mind. She had known he had a nice house and nice things. The property in Pleasant Hill had been an interesting revelation. This added yet another level to his overwhelming wealth that she wasn't expecting.

"The pack owns things. The companies own most of it, not only me," he told her, feeling how overwhelmed she was through the bond. His words did make her feel slightly better, but the knowledge that *he* owned the company, therefore he owned all of this tickled at her thoughts. "Every adult pack member has ownership in the companies I run. We make decisions together," Shane told her, seeming to follow her thoughts.

"And you all decided I needed one of these?" she asked, looking at the three vehicles that had been pulled forward.

"Just let me know which one, and I'll make sure it's all tuned up for you," Emily said, walking out of a room. Vee hadn't initially noticed her to the right, wearing some black coveralls. The three vehicles in question were all very different. One was a sedan, compact, but still had backseat and trunk room for supplies. One was a van, providing even more space for hauling all sorts of things, and one was an SUV.

"I can't... I've still got the Lumina... I'll..."

"You've been saving to get a more reliable vehicle, and quite honestly, it's the pack and pack business that keeps getting in your way," Shane told her, pulling her a little more forward to look at them.

"These are a lot more money than I've lost," she said, looking at the shiny black paint on each of them, knowing they had all sorts of luxurious gadgets and buttons on the inside.

"They are used," Shane said, raising his eyebrows at her, hoping that might entice her more. If he knew anything, she was frugal. Things of great expense made her uncomfortable, since she didn't grow up with anything nor did she have much now that she was an adult.

She looked at him, feeling out his emotions. He was only trying to help, and there was a little protectiveness there, which she assumed was because her Lumina was not exactly the most reliable vehicle. It was also going to be a lot harder for her to get to and from the shop from Shane's house without a vehicle. She sighed, letting go of is hand to walk to them. Shane wasn't trying to control or coddle her. He was giving her back some of her freedom by making sure she had a way to get around.

Vee circled each vehicle, looking at the slick paint. She got in each one, putting her hands on the wheel and looking around to see if any of them *felt* right. For some reason when she got into the van, she just knew it was the one. It had everything she had envisioned for her work vehicle and then some. There was plenty of space for tools and supplies. She could even keep a small stash of inventory in there, so she wouldn't have to leave a house call to go to a nearby hardware store if she unexpectedly needed an additional part.

She glanced out the windshield at Shane, who had been watching her, hopefully.

"This one would be nice," she murmured as she got out, getting a grin out of both Emily and Shane.

"Perfect. I'll get it to the house by tonight," Emily told them, clapping Shane on the shoulder before heading back to the side room.

"Do you have any more surprises for me today?" Vee asked Shane, still rather mystified by this large room full of cars.

"They can wait," he said, half joking. She narrowed her eyes but decided not to pursue it. "The apartment or the shop?" he asked as they walked back through to the front office.

"Apartment would probably be best. Who knows what Lori and Patrick are doing with my stuff," she told him, waving at Tommy and Thomas on their way out.

The much shorter drive to the apartment filled Vee with dread again. She knew what it looked like in there, and the idea of having to piece through all her things to see what was salvageable was daunting. She didn't want to think about how many of her possessions she'd have to throw away. All her things were practically worthless to begin with. Their only real value was to her.

As they pulled up, she recognized the buzz of Lori and Patrick, but there was a little twinge of desire from them as well. She raised her eyebrows and turned to Shane.

"Maybe you should just wait here for a minute," she said, staring at Shane and trying to hide her surprise.

"What is it?" he asked, very confused about her sudden emotional change.

"I think it would be better if it was just me that went up there first," Vee said, looking into his eyes, willing him to understand. He didn't quite seem to grasp her unspoken words, which she was mildly thankful for. She managed to convince him to just stay put in the car for a few more minutes before she hopped out, rushing up the stairs and opening her apartment. The desire she felt between them was still small, so she wasn't about to walk in on something she didn't want to see. She knew this would embarrass them though.

Opening the unlocked door tentatively, she saw Lori and Patrick sitting on her living room floor in front of her television, movies were in both of their hands and laps, but they were leaned forward, lips locked in a sweet and innocent kiss. She cleared her throat, causing them to separate instantly.

"Haven't gotten much done, I see," she said, smirking a little at them as they seemed to move as quickly away from one another as possible but still on the floor, color flooding both of their cheeks.

"No, no... I, um... I got your kitchen stuff packed away," Lori said, pointing to a box on the floor, trying to slow her heartbeat.

"My dad?" Patrick asked in a pained voice, knowing it was pointless to try to hide what had just been happening.

"I told him to wait a minute before he came up," she told them, causing both teenagers to sigh in relief.

They had actually gotten quite a bit accomplished, Vee realized as she looked around. Her books were packed away and shelves bare. The broken and unusable furniture was stacked at the front windows, including her mattress, which made her blush a little, thinking about what it had to have smelled like in that room to them. There were trash bags filled with smaller broken things to get hauled out, and they had been packing up her movies when they got … distracted.

She heard Shane coming up the stairs behind her as she looked at the progress. He still looked rather confused, but he let it wash away when he saw how much they had already accomplished.

"What's ready to take?" he asked, instead of the question he wanted to ask, which was what happened in there that had Vee wanting him to pause. No one was going to jump to answer that unspoken question.

The three of them loaded up the car, while Vee went to her bedroom to grab the remaining clothes she had left there. She filled her laundry bag with her dirty things and emptied the drawers of her few remaining clean clothes. Tomorrow she would have a lot of phone calls to make, she realized. She had to try to figure out who was dealing with Eliza's affairs as well as call her landlord of the last decade and tell them she was moving out.

Thankfully the only damage to the apartment had been the door Durran and Shane had demolished, but the new door that Thomas had had installed for her took care of that problem. She was pleased she didn't have to explain that her apartment had been destroyed to the landlord, who would definitely question why she was leaving on such short notice. It seemed odd that she would have to tell them she … what? Fell in love?

She stood alone for a moment in her mostly empty apartment, listening to Lori, Patrick, and Shane as they took her things to the two cars parked in front. Her feeling before they left for the property hadn't been wrong, she realized. She had been, in a way, saying goodbye to her old life. While the changes in her life were numerous and overwhelming, it wasn't as scary as it had felt before she'd warmed to the idea. And being around Shane consistently for the past few days, even when she was in a much weaker state, proved to her she could live with others. She smiled a little before following them out, plopping her bags in the back of Shane's car.

Patrick and Lori had headed back to drop off the boxes and bags at Shane's house, while Vee and Shane went to her shop to check on it. She had been a little worried the coven had also destroyed that, but the front door and showroom were still untouched. She opened the front door, scurrying to the alarm panel and turning it off as Shane entered behind her. She glanced at the blinking red light of her answering machine. There were plenty of messages waiting for her, one from Frank's lawyers, who Vee didn't particularly care to call back presently. That was a tomorrow problem.

Shane sat quietly, looking at the wall of keys behind the main counter as she scribbled notes to herself to call the other customers back. It felt nice that they all seemed very understanding of her need to take time away, given what her changed answering recording said, but still wanted to work with her when she came back.

Shane stood to go look at one key in particular. It, like the other keys on the wall, had no notches or teeth on the blade yet, being that it was just on display, but the bow of the key was intricate. Of course, Vee had many normal shaped key blanks on the wall, but since he had the time he seemed to finally notice that several of them were handmade designs. He had seen her other handy work of course; Vee made beautiful heart-shaped locks and the hand-crafted safes. If she were to have enough time to create custom pieces that she clearly was talented at making, she would probably be happier for it.

He pulled one of the custom blanks from the wall, a wolf head. It reminded him of the pendant Patrick had started wearing last summer when Ethan came home.

"When did you make this?" Shane asked, coming over to where she still sat by the counter and placed it on the calendar before her. She looked at it, blushing ever so slightly before she met his eyes.

"Last summer," she admitted. "I made it for you."

"Why didn't you give it to me?" he asked.

"We weren't anything, then. It felt strange to offer you a custom key, when I wasn't even sure how I felt about you yet," she told him, picking it up and twirling it in her fingers. That was understandable. He had tip-toed around for many months, trying to find reasons to be around her. She had come to his house on many occasions to look over a child or two that Shane was quite certain would be a Were just to have an excuse to talk to her for a moment.

"Would you make it for me?" he asked, watching her as her face and her feelings through the bond showed her surprise, but also excitement.

"I can do that," she said with a smile, turning to the back room to unlock it. There she had her tools for cutting keys. She flipped on the light finding the back

room to be not nearly as spic and span as she had left it. No, it looked worse than when Lori had her first change, lacking blood and gore. Vee's breath caught in her throat. She could have thrown up at the sight of it.

The back door stood wide open to the alley, as it had been for at least a day. How had the door been open, and the alarm still set? She stood before the wreckage mouth opening and closing like a fish out of water for a few moments as Shane moved around the counter to the door where she stood, looking at it from behind her.

"They were searching here too," she finally croaked, her eyes burning.

"So, it seems," Shane murmured, stepping past her into the destruction.

At least the locks hadn't been ripped apart or damaged like they had been the last time it had been torn apart, but the mess… Vee took in a shaky breath, remembering the work it took to get it back where it needed to be. She shook her head, trying to rid herself of the feeling of dread as Shane shut the back door, barring it.

"I guess Patrick and Lori will be busy the rest of spring break," she said, trying to lighten the mood, but the undercurrent of her emotions told a different story as did the way her voice quaked.

"We can send them to start working on it once we get back," Shane told her, stepping closer.

"They've done enough today," she said, turning her back on the room and walking into the showroom. He followed her, closing the door behind him and circling his arms around her waist from behind.

"It will be fixed," he whispered into her ear.

"I know," she said softly, leaning back into him.

There was no other reason to stay there, now. That room was far too overwhelming for her to even look at, let alone begin to do anything about currently. She felt the weight of her messenger bag on her leg, the envelope with the papers that had caused all this destruction hidden within it. They needed to open it, which would most likely prove to be far more tremendous than the idea of putting her inventory room together again would ever be.

They left the shop once again. The temperature not nearly as cold as it had been for the last week with the promise of spring just around the corner.

[Vee: Within the hour?]

Vee had texted Durran as they drove back to Shane's house.

[Durran: I'll be there.]

They came in the door to a mountain of boxes and bags, all piled in the entry way. She was honestly surprised how many there were, seeing all that was left of her worldly possessions stacked together. And they didn't even include the things in Shane's car. Her tiny apartment had held a lot more than she thought.

"I'm not sure where I'll even put any of this," she murmured, stepping up to the box on top which held her movies.

"I don't think you've seen the whole house yet, have you?" Shane asked, taking his coat off.

"I've seen most of it," she said, now crouching to look at her box of kitchen supplies, most which could be donated. Well, perhaps not her mugs.

"We have room," Shane told her confidently. He had been musing on their way home about getting her the space she needed to create things, not tied down to her operating hours at the shop. There was one place in the house that was completely untouched, a blank canvas. The attic. Years ago, he had thought to finish it and make it an additional bedroom for pack members who needed to stay overnight, but now it would be perfect to give Vee a little place completely her own that she could escape to.

"What are you thinking about? You seem to have become inspired and excited all of a sudden," she said, pulling herself away from her boxes to remove her own coat.

"I had an idea for something, that's all," he murmured. She narrowed her eyes at him but let him have his excitement. It was clear whatever it was wouldn't be surprising her today.

"Durran should be here soon," she said, moving to the dining room to set her bag on the table.

Now that they had made it back to Shane's house, she knew she had to open the package. There were too many questions surrounding what ever happened to be in the contents of that envelope. Who were her parents? *What* were her parents? Why had they given her up? Why would Gwen have wanted to know? So many questions could be answered, if she simply opened it. Or it would at least give a direction to find out more.

Vee was slipping the envelope from the bag and setting it on the table when she felt Durran at the door. She looked up at Shane, and he opened it, not even needing the knock that sounded as he approached.

"Come in," Shane said, opening it wide enough for Durran to walk through. There was still tension between them Vee noted. She could sense them both grow rigid in each other's presence, but it didn't feel nearly as hostile as it did a few days before. Perhaps there was a bit of comradery formed when they were fighting for the same goal.

Vee, Shane and Durran all sat at the large dining room table; the sealed envelope was in the middle. A pregnant silence had filled the room as Vee stared at it. Neither Shane nor Durran wanted to rush her, but everyone was eager to know what secrets were held inside. She finally reached out, the silence between them all growing too uncomfortable, and she carefully removed the bracket holding it together.

"We'll be fine, no matter what it says," Shane told her as she slipped the huge stack of papers out. She didn't say anything. She had no idea if she would be fine. She didn't know what was held in there.

Vee's eyes skimmed the first page. It was a birth certificate. She had seen her birth certificate many times. Her mother and father were listed there with her name very clearly being Victoria Muraco Malone, but here there was Muraco O'Morrigan. She furrowed her brow, looking at it. Her birthdate was on there, but that name couldn't have been hers. The formatting was wrong. It looked odd. It was completely unlike the Missouri certificate she had used for her whole life.

"Let me see," Durran said, holding her hand out. Vee handed the birth certificate over, looking now at the second page. It was a copy of the certificate she had always known to be hers. She let her eyes rest on her parents' names, Sarah and Graham.

"What are the other names on that?" Vee asked, holding her hand back out, realizing she missed the names of her real parents on her first look at the foreign document.

"There's only one other name... your mother," Durran said, handing it back to her.

Emerald eyes looked over the name with curiosity and confusion. It wasn't anyone she knew of. Fiona O'Morrigan.

"Who in the world is that?" Vee said in a hoarse whisper.

"That last name..." Durran said quietly, eyes glowing red.

"It sounds like... Irish tales," Shane murmured.

"Yes. Morrigan. The Faes of Fate," Durran said, confirming what Shane had been thinking. Vee failed to stifle a laugh, the sound coming out as more of a snort, making them look over at her.

"I'm sorry," Vee said, her voice rough as she tried to collect herself. "Fae? The Fates? Like the actual Fates?" she asked, dumbfounded. She knew about the Greek Fates but she had never really tied her knowledge of the Fae with actual history and mythology, so she found herself reeling a little. The line between human-told history and fairy tales was far more blurred than the humans liked to let on. She knew mythologies overlapped and were woven together more like an intricate tapestry, instead of distinct and different for each culture.

"Yes. All the cultures who have Fates in their myths are actually talking about the Morrigan. The Fae sisters. Daughters of the Fae who was once the king, Dagda," Durran told her. It didn't help.

"So, I'm somehow associated with the Fae," Vee said, briefly looking at her hands as if they would change now that she knew this. She had no glamor and no impulse to bargain. She could feel emotions. That was it. Well, that was all she *thought* she could do previously.

"Not by much, I wouldn't think. You don't smell like Fae," Durran said.

"She doesn't smell like any preternatural," Shane commented, making Durran nod with raised brows, conceding that point.

"But Muraco?" Vee asked, scrutinizing that name. She had always thought her middle name was selected because her mother had a small amount of Native American in her. That was how she thought she got some of her darker coloring when the rest of her family was much paler in comparison. Now that she knew her mother, or the mother she had always thought was hers, hadn't chosen it, she was questioning everything she had previously thought about herself.

"I believe that means…" Durran started, brows pulling together trying to remember.

"White Moon," Vee said, having looked it up when she was young. She looked down at the stack of remaining papers. She had no idea what they could possibly hold, but she couldn't help the pit that was forming in the bottom of her stomach.

AUTHOR BIO

Chelsea Burton Dunn is a Kansas City native—the Missouri side not the Kansas side. That matters to locals. Where is that you might ask? Right, smack-dab in the middle of the country. She has two beautiful children and is married to a superb partner, but let's not forget their two snuggly cats and eager eater of a dog.

Having always been a little strange herself, she instantly fell in love with paranormal, supernatural, and fantasy books, movies, and tv shows as a child. Did everyone think it was a phase? Absolutely. Was it? Absolutely not. Being weird is a blessing, not a curse. She's always embraced that part of herself and those around her.

She started writing from a very early age, finishing a Vampire novel in high school but had a bad

experience with self-publishing and has since left that world she created behind. Though she does boast a tattoo of a spade on her finger in its honor. She is a lover of music, having her other love and talent be for singing. She performed on main stage operas in the children's chorus from grade school to high school.

Chelsea loves to delve into the difficulties of life, love, and loss, while spicing it up with a little magic and monsters. As she liked to say when she was younger, "the monsters in my head need to come out to play every once in a while," so giving them life on the page seemed appropriate.

You can see more about Chelsea, her projects, and find her social medias by going to www.chelseaburtondunn.com

Sneak Peek at White Moon
Book 3 of the By Moonlight Series

This lock was being difficult. Years of wear had stripped the screws holding it in place, not to mention the rust crusting it to where it sat within the door. The house was a little over one hundred years old, like the majority of buildings in the area. But while most of them had been updated, this particular house had last seen an update in the late sixties, and this lock had not been replaced in many years.

Vee struggled with the lock, a fine layer of sweat collecting on her forehead as she continued to work at the metal carefully. She was also having a harder time holding back the sickly feeling she got from the minds below. Her brain felt like it was being doused in ice water repeatedly. Not that they were feeling anything bad necessarily, but she just so happened to be changing the locks on a Vampire nest.

She had been ousted to the preternatural world as a true Empath, so she found she had been getting more and more clients of all varieties. She didn't mind the extra income, but she did mind the unease she

With a sigh she pulled out her phone, dialing Lori's number. Lori was part of the reason Vee was in this particular predicament with the preternatural world. Vee had saved the sweet teenage girl from savagely murdering her friends when she unexpectedly turned into a Werewolf one night a little over a year before. Vee had exposed herself to protect people she didn't even know, but she wouldn't have done anything differently if she had to do it all over again.

Lori and Patrick were diligently watching the shop as she went on her run in the field. Patrick was Shane's younger son and her almost-stepson. The two teenagers had worked for her all summer, as they had the summer before, and there were only a few weeks left before she only had their help after school.

"*Hey, Vee. What's up?*" Patrick answered on the second ring.

"I thought I called Lori," Vee said, raising her eyebrow, not that he could see it, but she was sure he'd be able to hear it in her voice.

"*I was closer,*" Patrick said. Vee could hear Lori's giggle in the background, even though she had tried to stifle it. They weren't officially dating, but there was certainly a spark between them. It made sense, not only were they close in age, but they were also both Werewolves. They didn't have many friends to confide that part of their life in.

"I'm not going to make it back to the shop before lunch is over, so I'm just going to grab something quick at your house before I head back," she said, taking the few turns and stopping at a four-way stop.

"You mean 'home', Vee?" Patrick asked, his voice not hiding the smirk she could imagine forming on his lips. She rolled her eyes.

"Hard habit to kill," she said, still uncomfortable calling Patrick and Shane's house hers, even after five months. Patrick loved to remind her of it.

"We'll close down for lunch and see you in a bit. Everything is good here."

"We're fine, Vee!" Lori said in the background.

"Okay, okay…" Vee murmured, hanging up the phone as she pulled up to Shane's house.

She had made the space in front of the house hers, Shane and Patrick usually parking in back. The pack even steered clear of parking there, so she would have a place if they arrived before she did. She climbed out of the van, wandering through the grass to the front door, always feeling uneasy as she looked on the large colonial from the outside. It still felt strange that she was coming here of her own accord, instead of being summoned.

But as she placed her key in the lock, the unease seemed to melt away, feeling much more comfortable once she stepped through the threshold. The house had definitely taken on some of her attributes; a few books stacked on the side table in the living room, her little planter sitting on a narrow table just inside the door. The planter was where she had always stashed her keys at her apartment, so it felt natural to have it here now.

It still wasn't *hers*, and that was part of the reason she felt such an aversion to calling it that. She was comfortable there, yes, but the general feel of the house was still definitively Shane's.

BOOK CLUB QUESTIONS:

1. What do you think the potential consequences of Vee being exposed in the preternatural community are?

2. What do you think Vee is, now that we know her power is greater than she thought before?

3. How do you think Vee will cope with her life changing, now that she has agreed to not only have a relationship with Shane but marry him?

4. What problems do you see arising between Durran and Vee or Durran and Shane, now that Vee is mated to Shane and Durran

confessed their true feelings? Do you think there be problems? Why?

5. Now that Vee's powers are more than she originally thought they were, could it be an indication that she has a larger role to play in the preternatural world? Do you think that's symbolic of Vee's allowing more people into her life? Why?

6. What do you think the correlation is between Vee's opening up herself and her life to others and her abilities?

More books from
4 Horsemen Publications

Fantasy, SciFi, & Paranormal Romance

Amanda Fasciano
Waking Up Dead
Dead Vessel
The Dead Show
Dead Revelations

Beau Lake
The Beast Beside Me
The Beast Within Me
Taming the Beast: Novella
The Beast After Me
Charming the Beast
The Beast Like Me
An Eye for Emeralds
Swimming in Sapphires
Pining for Pearls

Chelsea Burton Dunn
By Moonlight
Moonbound
Bloodthirsty

D. Lambert
Rydan
Celebrant
Northlander
Esparan
King

Traitor
His Last Name

Danielle Orsino
Locked Out of Heaven
Thine Eyes of Mercy
From the Ashes
Kingdom Come
Fire, Ice, Acid, & Heart
A Fae is Done

J.M. Paquette
Klauden's Ring
Solyn's Body
The Inbetween
Hannah's Heart
Call Me Forth
Invite Me In
Keep Me Close
Heart of Stone

Jessica Salina
Not My Time
To Be Normal

Kait Disney-Leugers
Antique Magic
Blood Magic

DISCOVER MORE AT
4HorsemenPublications.com